Limpic and the
Shadow of the Moon

Limpic and the Shadow of the Moon

Lewis McUllan

For my wife and daughter, my parents and my siblings. For those who remember the 'shack at the back.' And finally Limpic. Conceived in despair; inspired by a hope of better things to come.

The Kindness of Strangers

Strangers then who took me in,
And gathered up the broken pieces of my life.
Who watched me, bathed me, loved me,
During hardship, pain and strife.
Who listened to my heart, but
More than that, they listened to my dreams as well.
And sat beside me into
The night, for sometimes drugs and solitude are hell.
Strangers then who cooled my brow
And checked my pulse and stroked my hand in place of mum.
Who turned lonely days and long
Hard months into friendships with a smile and hum.
Who brought me news of all kinds
From outside, inside, bedside, whether good or bad.
Who kept me in the picture,
But strove to make it such that I was seldom sad.
Strangers then who carried me,
Not knowing that they carried me, or lifted me
With tea and toast and gossip
Never thinking that these simple actions set me free.
And so it's for these strangers
Who said, "Go live, return to kith and kin,"
That I live and breathe and say,
"Thank you, thank you, kind strangers then, who took me in."

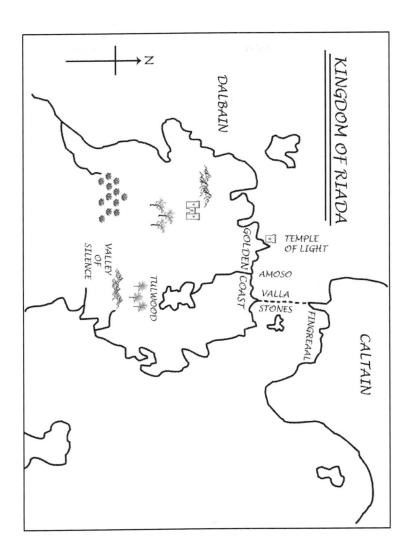

Table of Contents

Prologue

"Help me!" groaned the prisoner as he was lifted violently and freed from his anchor. His prison was dark – not that it mattered for he wore a hood over his head; a golden hood that sapped his strength and rendered him blind.

"No more!" he cried. "She can take no more!"

His captors merely chuckled and thrust him forward into the dust. He heard a door opening before he was dragged into a corridor, his feet trailing behind him.

"Move!" hissed a voice close by.

The prisoner received a vicious slap to the back of his head. He didn't care. It was all about her. They were killing her – didn't they see that?

He felt himself spinning around. *The floating stairs*. His ears popped and he was lifted quickly with awesome power by Obsidian Hewn. The cold bit at his feet and ankles as they left the uppermost room and went out to the spiral stairs.

"Go!" the voice commanded.

The prisoner refused; he dug his heels in and wouldn't budge, but his captors were stronger and he was hauled up the final steps, each one jolting every bone in his body. He knew what was about to happen. *The horror of it*!

He was thrown onto his knees and his head pulled sharply back. The wind whipped round his exposed throat.

"Nooooo," he moaned. "Not again, please! You're killing her!" There was a cackle and the prisoner's hair rose on the back of his neck. It was only then he truly realised his captors didn't care. The golden hood was ripped from his face and strong hands twisted his hair. Up above the sky boiled within itself and the clouds spat in disgust. A silvery light began to glow and then the moon appeared, lethargic and weak.

"Nooooo!" the prisoner wailed again, but it was hopeless.

There was a flash of light and a column of silver shot from his eyes into the heart of the moon. The whispers began in earnest, drilling into his brain and planting seeds of destruction. He saw her just before it happened – his mother, she was staring into the Pool of Reflections, searching for her son.

"Mother!" he cried, "Mother, I am sorry."

Her eyes opened wide and she reached out to him just before the silver took her. Like it had taken all the others.

The city shuddered to its foundations and then, slowly and with gasping hisses, began to sink.

Chapter 1

The moon drifted high overhead, pale and ghostly as tendrils of cloud brushed across her face. A gloomy mass moved from the west, swallowing the stars and smothering the moon. She fought behind the darkness and seemed to jostle and elbow her way through until her light shone out once more.

Limpic's whiskers tingled and a cold sensation ran up the back of his legs. He tried to speak but his jaw wouldn't move. He was standing at the tip of the Valla Stones, where they disappeared into the sea. He was staring at the inky black water with a sick, heavy feeling in the pit of his stomach. The moon's reflection changed, becoming swollen and bloated.

Suddenly a huge silver hand broke from the water and the reflection splintered. Limpic lashed out as his stomach heaved but he could not move. Flames sputtered from the flower that grew on his chest and then the door appeared; right in front of him, red and blistered and marked '22'. It opened and an intense heat hit Limpic in the face and drew sweat to his brow. A tongue of fire licked around the frame of the door.

Limpic tried to scream as the open door moved towards him like a gaping mouth. Inside was the room with the flowery wallpaper. He saw the chimney with the cawing crow. He saw the bed and the figure lying in it. Everything was on fire.

No! mouthed Limpic. He looked at his feet. They were on fire. Flames crept up his legs and the coldness from a moment ago fled. His flower was white-hot.

No! he tried to yell but nothing came.

"Ah!" Limpic jolted awake. He flapped all around his body trying to put out the flames, but as the memory of the dream faded so too did the fires.

"A nightmare," he panted, "just a nightmare." He swallowed and tried to catch his breath; his heart thudding against his ribs.

Pushing his limpet shell hat back from his forehead, Limpic leaned over the side of his boat – an enormous upturned limpet shell – and peered at the reflection of the moon. Sweat beaded on his coarse hair and dripped onto his temple before trickling towards his short stubby nose where it gathered on his whiskers. Giving them a twitch, he scooped some water in his hand and rubbed it over his face and down the back of his neck. Even though the liquid quickly ran off the short, thick pelt of brown hair that covered his entire body, he still felt somewhat refreshed and less feverish. He let a long, steady breath pass into the balmy summer's night.

To an observer he looked like a seal – his head, anyway. His chin was a little fuller than a seal's and his forehead a little higher. His torso was rather like that of a stoat or an otter and his legs were lean and muscular with feet like those of a wolf. Limpic had three toes on each foot, each very large and cushioned by thick leathery pads. They were also webbed for swimming. He stood on these toes now, just over five paces high, perfectly balanced and perfectly poised.

"It was just a nightmare," Limpic said. He shuddered. The same nightmare he'd been having for the past two weeks: the moon swollen up and bloated like it was sick and then everything turning to silver – even the sea. But tonight's nightmare had been the worst by far. It had been a long time since he had dreamt of the door marked '22'.

"Oh!" Limpic winced in pain. The wound surrounding the flower that grew from his chest was inflamed and hot to touch.

Old fears crept into his mind. Fears of fevers. Of burning up in the darkness and the loneliness of the night. Limpic sighed and stroked the flower, which had five petals, each white with purple veins. He had given up trying to conceal it because every time he did, the flower found a way to burrow its head through his clothes. Like a weed? No, that wasn't fair because Limpic knew it had saved his life. It had taken away the fire and the fever and protected him.

"So why are you burning now?" Limpic demanded, scratching savagely at the flesh around the flower stalk.

He ground his teeth and sank back down into the boat with a low moan, pulling his clothes away from his sweating body. Simple clothes. Seaweed that had been dried and stitched together with flax from his lint dam. It had been a tough year harvesting the flax; after the green lint had retted in his dam, it had taken an extra two weeks for it to dry enough to remove what was left of the useless outer casing. Only then could the flax be spun into thread. He bartered what was left for eggs or bread or whatever took his fancy with the Adameans whose farms and villages were scattered throughout Dalbain. The children of the earth were always willing to trade their goods for his thread. Children of the glar or muck more like, thought Limpic ruefully. They were feeling the strain of strange weather patterns and had only just survived an unseasonably wet spring.

Limpic drew his legs close to his chest and hugged them. He

brought his hand wearily across his eyes and bowed his head between his knees.

"The west," he muttered to himself. "The west!"

A recollection from his dream bubbled to the surface causing his heart to skip a beat. Scrabbling within the folds of his shirt, he withdrew a clam shell that hung around his neck – a gift from his parents. Limpic's hand trembled as he released the catch and the shell sprang open revealing the compass within. The needle floated in an iridescent liquid, giving the compass face a pearly glow. It bobbed to and fro and then drew still.

"North," gasped Limpic. "It points north. Phew!" Snapping the compass shut, he put it away and wiped his eyes. His compass was never wrong – the energy field still led north. "Heh, heh," he chuckled, chastising himself. "Limpic, Limpic, where did you think the needle would point – west?" He laughed at himself and then stilled. For some reason his mind continued to be restless.

He turned onto his stomach and peered curiously down into the murky depths of the ocean. His eyes moved a little to the left, to the reflection of the moon. It appeared to flicker and he immediately looked up. Although the night was cloudless and a million stars peppered the sky, the half-moon didn't appear as a solid, crisp body. Rather, it was smudged a little around the edges as though veiled by thin cloud.

Limpic stood up. His boat rocked a little, stirring up an odour of salt. "What's wrong?" he asked the moon. "What is it?"

Silence echoed back.

Strange, thought Limpic. He couldn't hear a thing. He was the only one of his kind, the only ullan, who could hear and interpret vibrations from everything around. It was his gift.

At first Limpic had found it hard to accept his 'gift' as

anything other than a curse. It had begun quite suddenly one night in autumn when he was around ten years old. He was awakened by an odd sensation deep within his ears – like something vibrating, or something opening and closing.

"It's just your sinuses," said his mother the following morning. By then the sensation had stopped and Limpic forgot all about it. A week later, Limpic's grandfather arrived from Caltain to stay with them. He was a scholarly ullan and had come to the family bothy in Lunaport by way of the Temple of Light, which housed thousands of books. He had brought many with him of all shapes and sizes and Limpic found them quite beguiling – even the smell of their pages and the creak of their leather.

The night before his grandfather was about to leave Limpic dropped to the kitchen floor grasping his head. "The lights are coming," he gasped, driving his fingers into his ears. Sparks danced behind his eyes and a strange, grating metallic sound threatened to burst his head open. He felt two large hands cupping his ears. There were two pops inside Limpic's head and just like that the sound stopped. He opened his eyes and found himself staring into the liquid, watery eyes of his grandfather.

"Better?" asked Grandfather. His grey whiskers twitched and he smiled reassuringly. Limpic's mother hovered in the background, wringing her hands and blinking rapidly.

"Wh ... what did you do?" stammered Limpic.

His grandfather lifted him to his feet. "I closed your inner ear." Before he could elaborate, Limpic's father came running into the kitchen unaware of what had just transpired.

"Follow me!" he shouted breathlessly. "They've come early – see." He gesticulated upwards as they gathered outside. Across the sky the northern lights danced and pulsed in various colours. Spirals of yellow here, wispy clouds of green there. Sudden bursts of colour like fireworks that left fading contours behind the eyelids of those who saw them.

"The lights are coming," murmured Limpic's mother, holding her hand to her mouth.

Later that night, with everyone in bed and while the small fire cast shadows around the room, Limpic sat on his grandfather's knee with a book opened. It was a large volume containing Limpic's family history.

"That," said Grandfather, tapping one of the pages, "is cousin Magragor." The page was a little yellow in colour and crumbling around the edges. The drawing was in charcoal and rather faded but it depicted a tall ullan with a strong defined jaw and piercing eyes. He was standing at an angle to the page. Over his shoulder was a length of tartan.

"As far as I can tell," said Grandfather in his deep, sonorous voice, "cousin Magragor is the only other ullan to have an inner ear. What it means is this. You can hear above and beyond the normal spectrum of sound. You have a frequency range exponentially greater than any creature on this planet. Everything that is vibrates right down to its tiniest part. Everything dances, everything sways, everything sings to the music of its being. And you, Limpic, oh, my boy, my beautiful boy, you can hear that music. See here." He opened another large book and pointed to a sentence that was underlined: *And then all creation sang. The stones, the sea, the sky, even the light. All that was rejoiced and their voices could not be quelled.*

"But how can *I* hear it?" said Limpic, and then he cried, "and how can I stop it?"

His grandfather held him close. "That sensation you felt in

your ears a while ago – like something opening and closing, those were your inner eardrums vibrating. As you are maturing so too are they. They're flexing their muscles. But just as you can close your nostrils when you swim underwater, so too can you close your inner ear."

"So I can block out the background noise then?" said Limpic, sitting up much straighter.

"If you want," chuckled Grandfather. "In time they will naturally close and you will have to open them when you want to listen beyond the normal range. And I believe you can do infinitely more. It was said that cousin Magragor even learned to communicate with things that had no lifeblood in them because he could manipulate frequency."

"So I can talk to the sea?"

"Maybe," said his grandfather laughing. He pulled Limpic close and kissed his head. "I believe you can do more than any ullan ever has. You have a gift – special ears, and a special brain to go along with those ears. One that can, and will with practice, decipher all the vibrations you hear until you can understand creation as though she herself were talking to you as I am. How else did you know that the northern lights were coming? You subconsciously unravelled the vibrations to receive the message within. Now off to bed for the both of us. I have a long journey back to Caltain tomorrow."

Limpic sniffed hard, recalling the night he learned of cousin Magragor and his inner ear. Perhaps that was why he had been given the Golden Coast to watch. Its accessible beaches and coves teaming with marine life had made it the crown of Dalbain – the glory of the Kingdom of Riada.

"Some ullan I am," he snorted gruffly. "The world's coming apart around me and I don't know why."

9

It was true. The Golden Coast was dying under his watch. On his travels from the Temple of Light in the west he'd seen the same thing over and over again: the golden beaches washed away, only to be replaced by shale and stone. He knew the same thing was happening on the shores of Caltain across the Northern Sea.

The ullans communicated through the Stone Thrones – portals that sent messages between Dalbain and Caltain. The chairs were set within basalt stones that led to a causeway beneath the waters of the Northern Sea. The throne of Caltain was perched at Fingreaal, a narrow peninsula that jutted south towards Dalbain. Limpic's High Throne was located within the Valla Stones. Once a month, when the moon was at her fullest, Limpic sat on his throne and spoke with Brona, of the clan of the Grey Whiskers. He was the head of all the clans of Caltain and wore a compass just like Limpic's. Brona's compass drew its power from the Southern Pole and always pointed south. Limpic's compass drew its power from the Northern Pole and always pointed north. Because the causeway that linked Dalbain and Caltain ran directly in line with this north–south energy line, Limpic and Brona were able to use their opposing compass directions to send messages to each other. They would sit in their thrones and their voices were carried north and south.

Of late, the messages Limpic had received were grim. Brona had been the first to report something amiss. About six orbits ago, not long after new year, on a visit to the most northern clans, Brona had witnessed strange silvery lights out in the west. He was to investigate further but each orbit brought about the same news. When Limpic suggested he send over his brothers to help, the answer had been a resounding no: Brona was head of the clans of Caltain and Brona would find out what was happening. The last time Limpic had communicated with him, Brona was a little on edge. He had witnessed the same phenomenon as before only this time much further south. And he had seen something else: a dark rider on a black steed wandering aimlessly across the sea on a cloud of shadows.

At the last full moon Brona had not returned to his post. Caltain, it seemed, had gone silent. That was when Limpic sent his two older brothers across the sea to find out what was going on. He also sent his sister south to find out what was happening around the southern shores of Dalbain. The gnawing feeling of unease only increased when his siblings never returned. Limpic's stomach turned over and over and he felt acid climbing into his throat. He should have acted sooner. He should have defied Brona's stubbornness and sent his brothers earlier – or maybe he should have gone himself?

Limpic shook his head and groaned. A feeling of helplessness swept over him and he wondered, not for the first, why he had been chosen to watch the Golden Coast. Brona was stronger by far; Limpic had watched him pick up the trunk of a pine tree at the Great Getherin' of the clans. He had tossed it aside as though it were merely a piece of balsa wood … but then he had been the first to fall under this terrible, silent curse.

"Clarity is what I need right now," Limpic muttered to himself, his head throbbing in the darkness. "I need to do my job and forget these troubles until I can talk to someone who has dwelt in the world longer than the watch of the ullans. Tomorrow I will visit Amoso. Now that it is nearing the summer solstice, he might speak with me."

With that small decision made he picked up his oars and headed for shore. He wanted to check on the little huddle of limpets he'd come across yesterday. He'd found them isolated in a small rock pool far from the water's edge. Having gently teased the tiny crustaceans to lower pools of water he wanted to make sure that they were adapting to their new surroundings. Somehow doing his job and shepherding the coast eased his worries a little.

He pulled efficiently on the oars but got nowhere – all of a sudden the sea didn't seem to know if it should ebb or flow. Limpic was only a hundred paces from shore and expected to row in easily on the incoming tide, but the waves began to swamp his little craft. His flower grew crimson and the skin burned.

"Whoa!" cried Limpic, abandoning his futile attempts to steer the boat. Instead he clung onto the lip of the shell until his fingers numbed. Swoosh! The sea fled into the night, taking Limpic's shell with it. With a violent lurch, Limpic somersaulted backwards and landed on the back of his neck with a bone-jarring thud.

"Oomph!" he grunted. He lay among swards of slimy seaweed trying to catch his breath. Staring up at the sky he saw the moon shuddering and growing larger and larger. A column of light reached out to it from the west.

"What the—" Limpic's scream jammed in his mouth and his stomach juices squeezed into his throat, souring his tongue. For a brief second he'd seen the sight that had cowed Brona – silhouetted against the moon was a dark rider on a black horse. The awful spectacle passed and Limpic was left with his heart hammering against his chest.

Scrambling to his feet he stood in ankle-deep water staring about him dumbly. "This … this can't be," he stammered. Crabs scuttled fearfully around his feet, scratching over the rocks and clicking their claws as they fell haphazardly among the seaweed. Limpic's mouth went dry. He peered saucer-eyed at the carnage all around as fish leapt into the air and thrashed blindly through the shallows. The air was filled with a sort of madness.

A thought flickered briefly through his mind and his stomach lurched again – his compass! Limpic withdrew the shell and snapped it open. His hand flew to his mouth and he started to shake. The needle was pointing west. Reeling, Limpic's legs buckled beneath him and he found himself kneeling in the water. He'd left it too late!

"Quickly! Quickly!" he screamed. His webbed hands seemed to clap together slowly, like they were moving in air as thick as treacle. "Come on, limpets, you have to move!" The futility of this statement wasn't lost on Limpic. The world was ending. Where was there to go?

He felt a sharp clicking sensation behind his nose and opened his inner ear. "Oh!" he gasped, cradling his head in his hands. A barrage of garbled sounds ricocheted around his skull like shards of broken glass. It seemed impossible to decipher any one on its own. Limpic slumped into the cold water and gritted his teeth. His eyes were streaming. With a deep breath he began to pick the sounds apart, isolating each into its own frequency by moving his inner eardrums. What he unravelled was a tale of woe.

"No!" cried the old, obdurate limpets. "We're limpets, I tell you! We stick to rocks. We don't swim much! Leave us be!"

Limpic clamoured to his feet and wrung his hands in frustration. He turned in circles overcome by the anguished voices all around him.

"Help us!" pleaded the crabs. He turned to grab them.

"No, us!" shouted the fish. He spun to reach one.

13

"I can't find my way!" cried a young lone limpet that had fallen from the rock face onto the tip of its shell. It was floundering helplessly and its fleshy body was vulnerable to the elements. Limpic pounced on it quickly and held it gently between his fingers.

"There, there," he panted, consoling the limpet and nestling it into a small fissure between some low-lying rocks. The limpet immediately stuck tightly to the rock and sealed itself off from the world outside. One safe but many still exposed.

Alarmingly, the flaps and splashes died away and the silence of death crept pitifully into the void. Limpic threw his arms about his face and sank to his knees.

"Ach, no!" he sobbed.

But another noise punctured his grief and caused his whiskers to tingle. He looked up and his breath caught. Waves. Legions of pounding, surging, frothing waves sweeping back to shore – and he was still a hundred paces from safety.

The first of them hit Limpic before he could even move. He was lifted from his knees and sent tumbling over and over in a pitch-black world of never-ending currents and bubbles. The cold cut through his face like blunt sawing knives. For a second or two he panicked and tried to fight back, disoriented and blind, heart pumping, head swirling. Seawater bit at the back of his throat and burrowed its way inside his ears – there hadn't been time to seal them properly or use the gills beneath his chin.

Focus! screamed his brain. *Don't fight the sea. Never fight the sea*! He forced himself to relax and pulled his hands across his forehead, shoving the heel of them into his eyes so he could close his second pair of eyelids; a transparent membrane that allowed him to see underwater.

His lungs, though bursting, were still full of air. Enough to

14

get him to the surface. He rolled onto his back and popped up out of the water like a cork from a bottle. He saw the moon briefly, swollen and sick, but alive, still alive and still in the sky. *No*! He fell back into the depths and brushed along the ocean floor. *Grab something*, his mind pleaded. *Grab a rock*. He found one but couldn't hold onto it – it was too smooth. Like it was made of ... silver! The entire seabed sparkled with it. Limpic gaped in horror. No wonder the sea was so ill – its very feet were turning into cold hard metal. His dreams were coming true! *Wrong*. His nightmares were coming true.

Just then, out of the corner of his eye, something raced towards him from the ocean bed. A flash of light erupted behind his eyes as his boat struck a glancing blow across his forehead.

"Oomph," he groaned and his mind fled and darkness rolled in. The sea ran away and the waves laughed. Like a rag doll, Limpic was carelessly tossed towards the shore.

The last thing he saw in his mind's eye was the dark figure silhouetted against a sickly, shuddering moon.

Chapter 2

When he came to, cool fingers were playing at his side, caressing him, stroking him.

"We're sorry, Limpic," said voices. Lots and lots of voices.

Limpic moaned in his semi-conscious state and rolled over, the sea gently lapping at his feet. The familiar smell of rotting seaweed filled his nostrils. He rose carefully then shrank back into the sand.

"Ow," he groaned. Pain throbbed in his head and when he closed his eyes bright colours pulsed behind his lids with every beat of his heart. A huge lump protruded on the right of his forehead. He touched the bump gingerly and winced. Immediately the sea gently swelled around his legs.

"There, there, sea," said Limpic, letting the water spill between his webbed fingers. "Do not trouble yourself so. I am well, and the bump has not opened into a wound."

This placated the sea sufficiently and it drew back to play with some gulls that had been hopping along the water's edge. It was back where it should be, covering the rocks and sandbars. The wind lifted briefly and sent tiny swirling columns of sand racing across the beach. A wave crashed with a great smack and fizzed and foamed before receding. Cloud shadows raced down the vast grassy banks that rose from the dunes to the land above and gulls wheeled and cried. Everything seemed normal.

"Aye, aye, aye," said Limpic cupping the last of the seawater dribbling through his fingers. He opened his inner ear fully and listened for vibrations. A cold flash of silver light exploded in his head.

"Oh!" he gasped, throwing what was left of the water to the sand. His brain froze and he forced his tongue to the roof his mouth. It was like he'd just eaten a mouthful of snow. He sat for a moment with his head in his hands, his breath hissing between his teeth in short, sharp bursts.

"Thank goodness," panted Limpic after a few moments had passed and his brain began to thaw. He lifted his eyes towards the sea, squinting as the sun reflected off its surface. Innocent and playful, it seemed like its old self.

"How can you be so normal?" he lamented. And then he said aloud the thought that had been rattling through his head. "You're turning to silver."

Limpic's stomach heaved and he dry retched on the sand. Wiping his mouth, he drew in a long, steady breath and held it. He let it out slowly and rubbed his stomach. "I must get to Amoso," he said. "Maybe he can tell me what to do." He found his hat lying next to him and put it on carefully, feeling very much like a small battered island after a storm.

"That's better," he said running his fingers over the hard rippled surface.

But how am I going to reach Amoso? he wondered, and his shoulders drooped. He stood in Crescent Bay and could easily see either end of the beach curling northwards. He scanned to the west, hoping he might find his boat. Nothing but sand, sea and dead fish. "I guess I'll have to walk," he said dejectedly. He glanced to the east and his eyes alighted on something whitish that was snagged beneath Mammoth Rock, a little way offshore. His boat!

Limpic's eyes crinkled in delight. Against all the odds he had found his hat *and* his boat. Small victories.

He pushed his hands into the wet sand and levered himself upright. His back creaked as he arched it. Now on his feet he was able to get a better picture of the shoreline to the east.

"I don't believe it," he muttered. His path to Mammoth Rock was barred by mountains of rocks and stones. The once golden sand was gone.

Limpic rubbed his jaw and made his way gingerly to the dunes behind the rocks.

"Ow!" he moaned, stubbing his toe on a rather sharp stone. He crawled up the embankment of sand that led to the dunes and checked his foot. The nail had lifted a little and a small blob of dark red blood oozed out. It throbbed painfully. He hobbled on.

The storm had cut great gouges into the shoreline and some of the dunes had been forced back so far that earth was appearing within the sand. Limpic picked an undulating path through the prickly hard grass, careful to avoid twisting his ankle in a rabbit hole. Every so often the wind lifted a little and Limpic could taste salt in the air. His stomach rumbled and he tried to remember when he had last eaten.

He emerged near Mammoth Rock, headed to the water's edge and carefully waded out. "Ouch," he yelped as the salt water attacked his damaged toenail, but soon the cold began to numb the pain.

The water was only just reaching his waist when he drew up alongside the bobbing limpet shell. It was upside down and snagged on a rock. Limpic counted the swells and waited until the seventh in a series. He jumped with the water and planted his feet firmly on the submerged rock face. In the same moment, just as the swell was at its highest and had lifted the limpet shell upwards, Limpic twisted it sideways. The boat righted itself immediately and Limpic allowed the sea to take it ashore while he followed behind.

Firmly back on dry land, Limpic gave his vessel a good checking over. He ran his hands around the lip and found one or two chips. The contours of the shell were rough and ridged and comforting beneath his fingers. A rumble in his stomach highlighted his hunger again. He leaned into the boat and opened the trapdoor at the very tip of the shell looking for his supply of dried seaweed stored in preparation for many days and nights of ocean dwelling. Limpic took a few handfuls and ate thoughtfully, chewing until the seaweed had all but dissolved in his mouth. It was tasteless. His tongue was still coated in stomach juice. He needed to find his oars if he was to reach Amoso. He walked around scanning here and there in case they had become trapped underneath the rocks and stones. He knew it was like finding a needle in a haystack.

Coming across a stream further into the sand dunes, he bent down and gargled until his tongue was clean. Then he eagerly lapped up the cool clear water until his thirst was sated. As luck would have it he found a lump of driftwood near the stream that would steer his shell admirably.

With practised fluidity, Limpic had his shell in the water and took his place at the helm in one easy movement. He sat up high near the front, sculling his craft competently with his makeshift oar. Before moving westward, he took a quick check of the limpet flock he had been nursing and found them to be relatively settled. They were still firmly attached to the rock where he had left them. A sure sign that they were alive and well.

"I'll be back soon," he promised them. Then, with a quick flick of his oar, he twisted his boat into the Westward Path, a channel of fast-moving water that was all but invisible to less-trained eyes. A tangible force took over the momentum of the boat and it sped along without any assistance. Swiftly Limpic left Crescent Bay behind and raced steadily west. He settled down, content to watch the shore roll by.

But the further west he travelled, the darker his thoughts became. The storm had given the coastline a thorough battering. Cliffs had collapsed, beaches were completely submerged beneath rocks and boulders, and carcasses of many sea creatures littered the little coves and bays. Above the surf the ominous thrum of a million flies filled the air. Limpic chewed his fingers and dreaded the coming of night. What if another storm hit? He quaked to think of it and hoped he reached Amoso before evening fell.

Upon rounding Devil's Toe, a treacherous outcrop of partially submerged rock, Limpic sailed past the Grand Cauldron, a large, sheltered cove surrounded on three sides by insurmountable basalt cliffs. On the western point of the cove the cliffs fell sharply into the sea to form the Valla Stones, where the High Throne sat. These stones were hexagonal in shape and created a narrow pathway that disappeared into the ocean only to reappear on the shores of Caltain at Fingreaal. Once a year, when the tide fell particularly low, this causeway was crossable on foot and that was when the Great Getherin' occurred.

"Humph," snorted Limpic with a smile as he remembered

the previous summer's festivities and all the laughter and fun that went with it. It felt like a lifetime ago already. His smile faded.

A shout roused him from his daydream, and when he looked towards the sound he saw a tiny figure jumping up and down on the Valla Stones. He threw out his oar and steered his little craft nearer to get a closer look. The figure on the rocks must have noticed his deviation for he relaxed and stood solemn and quiet with his hands folded behind his back. At closer quarters Limpic could see he was slightly taller than himself with a thin face and a rather sharp nose. His skin was pale – almost a light shade of grey, and he wore a band of red material around his forehead that kept his fair hair from falling into his eyes. He wore a shirt of chain mail over his dark red clothing and it was bound at the waist by a large red leather belt with a moon-shaped buckle. His legs were clad in more chain mail but his arms were bare. Two swords were strapped across his back.

"I am Truvius," called the pale stranger, stepping forward, "messenger of the elvern race. We need your help, Limpic. We need it desperately!"

Elverns this far north and needing his help? Curious. Limpic dug his oar into the water and drew himself as close to the Valla Stones as he could.

"How do you know my name?" he asked.

Just then his flower turned red and a great tongue of water reached out from the placid ocean and swept the elvern into the briny depths. Limpic jumped up, rocking his boat violently. Aghast, he stared disbelievingly at the empty space where the figure had been a moment before.

The sea had taken him.

Chapter 3

Without thinking, Limpic dived into the hungry waves. Unlike the previous evening he had time to seal off his eyes and ears, close his mouth and nose and allow the gills beneath his chin to feed him oxygen. He propelled himself towards the seabed and hooked his feet into a snag between the rocks.

A cacophony of creaking sounds swirled around him and silt lifted from the ocean floor to create a thick, gritty soup that whipped at his face. Even in the confusion of the noise and silt, Limpic knew he was somewhere near the mouth of the causeway, where he hoped that whatever the sea had in its belly would be regurgitated.

He rolled his eyes around frantically but saw nothing. He was just about to leave the safety of the rock bed when something rushed at him out of the gloom: another set of eyes – wide, terrified and bulging from their sockets. It was Truvius, the elvern. Limpic reached for him but the sea doubled back on itself and Truvius was whipped from his grasp.

Limpic steeled himself and crouched into a tiny ball so that the water couldn't sway him so easily; all the while keeping his eyes straining upwards through the churning sea, waiting for his chance to pounce. He could feel his heart beating wildly as the cruel waters tumbled over his head and pressed savagely around his ears. A small form appeared above, limply twisting in the merciless currents. With all his strength Limpic pushed off the seabed and thrust himself upwards. He grabbed hold of Truvius, cold and unresponsive, on his way to the surface and launched them both into the air.

"PAH!" he cried upon breaching. Thunderous booms replaced the muffled groans of the underwater world.

Limpic rolled onto his back, carrying the weak bundle on his stomach. White foam and spray stung his face and waves bubbled and fizzed around his ears. He waited for a wave to dash for the rocky shore and then followed along behind it, hoping he could get a footing before the next wave swept in.

As soon as he felt the cold, hard surface of the Valla Stones beneath his feet, Limpic turned and dragged his companion away from the water's edge, breathless with his exertions. Despite his chain mail, Truvius was far lighter than Limpic would have expected but he was still a dead weight. A huge wave pulled at Limpic's ankles but he stood strong, continuing his arduous tramp across the stones. By now his legs were burning and his throat was raw. Truvius began to choke and cough but Limpic didn't set him down until he was safely away from the reach of the sea.

Limpic bolted back to the water's edge and waited while the waves piled up all around him. He was in a precarious position, standing on the Valla Stones with the sea on three sides, but he didn't care. His head throbbed and his lungs burned. He balled his fists and raised them towards the elements, screaming.

"What's wrong with you? How dare you! *How dare you*!"

The sea continued to roll into shore, raising up lumbering

brutes of waves that arched for an eternity before exploding over the rocks. Their spray stung Limpic's face like fiery darts. It was as if the very powers that had created the world had been unleashed to destroy it. The wind howled, the sea roared and foam whipped into the air like little flecks of ash straining to leave an uncontrollable fire.

Waves seethed around Limpic's feet and rose up towards his knees. He was being pulled closer and closer towards the frothing writhing waters and *still* he shouted.

"How dare you, sea! How could you! What's wrong?" Tears blurred his vision and rolled down his cheeks. His shoulders tightened as he felt the shadow of an enormous wave rise up behind him, ready to cast him to his death.

But it didn't. Instead, the sea fell calm and shrank away.

Limpic drew in a large shuddering breath, staggered to his knees and fell onto his back on the firm surface of the Valla Stones. Exhaustion rolled in and washed away his seething anger.

"Oh," he sighed.

The pain in his head tried to rise from the depths but a trickle of sunlight fell on his face and drew it away. Somewhere close by an oystercatcher called, "Peep, peep," but by then Limpic was unconscious.

* * *

Limpic woke before Truvius. He blinked a few times and swallowed.

"Ugh," he moaned. His throat was on fire and there was sand and grit between his teeth. Then he remembered where he was and rolled over to sit up, his limbs heavy and the lump on his head pulsing. "I have to stop waking up like this," he croaked. He heard the elvern sleeping close by – his breath was laboured and his body clenched and relaxed repeatedly.

"Silver," muttered Truvius over and over and his eyelids twitched as he fought with some inner turmoil in his sleep.

Limpic's stomach tightened at the mention of silver and suddenly his plans were thrown into disarray. If the elvern knew something about silver, then Limpic would have to hear his story, but he couldn't just sit and wait for him to wake and he hadn't the heart to rouse him. And, anyway, it was getting late and Limpic dreaded venturing onto the water as night fell. But then the sea had taken the elvern during the day. It was almost like it had gone after Truvius.

Limpic got up quickly and scoured the cove looking for his boat. If he sat any longer dwelling on his thoughts and listening to the pathetic whimpering of the sleeping elvern, he thought he would go mad. He located his boat in the Grand Cauldron, halfway up the rocky shore. It had been completely upended and was now wedged tightly over a rock known locally as the Giant's Foot.

"Get over!" he panted through clenched teeth, using his pent-up frustrations to dislodge the shell and leave it the right way up. "Aye, aye, aye," he sighed wearily as he ran his hands over his little vessel. "You look like I feel – rough and battered but still seaworthy."

It was too far away from the sea for him to launch himself and the way was unsteady and full of boulders and rocks. It would have to wait till the morning when Truvius could help. At least it would be safe until then … unless the sea went mad again. A sobering thought.

Limpic opened the hatch and retrieved fishing line made

from his lint. He also found a hook, a float made from cork and a small weight. He would set his hands to work and perhaps his mind would rest.

His anger had fled. Now fear and a strange numbness gnawed in the pit of his stomach. Settling on the smooth contours of the Giant's Foot, he worked at the fishing line, forcing his nimble, trembling fingers to calm and repeat a procedure he'd practised a million times before. He struggled with the bait, held his breath, sighed and then resumed. His mind kept racing back to the sea, the moon and the elvern. What help did he require? If it concerned silver, then it concerned Limpic.

"Ouch!" he cried. Dark red blood welled from a prick on his finger. He sucked it and glared at the hook in his other hand. Muttering under his breath, he gingerly picked his way down to the water's edge and cast the line. There was an audible plop as it hit the water and the float bobbed on the surface.

Satisfied that dinner was near, Limpic turned his attention to gathering some kindling and driftwood, which seemed plentiful after another storm. He decided to set the fire on the Valla Stones so that he could keep an eye on the elvern and the sea. He also retrieved a leather skin from his boat and filled it with water from a small pool near the base of the basalt cliffs behind the Valla Stones. He quickly washed his face and gargled some fresh water to remove the grit from his mouth and cool his burning throat. Then he returned to where the elvern slept.

Within minutes the fire was glowing, two fish were caught, made ready and were slung over the flames. Now all Limpic could do was wait. He had already decided that in the morning he would take Truvius with him to see Amoso. Yes, that's what he would do – hopefully. He desperately wanted Truvius to wake up, to tell him why the elverns needed him. Too restless to just sit, he took out his bone knife and used it to file his fingernails, every so often glancing up to see if the sleeping elvern had woken.

Thankfully the smell of food was enough to soon rouse Truvius from his slumber and he hesitantly approached the small camp, stretching his shoulders and twisting his neck. He sat down beside Limpic and pulled his knees in towards his chest. Limpic forced himself not to look up in an effort to hide his distress. Instead, he leaned forward and poked a piece of the fish with his knife. When it broke away easily he grunted in satisfaction and removed it from the embers, setting it on a pan between himself and the elvern.

"Eat," he said with a nod.

Truvius looked at the dish suspiciously before following his host's example. He lifted up chunks of the fish, still hot from the fire, blowing them as they reached his mouth. Soon he was licking his fingers greedily and wiping grease from the side of his mouth and nose.

Limpic only pretended to eat. His stomach was in knots. He watched the elvern out of the corner of his eye. Truvius was eating quickly, apparently oblivious to his surroundings, but every so often Limpic caught him staring at his flower. Limpic pushed the pan towards Truvius, motioning for him to help himself to the rest of his fish. He angled his body away from the elvern's gaze and cast a few more pieces of wood onto the fire to stir it from slumber.

The hills to the west of the next cove, known as the Little Cauldron, had caused a premature twilight to descend across the Valla Stones. The Little Cauldron was just a smaller version of the Grand Cauldron, but its western point was made of two grass-covered mounds.

Soon a warm glow fell across their faces. Limpic crossed his legs and watched the flames rise higher and higher. Darkness was falling fast and the sea was simply a murmur in the wilderness. The night was warm but both Limpic and his visitor were reluctant to move back from the heat of the fire. There was a coldness hanging about that had nothing to do with the air temperature.

"Thank you," said the elvern when he had finished eating. "You saved my life."

Limpic drew his hands close and wiggled his fingers.

"Has it ever done anything like that before?" Truvius enquired. "I mean, the sea."

Limpic shook his head sadly and looked to where the sea was ebbing gently. His sea – or so it used to be.

"It was an incredibly brave thing you did. You know that, don't you?" insisted Truvius.

Limpic mumbled, unsure what to say and not used to praise. He jabbed at the fire with a piece of wood and then twiddled his thumbs. After a few minutes he cleared his throat and tried to keep his voice calm.

"The sea has been acting strangely. I have had to move limpets more times these past few months than I did *all* of last year." He turned to Truvius, his eyes wide and fearful, and placed a hand on the elvern's arm. "Please don't blame the sea," he whispered hoarsely. "It's my friend and I don't think it knows what it's doing. I think it's sick. I've never seen it act so unusually. I've never known the sands of the Golden Coast to disappear so quickly. I've checked the annals of history at the Temple of Light – it has never been recorded. *Never* in the history of the watch of the ullans!"

He turned back to the fire, sharply withdrawing his hand. If only his parents were still here. If only they hadn't sailed west on the great pilgrimage that all ullans take across the Pondus. He needed them now more than ever. His fingers scratched at the flesh around his flower.

Truvius squirmed uncomfortably.

"You must love the ocean very much, Limpic," he said in a low voice. "But you're right, the sea *is* sick, and it's not its fault."

Limpic furrowed his brow. "What is it?" he asked, turning his torso back round to face Truvius.

The elvern sighed long and hard and wiped his chin. "It's our fault, really. It's all our faults. Poor sea."

"What?" insisted Limpic. "What is it? What's wrong? Tell me!" He was trembling. Though they seldom nested by the shore, somewhere nearby a crow rasped. Limpic's stomach turned over and his teeth chattered.

Truvius played with his fingers and coughed nervously. "It's the moon," he whispered. "The moon is dying."

Chapter 4

"But ... but how?" stammered Limpic. He felt the bump on his head throbbing in the darkness. "I mean, why – what happened? How do you know?" His heart was pumping and adrenaline coursed through his veins. He knew the moon was sick ... *but dying.*

Truvius shifted uneasily and cleared his throat. "It began a few months ago, just after the new year – but first I have another story to tell you that goes back further still." He relaxed and settled himself into a more comfortable position, visibly relieved to finally say what he had come to say.

"We elvern folk are descendants of the High Elves. We've lived in forests our whole lives," began Truvius. "We love the woods, the trees, the open glades and shaded pools. We work the land anywhere we can, grow most of our own food and even keep beasts for milk and meat. We have a king, Zenith the thirteenth, and a queen who reign over our people, and for the most part we are a kind, peaceful and relatively simple folk. We have our sages – elders and heralds who advise the king. It is their gift. Zarkus, the king's closest advisor, is in charge."

Truvius gnawed on his lower lip for some time as though in quiet contemplation. He turned to Limpic. "Have you something to drink? My throat becomes dry."

Limpic nodded and handed him the skin of water. Truvius swallowed it greedily and the water ran down his chin. He did not wipe it away.

"All elverns have particular gifts that we use to help our people," he continued. "There are those who can study the way of the clouds and the air and so predict the weather patterns for our crops. There are others who grow our food and manage our way of life. I, for my part, have a military mind. I command the armies of the elverns. Though we are peaceful in general, we have our borders, and those outside them are not always as obliging as ourselves. We do not look for war, but if it comes," Truvius spread his hands across his knees, "we are ready." In the blink of an eye he pulled a long slender blade from his back and stuck it deftly into a small log that had rolled from the heat of the fire.

Limpic lifted his eyebrows in surprise at the speed and fluidity of the movement. "That is all very well," he said quietly, "but you have yet to explain anything about the moon."

Truvius snorted and a thin smile crossed his lips. "It's the gifts, you see," he said. "Our craftspeople can make the most sublime artefacts from almost any material – rock, wood, it doesn't matter. Why, we even have some women who can sew the very petals of roses together—"

"What about the *moon*?" insisted Limpic.

"Ah, well, I was just getting to that," said Truvius with a sniff. "The one material our smithies, miners and metalworkers love more than any other, in fact the one material *all* elverns revere more than any other is silver."

Limpic leaned closer. "Silver?"

Now they were getting somewhere.

31

Truvius held his hands to the firelight. "Look," he said, wiggling his fingers. There were four fingers on each hand, long and slender, ending in neatly trimmed nails. "Forget about my ring for now, silver though it may be. Look closely, what do you see? The colour of my hands, I mean."

Limpic peered closer and then sat back quickly, his eyes wide.

"Your skin! It's almost the colour of—"

"Silver," said Truvius. "Yes, Limpic, silver is in our blood. Quite literally. Small sediments of it are deposited there keeping us alive and giving our skin a silvery hue, especially under direct light. It gives us strength and speed beyond that of our enemies."

With a deft twist of his wrist, Truvius pricked the tip of one of his fingers so that blood oozed out. He held it up for Limpic to see.

"It's silver!" exclaimed Limpic.

Truvius smiled. "Yes, it is. Believe it or not, you also have metal in your blood – iron. That's why it's red. It keeps you alive. So it's not altogether so unbelievable to think that silver flows through the veins of my people. The High Elves revere the moon. We elverns *need* her to survive. We are children of the moon. Without silver, our bodies would collapse and die. It is the silver that fights off infections and diseases. Even some of your people use silver powder in their bandages to heal wounds."

"I suppose," said Limpic. "But, still, how does it get there?"

"Through our food." Truvius threw his head back and laughed when he saw the look on Limpic's face. "Don't worry, we don't eat bars of silver if that's what you're thinking!"

After putting his sword away Truvius continued. "We

harvest our food, hunt and fish at night-time. Then, once a month, when the moon has reached her zenith, we bring our food to her. She infuses it with her silvery light. Only a little, mind you – it isn't turned to solid silver, the same way the sun doesn't turn things to solid gold."

Dumbfounded, Limpic sat forward. "But, but," he stammered, "doesn't that mean *you're* killing the moon when you take her silver?"

Truvius shook his head. "No, the silver is only available on this one night, and we're only allowed to bring what food is required to sustain us for the coming month. The rest of the time the moon is free to replenish herself."

"Then what's gone wrong?" Limpic asked.

"Someone is taking more silver than can be sustained," said Truvius grimly. He fingered a white scar on his right cheek.

"Who?" said Limpic, narrowing his eyes. "And how?"

Truvius stared back. His own pupils were dark. His eyes were grey. "King Zenith's son. Our king-in-waiting, Prince Peruvius.

"The prince!" exclaimed Limpic with a furrowed brow. He was flabbergasted. "Why?"

"It's his particular gift," replied Truvius, peering into the embers of the fire. There was pain in his eyes. "He can turn anything to silver – solid silver. The moon herself bestowed the gift upon him on his sixteenth birthday in the Pool of Reflections by the River Shiman."

Limpic tugged at his whiskers. He couldn't believe what he was hearing. And yet ...

"I've told you the who and the how," whispered Truvius. "As to the why, our prince was betrayed and captured shortly after the new year celebrations. He'd gone out to seek some silver as a gift for his mother, our queen." Truvius stopped to catch his breath. His voice was thick with emotion. "I went with him, or at least I trailed behind. He's too fast even for me. The moon has given him strength and speed beyond that of *any* elvern I have ever known. Any elvern except Zarkus, of course. And Peruvius can see in the dark. He can see in the dark as though it were the middle of the day, so I lost him." Truvius stood up and began to pace. The scar on his cheek was getting whiter. "By the time I reached him he was already bound and gagged with a veil of gold over his eyes, unconscious on the forest floor. He would never have been vanquished so easily under normal circumstances."

Truvius's voice quivered. He turned back to Limpic and the firelight picked out tears in his eyes. "He was betrayed, you see. They knew the veil would take away his strength. Marah, his own uncle, the king's brother betrayed him." Truvius ran his fingers through his hair. "Marah is Zarkus's father so the treachery was even more keenly felt. He has always lusted after silver and was jealous of Peruvius's gift. That night I tried to help. I tried to save my prince but there were too many for me. All hooded and well-armed they took him … and left me to face my disgrace."

Now it was Limpic's turn to stand. He walked to and fro, his mind churning over what Truvius had just said. The prince was taken after the new year, which was when Brona had first reported strange lights to the west. Surely the two must be linked?

"Well, then, we must find the prince," he mumbled, more to himself than anyone else. "We'll leave in the morning – at once. We'll go to Amoso, the old man in the cliff – he'll know what to do. We have to."

"You must come with me first!" Truvius blurted out, gathering his wits. He grabbed Limpic's arm, squeezing until his knuckles turned white. "You must come to the elvern realm – to Tulwood. There are things I need to show you. Things you need to see. Then, together we'll go to this old man if you want. We'll need to gather supplies first anyway."

Limpic stared back at him. The elvern's eyes were dark and his thin mouth twitched uncontrollably. But what he said made sense. "I ... I will come with you." He prised Truvius's hands from his wrist. His long, slender fingers belied a grip of steel.

"Yes, yes, thank you. Sorry," mumbled Truvius. He took a deep, steadying breath and wiped his face with the back of his hand. "We can leave immediately – we must – using this." He removed something small from his pocket and held it up. "It's a Starstone. Our people make them from the dying embers of shooting stars. When you suck it and think of somewhere, you'll be transported there, but it can only take you somewhere you can picture in your mind. When I came to find you on the Golden Coast, the only place I could really remember were the Valla Stones. I only hoped that once I was here I would be able to track you down."

Limpic took the stone and held it to his eye. It was almost translucent and smelled like frost on a winter morning. He handed it back and shook his head.

"W... we'll leave in the morning," he stammered.

"But—"

"How did you even know to find me?" Limpic blurted out. He began to back away from Truvius, trying to find a reason to offload the burden laid at his feet. "You come here with this incredible story, and you know I live on the Golden Coast and you know my name. I mean, how can *I* even help?"

"My queen sent me," replied Truvius. He took a step toward Limpic. "She told me your name. She told me where to find you. She said I would know you by one thing." He raised his finger and pointed at Limpic's chest. "She said you would be wearing a white flower with five petals."

"But ... how could she know that?" whispered Limpic hoarsely. He sagged to his knees. His throat began to constrict and the muscles around his mouth twitched.

"I honestly don't know, Limpic. But my queen is wise. If she says you can help, then you can help. And I think your flower has a lot to do with it."

Limpic opened his mouth but nothing came out. He fingered the petals of his flower. "Give me a few moments to gather my thoughts," he croaked.

Truvius's shoulders tightened. "Very well, then," he conceded. He turned abruptly and sat by the fire, staring blankly into the dying embers.

Limpic left him and walked down to the northern tip of the Valla Stones where they dipped into the water. He shivered even though the night was warm. How could the elvern queen know him? How could she know about his flower?

"Aye, aye, aye," he murmured. He drew out his compass and flicked it open, rubbing his thumb over the smooth glass cover. He thought about his parents and his siblings. They knew as much about the flower as he did, which wasn't very much at all. There was a memory of the fire and the terrible fevers Limpic suffered, and then it was like they had all fallen asleep and woken after the storm had passed.

The needle of Limpic's compass bobbed to the west. He sighed and put it away and peered into the sky. A lighter patch of cloud was the only evidence that the moon had risen.

"I wonder if I dare open my inner ear again?" mumbled Limpic. "Just to hear the moon." He began to open his ears slowly, listening for the tell-tale buzz of vibrations. A small crackling was the only sound beyond the ebb of the water sucking and slurping around his feet.

"Nothing," said Limpic. At least there was no brain-freezing coldness this time. Maybe that was a good sign? The moon was up and nothing strange had happened. He dabbled his toe in the water. "Ouch!" he winced. His toenail smarted and the pain brought him to his senses. "We need to leave right now. I have tarried far too long."

A flash of light erupted from the west and the obscured moon began to burn through the cloud.

"My eyes," gasped Limpic. Silver sparks danced across his retina and he tried to blink them away. Through tears he saw a shaft of light falling from the moon and touching land somewhere north, roughly in the area of Fingreaal. Limpic's mouth fell open as a beam of silver light sped towards him under the sea. His blood ran cold. It was following the causeway from Caltain!

"No!" cried Limpic. The silver was about to take the Golden Coast. The flower on his chest turned red and began to smoulder and spit out a few flames like dry kindling. Limpic stared at it in horror.

"My nightmare!" he gasped. His chest muscles constricted until he struggled to catch a breath. An intense heat welled in Limpic's core and spread through his entire body. It roared through his head, down his arms and into his hands. It billowed through every part of him like a hot wind and he felt himself rising up onto the very tips of his toes as butterflies swirled around his stomach.

And then he felt strangely calm.

Limpic planted both his feet on the Valla Stones and squared his shoulders just as liquid silver, in the form of a grasping hand, burst from the sea. Water hissed from its gleaming surface.

"Stop," said Limpic, lifting both hands. His voice was steady. The hand recoiled with a sound like water falling on hot coals and the silver solidified.

Limpic stood for another second or two with both hands still raised. Everything was quiet and calm. He yawned, feeling strangely at ease and comfortable; as though his body was simply air. Then he tumbled backwards and caught a glimpse of Truvius staring down at him, wide-eyed and mouthing something nonsensical.

Truvius, he tried to say, did you see that? My flower just stopped the silver.

Chapter 5

"Are you sure you're alright?" asked Truvius. It was just past dawn.

Limpic nodded. "I feel good," he said. That was a lie. He didn't just feel good – he felt great. But also a little afraid. Had his flower really stopped the silver? What if it burned so much that the flames from his dreams returned? The ones that left him so ill afterwards. He touched the bump on his head. Was it smaller? His toenail no longer ached, that was for sure. And somehow he felt calmer. His mind was clearer. He rose to his feet on legs that were light as air.

"I'm sorry, Truvius," said Limpic. He put his hand on the elvern's shoulder. "I should not have tarried so long. We will leave immediately and go to Tulwood. We'll gather supplies and then come back here and go to Amoso."

Truvius cocked his head. "Only if you're sure." He turned and stared at the giant silver hand frozen in time and space. Splinters and shards of metal jutted away from the fingers so that it looked like a wave driven back by strong winds. The early dawn cast its shadow far across the calm blue sea towards the west. The waters clanked and frothed around its base.

"What do you think stopped it?" said Truvius.

Limpic threw a cursory glance at his flower and then back to the hand.

"It's a good sign?" said Truvius. "I mean some power was able to drive it back. Something must be working in our favour – right?"

Limpic nodded. "Aye," was all he said. He stared far out to sea, to Fingreaal. The sun flashed on a thread of silver. Limpic knew his brothers were near Fingreaal.

"And you're sure you're alright?" said Truvius, turning to Limpic. His brow was furrowed. "Last night your body was hot to the touch. You must have fainted from shock."

"Aye," mumbled Limpic, "must have been the shock." The shock of finding out that the flower he knew nothing about has the ability to drive back a power that has swallowed everything in its path.

"We should go," said Limpic. "Right now."

"Hold my hand and empty your mind," said Truvius with a nod. The elvern took two Starstones from his bundle and placed them both in his mouth. Immediately his face contorted into a hideous shape and his eyes watered profusely. At the same time a white curtain enveloped both him and Limpic, and the Valla Stones and the Golden Coast fizzled away into the vapour trail of a shooting star.

It felt like someone had just shot saltwater straight up his nose and Limpic wasn't sure whether his stomach had come with him or not. There was a lurch of movement followed by a fizzing sensation in his ears and then everything just went quiet.

"Ugh! Those Starstones have a very sour shell," spluttered Truvius, sticking out his tongue. "It's tough using your imagination when the thing in your mouth tastes like your face is going to turn inside out!"

"Why did you use two?" asked Limpic, shaking his head from side to side as if to drain water from his ears.

"One for each of us," replied Truvius. "And that makes it even harder to concentrate because it's twice the potency."

"You'd think you could make them taste better," said Limpic.

Truvius grinned. "The shock of their bad taste is the catalyst needed to begin the transport," he explained.

He and Limpic stood beneath a canopy of trees, just outside an archway that led into a castle. The sun was leaving little pools of light on the forest floor behind them and should have been stirring nature into action. But the woodland was silent – no birdsong, no bees. Limpic peered around and gasped in astonishment. Everything was silver. *Everything*. Flowers stood to attention like little silver soldiers. Blades of grass were as stiff as nails in a board and a small stream nearby looked more like a silver path cut in the forest floor.

Limpic turned to look at Truvius but the elvern's eyes were downcast and his shoulders were slumped.

"You see why we are so desperate," he croaked. "Our world is destroyed."

Limpic moved forward and touched the trunk of an oak tree. He shivered at its coldness and marvelled that he could still make out the roughness of the bark. This suggested that it wasn't covered in silver: it *was* silver from inside to out.

"Come," said Truvius, beckoning for Limpic to follow him and adding over his shoulder, "the king will be in the throne room."

"And the queen?" enquired Limpic.

Truvius hesitated. "No, she won't be with him. Stay close and do as I do."

They entered the castle and passed through an enormous marble hall decorated with hangings and paintings that had somehow escaped the silvery fate of the castle walls. The air was stale and subdued, stirred only by their passing, the silence broken only by their footsteps.

There were many intricate statues carved from silver. One, more beautiful than all the others, stood at the mouth of a vast winding stairwell. Her arms were outstretched as though reaching for something; her face had been captured between a moment of profound sadness and great surprise. It moved something within Limpic and he marvelled at the elverns' expertise in metalworking.

They reached the doorway to the throne room and paused. Truvius drew in a deep breath and entered. The heavy silver door creaked on its hinges and set Limpic's teeth on edge. It was eerily quiet. The king sat on a throne at the far end of a large hallway that was flanked on either side by tall marble pillars cloaked in silver. An empty throne sat beside his. More beautifully sculpted statues were placed around the room rather haphazardly. Truvius and Limpic had to manoeuvre between them to reach the king. It was all extremely odd.

And something else disturbed Limpic: his inner ear clicked and he opened it. It was picking up something beyond the stillness; beyond the normal spectrum of sound. Whispers – hundreds of them. Limpic paused for a moment but as soon as he tried to listen his inner ear grew silent. At the same time his flower flushed slightly pink.

"Your Majesty," said Truvius, bowing low to the ground.

His voice echoed around the high vaulted ceilings bringing Limpic back from his thoughts. He removed his hat and followed Truvius's example with a cursory bow. King Zenith looked up slowly. His eyes were empty and misted over and there were dark rings beneath them. His skin was more grey than silver and his beard was unkempt, straggled beneath thick lips and round nose. He had a fuller frame than Truvius but similar eyes. Although he sat motionless, almost slumped in his throne, his fingers drummed silently. A plain silver band was the only thing adorning them. He wore white robes, a silver cloak and a silver belt with a buckle that clasped together to form a full moon. On his head was an intricate silver crown. In the middle of it was set a black onyx stone that continued to pass through the phases of the moon as a light from within moved across its contours.

"I have brought Limpic," began Truvius, "from the Golden Coast."

Limpic stepped forward timidly but the king's gaze went right through him.

"Limpic?" he muttered with a shake of his shaggy hair. He rubbed his eyes and mumbled to himself over and over again, "Limpic? Limpic?" Then some seed of recognition took root in his mind, his eyes cleared and he raised his shoulders. "Of course, Truvius, you had gone to seek the aid of Limpic and here he is."

The king leaned forward and held out his hand. Limpic, unprepared for court etiquette, thought the king wished to stand, so he took hold of the extended arm and pulled him to his feet. Truvius's eyes almost fell out of their sockets and the king's mouth dropped open in surprise. He threw back his head and laughed.

"Oh, wonderful creature!" he roared. "Wonderful, innocent Limpic. But you have served me well already. I had quite forgotten that I could stand upon these legs, such has been my despair."

"Thank you," said Limpic.

"You have heard of our trouble, then," said the king, his countenance becoming grave again. "It lies heavily upon me – the loss of my son, the betrayal by my brother."

"Begging your pardon, Your Majesty," said Limpic, "but why did your brother take the prince? Does he love silver that much?"

"Father is unwell," said a figure sliding silently from the shadows behind one of the marble pillars. His long cloak, belted at the waist, trailed along the floor. It gave the illusion that he was actually floating across the hall. His arms were folded behind his back as he drew up alongside the king.

"My advisor, Zarkus," said the king, nodding. "Truvius's older brother."

Brother! So that made Marah Truvius's father. Limpic peered across at his elvern companion but Truvius's eyes were firmly fixed on the floor.

The king, unsteady on his new-found feet, stumbled and Zarkus was forced to grasp him quickly and hold him upright. His fingers were long and slender like Truvius's, but his nails were not as neatly trimmed. In fact, they were rather long and crooked. He too wore a band of plain silver.

As soon as the king was steady, Zarkus withdrew his arm and folded it behind his back. He cast an appraising glance at Limpic who in turn met his stare. Zarkus's eyes were black, maybe the effect of the dark rings around them, and his head was egg-shaped, growing wider near his scalp. His hair was thin and the remainder of it was combed sideways. He sported a rather feeble beard that made his thin lips appear even slighter than they were, and he had an odd scar just above his right eye.

44

On seeing the two brothers together their similar features were clear: sharp noses and slender lips.

Limpic shivered a little under Zarkus's gaze. His eyes seemed sleepy or glazed over. Limpic was glad when he turned his attention to Truvius who was standing awkwardly with his head bowed.

"You disobeyed a direct order!" snapped Zarkus.

"I … I thought it best—" muttered Truvius, not lifting his head.

"You thought nothing!" shouted Zarkus. His voice was sharp and clear but there was a hint of something deeper in it as it reverberated around the capacious hall. "You are not here to *think*," he continued. His hand reappeared from behind his back and the long finger with the ragged nail stabbed the air. "You left our borders unprotected," said Zarkus with menace. "Goblins and hobgoblins are running amok. They've even been sighted as close as Mirror Lake." Zarkus began to pace, circling Truvius before making a beeline towards Limpic. "You ran off on some ill-conceived quest to find a creature that we know very little about – you didn't even know where he lived!"

Limpic smarted under Zarkus's glare and he felt the inside of his nose prickle. "I'm Limpic," he said and proffered his hand. "At least now you know my name. And to answer your question, I live everywhere and nowhere. The Golden Coast is my home."

Zarkus's gaze flitted from Limpic's face to the flower on his chest. He blinked rapidly and stepped back, ignoring Limpic's hand. He snorted and turned away abruptly. But Limpic had seen the change, fleeting though it was: Zarkus's eyes had momentarily come to life. Limpic stroked the flower petals.

"He had my permission to go," said King Zenith

breathlessly, his voice low, almost breaking. "We must explore every available option, Zarkus, please—" He began to cough so forcefully that Truvius stepped forward to take hold of him.

Zarkus's features remained hard. He licked his lips, picked at the scar above his right eye and shrugged. "Very good, Your Majesty," was all he managed to say before disappearing into the shadows as quickly as he had appeared.

The king sighed. "Walk with me, Limpic," he said, "for I haven't stretched these legs of mine in such a long time. Truvius, you will come too."

They moved slowly through the myriad of statues forcing them to walk one in front of the other.

"Truvius has informed you of our links with the moon?" said the king, shuffling at the head of the line. His feet made little swooshing noises on the smooth floor. He stopped and turned.

Limpic looked up and met the king's eye, giving a brief nod. He guessed he would be as tall as Zarkus if he stood at his full height, but he was stooped over and his arms were wrapped across his stomach like he was hugging himself.

"I am Zenith the thirteenth," continued the king sullenly, "but I sit on the throne of my brother, Marah. My father, the twelfth Zenith, placed the Kingdom of Tulwood into my hands because he feared that Marah's heart was too cold – that it had become like the silver he so badly wanted." The king shuffled off once more. "My father was wise. While the rest of us revered the moon and gave thanks for her sustenance, Marah gazed upon her lustfully. A heart like that could never rule over a land and a people so connected with silver."

King Zenith shook his head sadly. "My father was wise but perhaps a little tactless at times. He knew that Marah was flirting with the darker side of life. Tragedy, yes, great tragedy had befallen him, all of us, but it had also given birth to great beauty." The king glanced kindly at Truvius. "Marah could not see that beauty, only injustice. He abandoned his family and invited misery upon himself. He found fault and error everywhere, sought solace in all the wrong places. He dwelt on a past that could not be changed. He destroyed a future that could have been wonderful. Losing the throne only compounded his misery." He halted and his chin settled on his chest.

"He conspired with our enemies, Your Majesty," said Truvius sharply. "He tried to buy their allegiance so that he could take your throne. That's why he wants the silver so badly. That's why he took Peruvius."

Limpic was taken aback by Truvius's apparent indifference to his own father. King Zenith, however, waved off Truvius's attack. He began to shuffle again, out into the large hall. "Yes, yes, I know, Truvius. I know all that. I can hardly believe it. My own brother conspiring with goblins and hobgoblins and goodness knows what other creatures of the night."

"But he did," insisted Truvius. "And he does. Goblins are rampaging through our borders unmolested, and our armies aren't fit to hold them off. Our people weaken. Silver no longer flows through our veins as it once did. We are dying, Your Majesty. We are dying with the moon."

The king groaned and his shoulders sagged. He leaned up against the statue at the bottom of the huge stairwell, tears in his eyes. "I know, Truvius. I know. But I have little fight left in me. I feel old, cold. Where do we go? Where do we start? Marah has taken Peruvius somewhere we cannot find. Somewhere so powerful that he can turn things to silver from great distances and almost at will. Such destructive forces have never been wielded before. The moon will not reach her zenith. She cannot sustain the loss."

"Limpic will show us the way, Your Majesty," insisted Truvius. He placed a hand on the king's shoulder. "Limpic has a plan – a place to start."

The king turned to Limpic, faint hope rising in his tired old eyes. "Do you?"

Limpic licked his lips and stepped forward. "I know somewhere we can start," he said kindly. "Someone, actually. The one we call Amoso. He knows … things. I was on my way to meet him when I bumped into Truvius—"

"He saved my life," interrupted Truvius. "He pulled me from the sea, a wild sea."

The king straightened a little. "Is this true?" he asked.

Limpic looked at his feet. "I simply did what anyone would do," he mumbled.

The king peered long and hard at Limpic, searching him up and down until his gaze settled on his flower. A tiny flicker of light appeared in the depths of his eyes and he smiled.

"I believe you can help us, Limpic," he said. "I believe you can save us. I believe my queen and I have found our champion."

"Begging your pardon, Your Majesty," said Limpic. "But where *is* the queen?"

"Right here," whispered King Zenith, tenderly stroking the face of the figurine at the foot of the stairs. "Peruvius turned my queen to silver." Then he spread his arms, taking in all the other statues. "Along with most of my household."

Chapter 6

"Just throw it down there," snapped Truvius. It was a little past noon on the same day.

"Yes, Your Majesty," replied Brutonia affably. He grinned broadly and dumped his load beside an ever-increasing pile of cargo.

He was an enormous elvern. A good head and shoulders taller than Truvius with a great barrel chest and arms as thick as Truvius's neck. He had studded leather bands around his wrists and wore a long copper chain-mail vest that covered the tops of his legs and was secured in the middle by a broad black belt. A double-headed axe-like weapon was slung across his back. It was called Dunnehammer but Brutonia occasionally referred to it as "The Attitude Adjuster". It had an axe blade on one side and a blunt hammer on the other.

"A few more things to get and we can be off," he called over his shoulder before disappearing through a door just off the main hallway.

"He's big," said Limpic with a smile and a shake of his head.

Truvius chuckled. "Just don't say that to his face … and don't stare at him too much either. Brutonia hates that."

Limpic nodded. He gazed across at the statue of the queen

and sighed. What did she know?

"It's so quiet," he whispered.

Truvius didn't look up from sorting through their supplies. He merely grunted.

"It must have been awful," continued Limpic, still gazing at the statue, "for the king, I mean."

Truvius blew out his cheeks and rose slowly. He too peered at the figurine. "I had returned to the border along with Brutonia. He's my second in command. We were desperately trying to staunch the flow of goblins and hobgoblins marauding through our lands." Truvius fingered the scar on his cheek. "They have become more persistent and tenacious. They know we are weakening."

Truvius closed his eyes and his shoulders tightened. "There was nothing we could do. We saw a strange light out to the west and the column of silver reaching down from the moon. We knew it was near the palace, so I left our commanders and took Brutonia. We raced back as quickly as we could but we had to fight our way through small pockets of goblins, so it took us the whole night." Truvius opened his eyes. His mouth pursed and his nostrils flared.

"We found the king half mad, pawing at that statue and crying out for the queen. He was rambling about a silver mist. He said there was shouting and wailing and then … silence." Truvius shuddered. "I forbid any of my soldiers from carrying Starstones in case they take the easy way out in the heat of battle. That night, I sorely wished I hadn't passed that decree. Maybe if we'd gotten here sooner—"

"You would also be statues of silver in the king's castle," said Limpic.

Truvius lowered his head.

"And yet the king wasn't turned to silver," said Limpic, thinking aloud.

"He's no threat now," replied Truvius. "You've seen how he is yourself. A shadow of a once proud, noble elvern. He just sits and grieves."

"And Zarkus – your brother. He wasn't turned either?" said Limpic.

Truvius flinched. He opened his mouth to say something and then seemed to think better of it. In the end he simply shrugged and knelt by his bags, fiddling with something inside.

Limpic wondered about Zarkus. Truvius's relationship with him was strange to say the least. He looked at the queen. What do you know?

"The queen didn't sit idly by after Peruvius's disappearance," said Truvius. He was peering into his bag. "She was quick to send out scouting parties. Seven to the north, seven to the south, seven to the east and seven to the west. They all returned empty-handed after a few months ... except those who had headed—"

"West?" said Limpic.

Truvius raised his eyebrows and nodded slowly. "Those who headed west never returned – they just disappeared. But how do you know?"

Limpic drew out his compass. "Look," he said. "The needle is never wrong."

Truvius rose from his crouched position and peered at the compass.

"West," he murmured.

"West," confirmed Limpic, tucking the compass away again. "The energy field has shifted. Something powerful is happening out west. You've seen the light over there at night, as have I."

51

"But ... but the compass only points to the most powerful pole – the North Pole," stammered Truvius. "There is no Western Pole. Travel too far that direction and you only find the east."

"Aye," said Limpic. He began to pace the floor. "So what do we know? Put it all together and what do we know? Peruvius has a gift that enables him to take silver from the moon. He was kidnapped by an uncle jealous of this gift, possibly taken west – agreed?"

Truvius nodded.

Limpic folded his arms behind his back and continued to pace. "Since then silver has been flowing from the moon and turning things to solid silver. It's a fair guess to assume someone, most likely your father Marah, is manipulating Peruvius's gift to turn the moon into some kind of weapon. Agreed?"

"Agreed," said Truvius. "But the fact the king wasn't turned to silver indicates that Peruvius's gift can be manipulated to turn one person to silver and leave another."

Limpic stopped pacing. His shoulders slumped a little. "The west is a very big place, Truvius. I hope Amoso can give us a better lead."

Suddenly Truvius's eyes brightened. "Come to think of it, I know that the queen gave explicit instructions for each group of scouts to seek the guidance of a sage before embarking on their respective quests. I think the western scouts were to begin searching at the Valla Stones. It would have been around the spring equinox."

"Well, Amoso is the only sage I know west of there," said Limpic, smiling eagerly. "And Amoso only speaks at certain times of the year. The spring equinox being one of them and the summer solstice another, so maybe we are on the right track already."

Truvius grinned. "No wonder the queen sent me to find you, Limpic. You've got us on our way and we haven't even left Tulwood."

Limpic's smile faded. The queen again. He stroked his flower.

Truvius cleared his throat awkwardly. "The queen was searching constantly, Limpic," he said. "Her only son had been kidnapped. After the household had been turned to silver, and after the king had composed himself a little, he gave me a note written in the queen's handwriting. It told me about you and your flower." Truvius's mouth twitched and he stared at the flower on Limpic's chest. Limpic knew what he wanted to ask.

Limpic took a deep breath. His mouth felt dry. "This flower—"

"There," said Brutonia, dumping the last of the things on the pile. He scratched below his chin with a large stubby finger. "Daggers, swords and bags for carrying things. And a bundle of fire rope forged in the mines of the dwarves. It's said it can't be broken, even by the sun itself!" Brutonia raised his shoulders sceptically only to shrug them back down. "But what do I know?"

He glanced over at Limpic and then at Truvius. "Phew, you could cut the atmosphere in here with a knife." He clapped Limpic on the back. "Come on, lad, as my father used to say, 'things will be better in the morning'. That's my motto."

"You're just saying that because you can't wait to leave," growled Truvius. "Things *will* be better for you in the morning. I've heard about Sophia and Andra bickering over you, so come on, Brutonia, which one is it? Which one gets the great honour of your betrothal?"

"Please," replied Brutonia waving off Truvius's question with mock sincerity. "We have more important things to take care of."

"Like what!" demanded a voice from behind.

Brutonia grimaced and muttered something under his breath. An elvern girl was standing in his shadow with her hands on her hips. Her plump cheeks were twitching and her green eyes burned. Whether it was Sophia or Andra, Limpic couldn't tell.

"Oh, for a diversion," said Brutonia sighing and turning slowly.

Limpic's flower glowed yellow and his chest felt hot. The air suddenly crackled and there was a bright flash of white light and the smell of winter frost. Limpic turned his face away to shield his eyes and stumbled backwards to the ground. When he looked round he saw a silver figure prostrate on the marble floor. Her right arm was outstretched and her hand was caught in the motion of throwing something. Her mouth was open in a soundless scream. The thing she had thrown rolled across the floor and only came to a stop when Brutonia put his foot on it – some kind of shell. The brief stunned silence that followed the clattering of the shell was punctuated by the screaming of the elvern girl.

"Tabitha!" shouted Truvius, rushing to the silver statue on the floor. He looked back over his shoulder. "One of the seven sent to the west. She must have come home using a Starstone – but she was turning to silver and it's daylight. The moon isn't even up! How can that be?"

Limpic swallowed and took his time getting to his feet. His knees felt quite wobbly, so much so that he almost tiptoed over to the shell to pick it up.

Brutonia had his arm around the sobbing elvern girl. "It's alright, Sophia, don't look," he murmured. The girl had her head buried deep into Brutonia's large chest. Her dark hair trembled with her shoulders.

"I won't let it get me! I won't!" she screamed, beating Brutonia's chest. "The silver took my father! I've nothing left!"

Brutonia looked at Limpic and jerked his head towards the door. He led Sophia away and her sobs retreated into the distance. A disconcerting silence fell again.

Limpic and Truvius stared at each other and then the silver elvern on the floor; an elvern who moments before had been flesh and blood.

"Look, one of her boots is missing," said Truvius.

Limpic gulped. "We need to get a move on," he said quietly. His heart was still thudding in his chest.

He glanced down at the shell. It sat comfortably in the palm of his hands, iridescent in the low light. One end was fatter than the other and contained a large opening. The shell spiralled into a point where there was another, smaller opening.

"Some kind of conch shell," said Limpic.

Truvius came and stood beside him. "I guess we'll be needing it."

"It must be important if she thought to return it to Tulwood," replied Limpic.

"Tabitha was a good elvern," said Truvius solemnly. "She fought nobly in the wars with the goblins."

"She *is* a good elvern," said Limpic. "She's another reason for us to figure out what's going on."

They quietly returned to their packing, although Limpic found himself constantly staring at Tabitha and wondering if the same fate lay in store for them.

***

"I found that weapon you asked for," said Brutonia, striding into the room later in the afternoon.

He carried a bow made of dark wood that sparkled like the night sky. The string was brilliantly white and strung to pieces of bone attached to either end of the bow. Limpic and Truvius were finishing some sandwiches. The bread was already stale as food was running short. What was left was already packed.

"I'm sorry we couldn't leave earlier," he muttered handing the bow to Truvius without making eye contact. "It's just, well, Sophia's resting in her room now." He glanced across at the stricken form of Tabitha. "She still feels guilty."

"Guilty?" Limpic asked.

Brutonia looked to his feet and pawed the floor with his foot. "She was far away in the forest when the silver column hit, so she wasn't turned."

"But that's nothing to feel guilty about," said Limpic.

Brutonia smiled sheepishly. "She'd been fighting with her father … about me. Her father said I was only toying with her, that she deserved better. Sophia had defended me."

"Ah," said Limpic. He scratched behind his ear.

"It's alright, Limpic," said Brutonia with a rueful grin. "I actually think her father's got a point."

"Humph!" snorted Truvius with a shake of his head. "Everything's a joke to you, Brutonia."

He lifted the bow in his left hand and grabbed the string as if to fire an arrow. Turning deftly, he aimed at the inside of the door, releasing an arrow that appeared from nowhere. It quivered for a second within the wood and then dissolved and fell away like dust. The bow glowed a little and gently hummed.

Truvius grinned at Limpic's surprise. "The Bow of the Nimue, always armed and always deadly." He handed it across. "A small comet once fell from the constellation of the Archer. It struck a tree not far from here. Past elverns crafted the tree into a bow and engrained it with stardust from the rock. Try it."

Limpic flexed the bow, lifted it to his eyes and drew back the string. Immediately, where there had been nothing, an arrow, straight and true, sat in his sight. Limpic released his fingers and the arrow hit the door a little way off Truvius's mark. No sooner had it stuck fast it fell away.

"Excellent shot!" bawled Brutonia. "He's nearly as good as you, Truvius!"

Truvius nodded approvingly. "Next time do not sight the arrow. Look to the spot you want to hit and the bow will do the rest."

Limpic nodded.

"Now, Brutonia, did you find the Solaars?" Truvius asked.

The big elvern grinned and rooted through one of the bags in the pile. He pulled out three large crystal-like pebbles, each about the size of Limpic's fist. He also drew out what appeared to be three batons. In one end of a baton he pushed a Solaar and handed it to Truvius. Truvius shook it and immediately the pebble glowed, casting out a bright shaft of light.

"Leave these stones in the sun for a day and they capture enough light to glow for a week," he mused.

"That could be very useful," said Limpic taking one of the Solaars and a baton.

"Right," said Truvius, heaving a bag over his shoulder. "Now that we're all ready let's go."

Limpic lingered. "I, ah, don't suppose you know anyone who

could keep an eye on some of my limpets while we're gone."

Brutonia creased his brow and thought for a moment. "Horas!" he said with a click of his fingers. "He just came back last night from collecting herbs on the mountain trails."

"Go and get him," Truvius commanded Brutonia, "and meet us at the Grand Cauldron. We'll take the supplies ahead. Quickly now!"

Chapter 7

Limpic helped Truvius gather the rest of the equipment before they stepped out into the silent silvery forest. They carried the canvas packs on their backs and two more between them. Truvius also had a small bag of Starstones attached to his belt. As they moved stealthily through the woods, Limpic kept peering over his shoulder. His inner ear was vibrating again; he was sure there were whispers behind him. And then he heard a crow caw and the skin around his flower smarted and the petals burned red.

"Not now," muttered Limpic. He placed his hand over the flower in case Truvius saw it. Then he had a thought. *What if it's a warning?*

"Here will do," said Truvius as they stepped into a clearing that was free from silver. "I just don't want to use the Starstones with all that silver around me." He took one and then handed the bag to Limpic. "See you at the Grand Cauldron." Just as he popped the Starstone in his mouth he cried out and pointed, "Limpic, look— " but before he could finish the sentence he disappeared in a shimmering flash.

Limpic instinctively threw himself to the ground. Something whizzed over his head and thudded dully into the trunk of a tree where Truvius had been standing merely seconds before – a black arrow. Limpic rolled onto his side and withdrew the Bow of the Nimue. Suddenly the other side of the clearing erupted and myriads of stooped and disjointed forms lurched from the undergrowth.

"Goblins!" cried Limpic. He loosed an arrow, remembering to sight it by looking to the target. It hit the lead goblin right between the eyes but rather than the creature falling forward stone dead, it vaporised, leaving a shadowy residue hanging in the air.

Limpic had no time to process it as something hit the ground right by his head – an axe. He rolled to his left and loosed another arrow only to see it go wide of its mark. With a sickly feeling he saw that the goblins had spread out around the clearing and were surrounding him. A shape moved to Limpic's right. He turned the bow's shaft and deflected a savage thrust of a rusty blade. Then he was entangled with a goblin and the two of them were rolling over and over. The smell was disgusting and the creature's breath was stale and rank. For a moment Limpic peered into its eyes. They were completely black. The goblin drew back its fat upper lip revealing large blunt teeth. It snarled and vaporised right before Limpic's eyes.

"Go!" commanded a voice.

"Zarkus!" gasped Limpic.

"Go, Limpic! Find Peruvius," shouted Zarkus. Something like silver lightning erupted from his fingers and half of the goblins vanished. He leapt into the air, spinning like a top, throwing shards of lightning to the right and left.

Limpic scrambled away. He found the Bow of the Nimue and his pack. He desperately scurried through the grass looking for the bag of Starstones that he had dropped in the panic. They had spilled open and scattered but he managed to find one and shoved it into his mouth just as a shadow fell across him. He turned and shielded his face as the ground lurched beneath him and he smelled frost.

"Limpic!" cried Truvius, clutching his face between his hands. "Are you hurt?"

Limpic took a deep breath. "No, no," he gasped, although his heart was rattling in his chest. "I think I'm fine." He sat up and shook his head. It felt full of water. He dusted bits of grass from his clothes and then sniffed. The air was salty and he heard gulls crying in the distance. He looked around. They were alone on the Valla Stones. The elvern's face was ghastly white and his hands were shaking violently. "I'm alright, Truvius, honestly," said Limpic, slowly rising. The stones were hard and cold beneath his feet in sharp contrast to the soft mossy forest he'd just left. "Zarkus saved me."

"Zarkus?" said Truvius quickly. His face darkened. "What was Zarkus doing there?"

"I don't know," replied Limpic, wiggling a finger in his ear. "But I'm glad he was or this quest might have been over very quickly."

Truvius made a clucking sound with his tongue. "Goblins," he muttered, "at the very gates of Tulwood." He shook his head.

"Unlike any goblins I've ever seen," said Limpic. "Their eyes were completely glazed over in darkness, and they didn't die the way they're supposed to either. They just kind of ... vaporised. I'd say there wasn't much goblin left in them."

Truvius turned and peered out to sea. His hands were behind his back, just like his brother. "It's the same on the borders." He sighed. "There is no love between goblins and elverns – in fact, there is no love of goblins at all. But recently these ... things.

They aren't like normal goblins."

"It's like they're possessed," said Limpic. "Like there is something driving them, something very dark." He watched Truvius closely. Limpic was sure the elvern knew more about the goblins than he was letting on.

Truvius didn't turn around but continued to look out into the blue. When he spoke his voice was flat. "You think me callous." he said. "You think I speak ill of my father."

"I know nothing of it," replied Limpic truthfully.

"I am the tragedy the king spoke of. I am the shadow that fell across my family. Mother died giving birth to me and Father went mad. I was raised by the king and the queen. Peruvius is like a brother to myself and Zarkus." He let his abrupt statement settle for a second and turned. "Perhaps that's why the king wasn't turned to silver. So he too could experience loss." Truvius blinked and then shook his head. "Shall we get your boat in the water?"

Limpic nodded, unsure of what to say. "The sooner we find Peruvius the better," was all he could muster.

The boat was where Limpic had left it and the two of them wrestled it down the rocky cove and into the sea. They placed all their things into the bottom of it, including the shell from Tabitha, the fallen elvern.

Truvius stuck out his bottom lip and scratched his chin. "Do you think it will carry the three of us?"

"Oh, aye," replied Limpic. "I once had two mermaids and a merman in it, nay problem."

"Very well then," said Truvius. He glanced up at the huge silver hand still reaching from the water. Sunlight filtered through its open fingers and danced on the surface of the sea, which fizzed around the peculiar structure as though it were simply a rock. Truvius raised his eyebrows and glanced at Limpic.

They looked up when a white light streaked past, taking them by surprise. It dashed off to the east, circled a column of stone just above the Devil's Toe and raced back towards them. Limpic's whiskers tingled and he instinctively ducked. At the last moment the light rose up and hit the grassy hills on the far side of the Little Cauldron.

"Horas has landed," said Truvius with a chuckle.

By the time Brutonia and Horas reached the Valla Stones they were a sorry sight indeed.

"You don't change your mind at the last minute!" Brutonia scowled, gingerly rubbing a bruise above his eye. "We could have ended up on the other side of the moon."

"Well, then, you should have taken your own Starstone instead of hitching a ride with me," replied Horas indignantly.

"You know I hate the taste!" grumbled Brutonia. "And, as my father used to say, 'if we were meant to fly we—'"

"Oh, bully for him!" snapped Horas. "He didn't *used* to say anything. He's *still* saying *everything*. That's why he was sent to the borders where he could *bore* the enemy to death!"

Truvius simply puffed out his cheeks and Brutonia looked to the heavens. Then Brutonia's eyes widened. "Was that always there!" He pointed at the silver hand.

"Yes," replied Truvius. "Yes, a huge silver hand has always towered over the Valla Stones."

Brutonia grinned and held up his hands. "Point taken, Truvius, but as my father used to say, 'sarcasm is the lowest form of wit'."

"Humph!" grunted Truvius.

Horas was rather portly and had a long thin nose that

sprouted into something similar to a broccoli crown. His fair hair was combed back off his forehead. He sniffed the air and gave himself a great shake, and the pots and pans that were tied around his neck clattered and banged in unison.

"Well?" he demanded.

"*Well*, what?" snapped Truvius.

"Where are these limpets I've been sent to babysit? After all, they're more important than my green vegetables."

"Oh, you'll have to walk back east," said Limpic. "Through the tunnel at Gid Point and across the beach. The limpets are in a little cove just the other side of Mammoth Rock. They shouldn't need too much attention if the sea behaves itself. They know how to find the food they want."

Horas sniffed and stared at Limpic as though seeing him for the first time. "Yes, I know where you're talking about. I once walked all the way from the Temple of Light in the west to the Dry Lake in the glens." His face changed from a scowl of contempt to a look of incredulity. "Where did you get that?" he gasped, pointing at Limpic's flower.

Limpic stepped back and turned his chest away. "It's, ah, I mean, I've always had it, ever since I was little." He was painfully aware of just how little his voice sounded.

"Sorry, I don't mean to point," replied Horas, positively dancing on the stones. "It's just flowers and plants are my passion. I might do a spot of research while I'm up here. Make medicines and the like, hence my pots and pans. I could still find some common scurvy grass, which is full of vitamin C. And I'll definitely want to take a look at the meadow cranesbill, which only grows behind Crescent Bay. But that flower of yours, well, I've never ever seen one – only in my books, and even then they were the stuff of myth and legend, just stories.

It's said they surround the land beyond the Western Pole. Fire flower, I think it's called, or at least that was one of the names. It looks identical to the periwinkle except it's white instead of purple."

"Oh," said Limpic, rubbing at the skin around the flower. He couldn't help but think about the flames that had spat from it last night. Fire flower – a fitting name.

"According to my books," said Horas, babbling on while still dancing on his toes, "wherever the fire flower grows, no weeds grow. It's like the flower won't let anything bad near it at all. Isn't that extraordinary? Imagine a land surrounded by them! Nothing bad could get in!"

Limpic was aware of Truvius's watchful gaze.

"Yeah, that sure *is* strange," said Brutonia rolling his eyes. "But perhaps you had better be off now, Horas."

Horas's face returned to its indignant state and he turned to leave before stopping and looking all around him. First to the Valla Stones that rose into the face of the high basalt cliffs, and then to their left where they fell steeply into the basin of the Grand Cauldron and finally to the right where they angled into the Little Cauldron.

"Hmm, how does one get out of here?" Horas enquired.

"You could use a Starstone," said Brutonia laughing.

"One Starstone a day is quite enough," snapped Horas. "And, anyway, one would rather perambulate through the fauna than fly over it."

"Go back across the stones to the pathway behind," said Limpic, pointing to the right. "Pass through the basalt gate that links the Little Cauldron to the Grand Cauldron. Follow the path until you reach the Clinging Steps. Take these to the top pathway and follow it east. It shouldn't take more than a couple of hours."

"Ah, the Clinging Steps," said Horas, as though remembering a bad dream. His face had gone a little pale. "You mean those wretched wooden slats that have been battered into the side of the cliff? Those horrid, hanging, rotten planks that are of little use to an ant never mind those of us who are, well, sufficiently weighed down with utensils, shall we say. I mean, clinging is all well and good until there's nothing left to cling *to*. And if memory serves me well, and it does—"

"They're fine now," insisted Limpic.

"Yes, well, I suppose I will be the judge of that," said Horas with a sniff.

"Starstone?" said Brutonia, with a wide grin.

Horas crinkled his nose in disgust and turned one way and then the other, muttering under his breath. Eventually he decided upon a route and soon the jangle of his saucepans, cups and saucers died away until only the three of them were left.

"The mind boggles," said Truvius with a shake of his head.

"I know," replied Brutonia. "Did you hear Horas? He actually said sorry to Limpic – I've never heard Horas apologise to anyone before!" Brutonia looked down and eyed the limpet boat suspiciously. "Are we going in that?" he asked, arching his eyebrows.

Limpic jumped in and steadied the boat. "Nothing wrong with my vessel," he assured him, glad of the opportunity to steer the conversation away from his flower. "Now get in one at a time."

Truvius stepped in first and seated himself near the front without any fuss. Brutonia was less spritely. The minute he put his large foot into the stern, he panicked and his arms windmilled frantically. His other foot was still on the Valla

Stones, and the gap of water in between was growing steadily wider.

"Any time you feel like bringing the rest of yourself aboard would be great," grunted Limpic, wrestling with his oar to keep the boat from floating away.

Brutonia was finally forced into a decision as his legs began to creak. Off balance, he fell stiffly into the bottom of the shell with both legs pedalling thin air.

"There you are," laughed Truvius. "You've finally got your sea legs!"

Chapter 8

"Aw!" groaned Brutonia. He clung to the side of the boat while his face took on a subtle shade of green. "It's not helping, you know."

"What?" replied Limpic absently.

"You said to stare at something on land to help my stomach."

"Well, what are you staring at?" asked Limpic.

"Those sheep over there," lamented Brutonia, "but they keep moving."

"You're supposed to look at something solid like a mountain or a cliff!" said Limpic chuckling. "Try over there, away in the distance. Do you see those rocks sticking up out of the surf?"

Brutonia turned his head slowly and faced the direction the boat was moving: west, following the contours of the coast.

"That's the Spine," said Limpic. "It definitely won't move! And we're heading that way anyway."

Brutonia nodded miserably, his eyes sunken and sickly.

"Poor elvern," said Limpic kindly. "It won't be long now."

Soon the current picked up and the basalt cliffs rose once more out of the sea. On top of one of the cliffs, on a small headland, stood the remnants of Castle Cairn. Beneath it was a large cave known as Mermaid's Rift, and, unsurprisingly, a mermaid sat on a rock near the entrance, fanning her ice-blue tail in the early-evening sun. The sea rose and fell just beneath her and she dabbled her fingers in it playfully.

"Is he in a good mood today?" called Limpic.

The mermaid laughed and plunged into the water reappearing by the side of the boat. Her eyes were as blue as her tail and her skin was the colour of the white rocks that littered the sandy beach further west. Her hair was black like a raven and her lips were as red as hawthorn berries and slightly parted to show teeth as white as snow. Even Truvius sat up and stared at her in wonder, having been quiet and still for the duration of the boat trip. The mermaid crossed both her arms on the side of the limpet shell and rested her chin on them.

"My dear Limpic," she sang, her voice so hauntingly beautiful that it always sounded musical. "What have you brought with you today?"

"They're my friends," Limpic replied, a little breathless. Mermaids always left his stomach in a flutter. "Elverns. Truvius and Brutonia. Brutonia is the green one."

The mermaid laughed merrily. "And are they supposed to be that colour?" She peered inquisitively at the 'green one'.

Limpic grinned and his pearly white teeth sparkled. "He's not too good on the water but that will improve."

"It better," the mermaid said giggling. Her face grew grave. "I have heard rumblings from the deep, Limpic. Strange tidings of dark riders and silver thieves. Whispers and gossip from my people to the west."

Just as quickly the mermaid's face changed again, becoming pleasant and convivial. She flipped herself backwards into the water and disappeared below the boat, reappearing on the other side much further out to sea.

69

"Oh, and, no," she called, "he's in a terrible mood ... as always. Be careful, sweet Limpic. The world would be a sorrier place without you."

"Who are you talking about?" Truvius asked as the mermaid disappeared under the surface.

The tiny boat had drifted languidly further to the west and it bumped up against a shelf of rock beneath a rugged limestone cliff. Bits of grass and some sturdy pinkish flowers sprouted from cracks and fissures. Limpic quickly jumped out and tapped the cliff face with his makeshift oar three times, muttering something under his breath. There was a rasping, crumbling, creaking sound and the limestone began to swell and recede. Bits of it crumbled and tumbled down onto the shelf and sent vibrations up Limpic's legs.

"Him," said Limpic, turning to look at them and thumbing over his shoulder as he did so.

Truvius and Brutonia stared slack-jawed and bug-eyed. A huge rugged face was staring down at them from the cliff. His eyes were sunken deep beneath a formidable temple and huge eyebrows of pure limestone added further depth to his face – an angry and disgruntled face at that.

"What do you want?" the craggy face demanded.

Truvius stepped off the boat and squared his shoulders. "We have come to seek your assistance."

The enormous eyebrows knitted together and great furrows split across the forehead. Every time he moved more lumps of limestone rock littered the trembling shelf.

"My assistance? Pah! I am Amoso, born of stone. What assistance could you require of me, little one?" His voice was deep and gravelly, like a landslide, and boomed out across the water.

Truvius thought for a moment. "Actually, I'm, ah, not quite sure. It was Limpic who brought us here."

"Limpic, eh. Where is the little fellow?"

Limpic shuffled forward and fell beneath the gaze of those stony eyes.

"Limpic!" thundered Amoso. Chalk dust plumed into the air. "I haven't spoken with you for quite some time. Not since you cleaned all that green scum off my face after the last great storm."

"Well, sir," said Limpic quietly. "That's the thing, you see. I think the storms are only going to get worse."

"And why would that be?" the cliff enquired.

"Well, you see, sir, it's really the moon—"

"Can you help us or not?" Truvius demanded, nudging Limpic out of the way.

"Have I been asleep so long that rudeness has become a virtue?" asked Amoso. "And might I enquire again, little impetuous one, what exactly it is that you *want*?"

Truvius clenched his fists into two trembling white balls. He said nothing but his face burned.

"Please, sir," muttered Limpic.

"Yes, yes, speak up, lad, I've got rocks for ears!"

Limpic drew closer. His head was bowed ever so slightly and he wrung his fingers together. The sight of him seemed to placate Amoso and his hardness mellowed somewhat.

"Please, sir," Limpic said again. "It's the moon, you see. The moon is sick. That's all I can really tell you. We three here," he spread his arms to include Brutonia who was still languishing in the boat, too sick and alarmed to get out, "we have to head west to rescue … someone, and hope that we can save the moon because it is desperately ill."

71

"I know it is," replied Amoso. "I can feel the anguish in the night air and I can hear the terror of the sea. I will not ask you any more about your plan but I know more than any of you could ever hope to understand. You are searching for a lost prince, one who is stealing silver from the moon. The kingdom of the elverns lies encased in a hoary shroud. The queen of that realm no longer moves and its waters no longer run."

Limpic stepped backwards and his mouth fell open. "How do you—"

"Heh! Heh! Come now, Limpic, you are in the presence of a great and powerful sage! I wouldn't be very great *or* powerful if I did not know what was going on."

The rock beneath Limpic's feet vibrated with the echo of Amoso's merriment.

Then Amoso stopped laughing and stared straight at Truvius. "Besides, I have met seven of *your* kind before. Seven elverns seeking my help to find Prince Peruvius."

Limpic turned to his friend. "Then we *are* on the right track."

Truvius's eyes glistened and he let out a short sharp breath. "So you know of our quest. Can you please help us?"

Amoso closed his eyes and gathered his eyebrows together so closely that they became one. He stayed like this for quite some time, until the three travellers thought he had gone back to sleep. And so did a gull, which settled on his nose. Limpic was about to clear his throat when the great face stirred and Amoso's eyes opened. The gull cried indignantly and wheeled away.

"I have thought deeply about your quest," he said as softly as was possible for his kind. "I cannot help you."

Limpic blinked and his breath caught in his throat. Had he heard right? He struggled to take it in. "Please, sir."

"Limpic, Limpic," said Amoso, his huge eyes softening. "It is not that I would not help you. It is that I *cannot* help you."

Limpic felt like the stones beneath his feet were about to give way. The bump on his head throbbed and his shoulders sagged. Clearly moved by Limpic's appearance, Amoso sought to explain his predicament.

"As I told the seven," he began, "your first journey is west, due west. You must seek the Golden Mile, where the sun creates a pathway as she nears the horizon. Be mindful that the true Golden Mile, the one that leads to the sun itself, can only be entered by passing through the Gates of Dusk, which can only be found by summoning the Gatekeeper. And here is my quandary, the Gatekeeper can only be summoned by blowing the Echo Shell when it begins to vibrate." Amoso drew his lips together so tightly that the rocks around them began to splinter and crumble. "And I gave the only Echo Shell in my possession to the seven to guard with their lives."

Limpic pursed his own lips. His shoulders began to tremble. His stomach began to shake. Soon he was quaking all over with his head thrown back in laughter.

"Limpic, my dear fellow," said Amoso, "please, there is no reason to become hysterical. Maybe …"

Limpic ran to his boat scrambling between Brutonia's feet. He pulled something out and held it up for Amoso to see.

"The Echo Shell!" bellowed Amoso, "But how?" His voice thundered out to sea and bits of stone and gravel peppered the surface of the water.

Limpic gathered himself. "The seven did indeed guard the shell with their lives. Only today one of them, Tabitha, returned this shell to Tulwood. Now she lies encased in silver in the king's castle."

"Then I can help you," said Amoso sighing in relief. "I must help you. I always reward those who are kind and compassionate, polite and trustworthy. Limpic, you are all of these things and more." He turned his gaze upon Truvius and his eyes became mere pinpricks. "You, on the other hand, must be careful that you do not embrace the very thing you wish to avoid."

Truvius pressed his lips so tightly together that they became a thin straight line. He touched the scar on his cheek. "I apologise for my rudeness," he said quietly. "I will heed your advice."

Amoso smiled and his features mellowed. Indeed, he looked rather splendid. "Little one, do not try and carry the entire burden on your own shoulders. Those who walk by your side can take their share too."

Truvius nodded and smiled. His own face softened.

"Now," said Amoso, "you first must cross the ocean before you even think about going beneath it. I have many friends down there but also many enemies."

"Ah, beneath the ocean?" exclaimed Brutonia from his perch in Limpic's shell. He was still hanging sickly over the side. "Who in their right mind would want to travel beneath the ocean? Truvius never said anything about going under the sea. As my father used to say—"

"Brutonia, not now!" hissed Truvius. He turned to Limpic. "Although he does make a valid point."

By now Amoso had closed his eyes and his breath was deep and slow. This time it really did look as if he had fallen asleep. Limpic and Truvius looked at each other and shrugged.

"Ahem!" coughed Limpic.

The cliff snorted and his eyes opened, vague and dusty.

"What is it?" he demanded. "What do you want? Can't you see I'm sleeping! I was dreaming, you know." He smiled a great big craggy smile and the shelf beneath Limpic's feet swelled. "I was dreaming that I was talking to an ullan who wanted to travel below the sea to catch the sun." His smile faded, his eyes closed and he snorted. "Dear me, what nonsense I am speaking."

It looked like he was about to go back to sleep when Limpic spoke up.

"Excuse me, sir," he said, "but you were about to help us travel across the ocean."

Amoso frowned a deep creaking frown. "Ah, yes," he thundered. "You want to travel across the sea. Well if you could summon a rainbow it would … ah no, you don't know what's at the other end of it. Well, yes, now let me think. The seven had a ship of their own, powered by Starstones, but you have no vessel other than that small shell, which will not do, dear me, no! Limpic, you have heard of the great ship *Polestar* that sleeps upon the ocean floor at the Devil's Toe?"

"Aye, sir, I know of her."

"Well, now, call her then, little Limpic. Call her from her slumber using the Echo Shell."

"But how?" Limpic asked.

"Place the Echo Shell in the water and blow," replied Amoso eagerly.

"Of course!" laughed Limpic, clicking his finger and thumb.

"Call her forth, little one," whispered Amoso gently.

Limpic went down onto his knees and dipped the bigger end of the shell into the water. He put his lips to the other end and blew with all his might. There was only the faintest echo of a sound that disappeared out to the eastern horizon. Limpic rose and stood silently, the shell hanging loosely in his hands. Truvius peered intently to the east, narrowing his eyes until they almost closed. Even Brutonia managed to lift his head out of the boat.

A soft early-evening breeze crept past and the late sunlight began to smudge away the edges of the shore. Everything was burning amber. Out to sea, three gulls flapped their wings and lifted themselves noisily from the surface of the water. Something had disrupted their evening nap. A line of bubbles drifted along the area the birds had just vacated, outlining an underwater current. The waters just in front of Amoso trembled and popped as large circles formed and wrestled with one another. As quickly as they became agitated they grew eerily quiet.

Suddenly the still surface exploded and a dark shimmering form burst forth, rocking and blinking in the orange sun. It was a dripping wet galleon. Water poured out of the great ship's saturated gunneries and off the top of the lookout mast, spewing through the dark seaweed that hung and winked in clumps around the deck and prow. Limpic's tiny boat flipped up and over, crashing onto the limestone ledge just beneath Amoso.

"Help!" cried Brutonia throwing his arms across his face as the boat clattered down on top of him.

Truvius stared at *Polestar* with large eyes and an unbridled smile appeared on his face.

Limpic jumped up and down and punched the air. "*Polestar*!" he exclaimed.

"She's a fair vessel, is she not?" said Amoso with a sniff. "She'll take you anywhere you want to go. Climb onto her forecastle and out onto her bowsprit and stare into the horizon and she will make for it."

"What about under the water?" Limpic enquired. "What did you mean by that?"

"When you catch the sun, you will be dragged beneath the sea as she descends to her rest," replied Amoso.

"That might prove difficult," said Limpic. His stomach fluttered at the thought.

"Not for *Polestar*," said Amoso laughing. "She's as much at home under the water as above it. That's where she lives, remember."

Limpic chewed his bottom lip and looked to his two companions. Brutonia was only now climbing furtively from beneath the limpet shell, staring at the galleon in dazed wonder.

"I'm not worried about the ship," Limpic murmured. "I'm more concerned about how two elverns could survive beneath the waves for more than a few minutes. They can't breathe like I can."

Amoso drew in a sharp breath. "I see your point," he conceded. "The elvern ship had a water tight cabin at the rear. Such is their fear of drowning. But *Polestar* … emm." He closed his eyes and from the sound of rocks churning within his brain, he was thinking.

"Bring me some seaweed at once!" he demanded abruptly.

Limpic rushed to do as he was told, helped by Truvius. They pulled swathes of slimy weeds from the lip of the shelf and laid them in a pile before the cliff.

"Now stand back," said Amoso. He licked his cracked lips and a huge tongue flicked out drawing all the seaweed into his mouth. He closed his eyes and chomped and chewed with swollen cheeks. He looked and sounded like an enormous rocky cow ruminating on the cud. Finally, he stopped chewing and began to blow. A bubble appeared between his lips, growing bigger and bigger so that Limpic and his companions had to step to one side to allow it room to expand. The bubble pushed Limpic's overturned limpet shell into the water and continued to expand until it was as high as *Polestar*'s poop deck.

Eventually, after much huffing and puffing, Amoso seemed satisfied. With a gentle pop he let the enormous bubble roll away from his mouth.

"My goodness!" he gasped. "That was tough. And to think some spiders do this all the time." His eyes were crossed with exertion. It took him some time to regain his breath and composure.

"That should take you to the bottom of the ocean, or even deep into space if you want. Just attach it to *Polestar* and tow it behind you. When the time comes to dive below the surface, anyone who cannot breathe underwater can get inside the bubble and be quite safe."

Amoso was rather pleased with himself. His eyes started to close and parts of his face began to solidify. "I can do no more to help you," he muttered as the limestone rocks hardened all around him. "Go and save your moon. It is time for me to sleep." In no time at all he was silent and his features were gone, hidden once again in the rock face. Moments later gulls returned and settled on a protuberance that had once been his nose.

"What now?" Brutonia asked.

"Now we have to attach the bubble to the ship," Truvius announced, wading into the water.

Chapter 9

"Yee-haw!" screeched Limpic as *Polestar* skipped like a giant pebble across the waves.

They'd been sailing all night and half a day and Limpic had barely left his perch on the bowsprit except to eat some breakfast as the sun first began to blink over the horizon. He was full of joy – the joy of the ocean. He could feel it surging through his veins. He threw a glance back across his shoulder and laughed. Truvius and Brutonia staggered haphazardly across the deck of the forecastle, trying vainly to discover their sea legs. Behind them the giant bubble appeared, rising higher than the poop deck as it tumbled over the uneven surface of the ocean. They had lashed it to the back of the ship with ropes and fishing net the night before and then set off promptly.

"Faster!" cried Limpic, rising to his feet, nimble-footed. His hair swept out behind him and his eyes were clear and deep, opened up and soothed by the vastness of the blue horizon. His face had a permanent smile and his teeth flashed in the white sunlight. There was a surge from behind as though some invisible hand had shunted them and *Polestar* lurched forward at a phenomenal pace. Truvius and Brutonia finally had to admit defeat and lie down as the angle of the deck chopped and changed.

Limpic turned back towards them and cackled, then he grabbed a rope from above his head and scurried lithely from the bowsprit to the mainmast. Up there every movement of the ship was magnified tenfold and the mast swung backwards and forwards like a pendulum. Limpic threw back his head and drank in the sounds and the taste of salt. The wind nipped at his cheeks and Limpic nipped back. It tugged at his clothes and wrestled with his hat. Sometimes it dropped to a barely a whisper. Just as suddenly it roared back to life and Limpic roared back, laughing till his belly ached.

"I'm alive!" he bellowed but the wind stole the words from his mouth and gave him a clip around the ears for good measure.

"Shouldn't we slow down?" Truvius yelled as he rolled one way and then the other.

Limpic barely heard him, his attention reserved for the wind and the sunlight glinting off the shallow waves like a billion tiny winking eyes. Eventually he felt the rigging of the mast jiggle as someone attempted to climb up to him. He peered down and grinned as Truvius abandoned his quest and lay panting within the folds of the netting.

"Limpic!" he bawled, "aren't we going too fast?"

"Guid day for it!" Limpic shouted over the din of the wind.

Truvius was being buffeted from every direction. "We're going too *fast*!" he yelled angrily.

Limpic furrowed his brow. The anger on his friend's face threatened to darken his own thoughts, but he pictured in his mind's eye the lifeless form of the queen and Tabitha and his own siblings.

"No, Truvius," he replied resolutely, "we're not going fast enough."

He turned and stared into the horizon wondering how close they could get before the silver found them. Drawing out his compass Limpic glanced at the needle.

"Due west," he murmured to himself snapping the compass closed. Right into the eye of the storm. Into the silvery light.

"How long will it take?" Truvius asked in a softer tone. He had managed to climb further up.

Limpic shook his head sucking the cool clear breeze through his nose. He smiled. "Maybe forever." He turned and stared into Truvius's eyes. "Part of me hopes it takes forever."

Truvius looked at him curiously. He muttered under his breath and carefully slid down the rigging, receiving several burns to his hands and legs for his efforts.

Limpic watched him go and shook his head. He turned and stared longingly into the eternal western horizon and allowed his cares to float away. There was something about being on the water – especially on a great ship like this, treading towards a horizon that never seemed to get any closer; beneath a sky that couldn't get any bigger. It seemed foolish to worry.

Limpic took another deep breath and reluctantly left his perch. He landed just behind the mainmast as quietly as a mouse. Truvius and Brutonia were sitting with their backs against it.

"I don't know what has gotten into him," he heard Truvius grumble. "You wouldn't think we were on a quest to save the entire world!"

"Limpic is where he was born to be, where he longs to be," replied Brutonia. "Out on the open sea he's as close to heaven as a creature can be while on Earth."

Oh, Brutonia, how right you are, thought Limpic and smiled, his whiskers twitching.

Truvius snorted, got up and stomped around the deck becoming grumpier every time he fell over with the rolling of the ship. "Well, we need to get things put away before they go off!" he snapped. He was referring to the cold meats that were still in bags on the main deck, along with most of the other things they had brought aboard.

"Well, let's put them away," replied Brutonia gently. "And, remember, none of us would even be here if it wasn't for Limpic."

"Humph," grunted Truvius sourly.

"Aye, aye, aye," sighed Limpic. "Time to pack everything away," he said, stepping out from behind the mast and rubbing his hands together. "Brutonia, take the weapons below deck to the stern. There should be a small armoury there. Truvius, take the food to the galley quarters on the prow. The meats would also be best stored below deck where the keel lies beneath the waterline."

"And what are you going to do?" Truvius asked, unused to taking orders.

"Well," said Limpic, "I need to get things ready for the storm and prepare to catch the rainwater."

"Storm?" said Truvius sceptically. "But the sky is clear in every direction."

"Oh, there'll be a storm alright," said Limpic gravely. "Mark my words. We cannot hope to sail these waters in peace." He could feel a dull ache begin to swell behind his nose and eyes – a sure sign that the weather was changing. Twice before the storms had caught him unawares but surely not this time.

He left a bemused Truvius and went about his business: he made sure everything that could be battened down was. He rolled wooden caskets over to the poop deck where the water ran down onto the main deck before eventually falling over the side of the ship. Here he fashioned some rolls of canvas into long tubes that he put into the kegs to collect fresh water. All they needed now was some rain. Next he rechecked the entire ship from prow to stern, making doubly sure that everything was fastened securely. While doing so his thoughts strayed to the bubble flying along behind them. He decided it should be drawn in closer and lashed to the back of the ship more firmly. When Limpic was satisfied all was in order, he checked on how the others were doing and found them midship.

"Everything sorted?" he enquired.

"Aye aye, Cap'n," replied Brutonia with a salute and an easy grin.

Truvius stared at his friend contemptuously. "Everything is as it should be but I still don't know where we are going."

Limpic pointed to the front of the ship. "We are sailing due west, leaving Dalbain to our backs." He turned one hundred and eighty degrees and pointed to the unrecognisable purple haze on the eastern horizon. "The world we know is far behind. We are entering the Pondus, the great ocean that cuts our world off from beyond the west. Somewhere out there our sun takes refuge from the darkness of the night. That is where we head now."

Limpic thought for a moment about his parents. They had journeyed into the Pondus when they came of age; when they heard the call of the ocean. The final pilgrimage. Maybe this would be his? And yet ... he had heard no call.

"And this storm – will it really come?" Truvius pushed.

Limpic looked to the sky and frowned. His whiskers trembled as he sniffed the air. The uncomfortable yet familiar pressure was steadily building behind his eyes and nose. "Yes, it will come, maybe not today or even tomorrow, but a storm is brewing, and it will not be light. In fact, I fear it may be greater than any I have ever seen. Things aren't right. But we have prepared ourselves as well as we can." He sniffed the air again and closed his eyes. His inner ear was clicking faintly, so he opened it. *Those whispers. I hear them even here.* He couldn't pinpoint the sound and it skirted around the peripheral of his inner ear like a movement at the edge of sight. His flower had turned from white to a faint pinkish colour. *Something was off* and his flower was sensing it. *Maybe the storm?*

"And what are we supposed to do now – just wait?" grumbled Truvius.

Limpic's eyes sparkled like the sun on the waves and his concern melted away. "Now? We sail, of course! And we relish every single moment that we are free to ride upon the greatest pathway on Earth! Taste the salt in the air." He put out his tongue. "Listen to the creak of the timbers and the slap of the waves." He threw back his head and yelled just for the sake of it.

Truvius's eyes darkened. He drew his lips into a thin straight line and ground his teeth before storming into the captain's cabin. The door slammed behind him with a sharp bang.

Brutonia looked at Limpic and rolled his eyes. He smiled and pointed at the almost transparent film of purple that was Dalbain. "I wonder what I'll look at now when my stomach feels off," he said.

Limpic clapped him on the back. "It's almost time for lunch. Being on the sea always makes me hungry, and it'll probably help your stomach to get some food, but first go and make your peace with the ship," he said. "I think you'll find your sea legs."

Brutonia shrugged. "Maybe I'll feel better in the morning!"

He wandered to starboard and sat staring out to sea with his chin resting in his folded arms.

Limpic watched him for a while before returning to the prow where he sat once more on the bowsprit with his legs dangling on either side. The emerald water slipped beneath his feet, split apart by the prow of *Polestar* with little more than a gentle hiss. A dolphin appeared riding the crest of the small wave that sat just forward of the prow. The sun dappled its back and every so often spouts of frothy foam fizzed from its blowhole. Limpic took out a small razor shell and played a tune. A beautiful yet haunting melody that mingled with the wind and the waves, complementing nature's every sound. After that he sat and contemplated his mission. Every moment brought them closer to Peruvius and Marah, the dark elvern.

"And when we find them, what will we do?" His question hung in the air unanswered. Limpic's stomach growled and he shook off his thoughts and returned to midship to find Brutonia fast asleep, his chin resting on top of the bulwarks. Limpic smiled and thought it best to let him nap. He retrieved some food and tried the cabin door but it was locked. Truvius was obviously still brooding. Limpic knocked and set some food by the door, as he did by Brutonia, and climbed into the folds of the rigging to take his own.

It was only supposed to be for a minute but the ship's movement swayed him gently this way and that. The sun's rays warmed his face and bathed his eyes. He heard the gentle slap of water far below and his eyelids grew heavy and he drifted off to sleep.

Limpic had beautiful dreams of floating across the sea on an old rocking chair, gently and freely, while the sun drifted beside him, leading him across the waves. He was playing music on his shell, which made the sea happy; it made everything happy. A sleepy haze hung across the never-ending horizon. His parents stood within the haze beckoning him. Limpic waved and laughed. Everything vibrated around him. The silver was gone and the forest had been set free. Birds cooed, bees hummed, rivers chattered and streams babbled. A honey, golden hue lay over all. The weight of war had been lifted and Limpic was free of any burden.

But then the sun began to fade and cry as a moon, dark and red, shifted like a ruby over the blackening horizon. He heard a terrible cacophony of frenzied whisperings. Suddenly his rocking chair thrashed backwards and forwards and water sprayed over his face. He fell onto the Valla Stones, which hummed as silver oozed up between their cracks. Limpic tried to run but his legs wouldn't work. The silver flowed over his feet and rooted him to the spot. It was cold, so cold. It rose up over his knees and onto his stomach. Limpic shuddered. The silver reached his chest and neck. He struggled to breathe. He opened his mouth to scream but the silver flowed inside. He could taste liquid metal. The last thing he saw, before his eyes turned cold and hard, were legions upon legions of silver figures marching up out of the water. Their faces were featureless and everywhere they stepped turned to silver. The Golden Coast was gone. Limpic's flower glowed red and spat fire.

"No, no, not again!" he shouted, trying to flap at the flames with arms that wouldn't move.

"Wake up, Limpic!" Brutonia stood over him, silhouetted against a sky that was threaded with sinuous snaking lightning bolts. Low, thunderous booms echoed across the vast and empty void all around.

"The storm has come!" bellowed Brutonia, clinging grimly

to the rigging.

Limpic gasped. He reached for his chest. His flower was glowing red. He was still half asleep but a huge mouthful of saltwater fully roused him.

"Urgh!" he spluttered, half choking, half retching.

Already – the storm has come already? How long had he slept? He took a deep breath and sprang up. He ushered Brutonia to the deck and, finding rope, lashed it to the mainmast. He cut off some for himself.

"Tie this around your waist!" he shouted over the wind.

Brutonia took the rope and fastened himself to it.

Limpic bundled him to starboard. "Stay here," he insisted. "Lie as flat as possible and do not try to cross the deck. I will come back for you and we'll make for the bubble."

Brutonia nodded dumbly and grabbed onto whatever he could find that was most solid. There was an enormous phosphorescent flash and the air crackled with energy. The thunder, which had echoed from far away, seemed menacingly close. Brutonia closed his eyes and turned his face away from the stinging waves that began breaking like wild foaming horses all over the deck.

Polestar heaved and groaned as she pitched and rolled in every conceivable direction. She was as if mad, unsure of what was up and what was down. Every so often the sky lit up and the lookout mast appeared for an instant, framed against a sky as angry and troubled as the waters beneath. Rain fell in icy sheets, driving across the main deck like continuous arrows of water.

Limpic stayed low and moved across the deck slowly and carefully. He kept his head beneath the side of the ship and moved aft, allowing the sea to break across his shoulders. He eventually made it to the cabin door. Every time he managed to open it a slither, the wind or a wave tore it from his grasp and lashed it closed again. A brief lull gave him enough time to get inside before the door slammed viciously behind him.

The cabin was dark and strangely quiet. The wind and the rain seemed very far away, as though battering against the edges of his mind. The whispering he'd heard earlier was palpable now – even without his inner ear. Limpic felt more afraid of the whispering than the storm.

"Truvius!" he hissed. "Truvius, are you in here?" There was no reply. Limpic crawled along the floor on all fours, feeling blindly in front of him. "Truvius, we have to get out of here, we have to reach the bubble. Those windows could shatter any moment and you don't want to be near them when they do."

Still there was no reply, but the wind and the rain were beginning to break through, growing louder and louder. The cabin magnified every creak, groan and shudder of the ship. And there was another sound too, like something hard crashing around in the dark.

Limpic continued to grope about in vain when a flash of lightning split the darkness in two. For a couple of seconds, the entire cabin lit up. Truvius lay unconscious beneath the windows while a cannonball ricocheted around the floor as if possessed. Limpic waited until it rolled to the other side of the room before he made a dart for Truvius as darkness fell again. He felt Truvius's warm face and fumbled around until he grasped his hand.

He held back until the ship lurched forward as it raced down the side of an enormous wave and then dragged Truvius towards the door. Unfortunately, the cannonball had the same idea and Limpic heard it come crashing towards him in the dark.

At the last moment he threw Truvius to one side and himself to the other as the cannonball splintered through the door as if just fired at the ship. The door burst outwards with a screech, only for the wind to catch it, twist it and cast it back into the cabin in an unquenchable rage. Rain and waves surged through the opening in rivers and it was some time before Limpic managed to find his feet. The chill of the water had roused the unconscious elvern somewhat and he groaned. Limpic cast his piece of rope between the two of them and pushed Truvius out into the storm.

"Keep your head down and your eyes closed!" Limpic shouted, but it sounded more like a whisper against the wind.

Truvius crawled in front of him, coughing and spluttering as saltwater swept around his knees and feet.

"Go right!" bellowed Limpic, pushing Truvius to one side. "We have to get Brutonia. He's on the starboard side!"

The wind was snarling now, biting at any who dared defy it. The icy fingers of the sea snapped, writhed and pulled at the two tiny figures huddled together for safety. They made their way up the entire starboard side but Brutonia was nowhere to be seen or felt.

"Are you sure this is where you left him?" yelled Truvius, sheltering under the bulwark.

"Aye!" Limpic shouted back. "I left him right here and told him not to get up."

"I can't feel him anywhere," Truvius shouted back.

Then Limpic felt something beneath his fingers and acid rose in the back of his throat. It was a piece of rope with nothing at the other end of it.

"Nooo!" he yelled, rising onto his knees.

A huge wave smashed him onto his back but he rose again

89

and scrambled to the side of the ship. "Brutonia!" he yelled as Truvius tried to wrestle him back.

"He's gone, Limpic! He's gone!"

Limpic wrenched himself free and stood right up on the deck and peered out into the storm, tears streaming down his face mingling with sea spray and rainwater.

"Brutonia!"

There was another flash, much further away. The sea was momentarily illuminated and Limpic could see something black bobbing in the water before sinking. Limpic planted a foot on top of the bulwark but was pulled back by Truvius.

"Don't be a fool, Limpic! Not even you could survive that."

"I have to save him!" cried Limpic. "I'm his captain!"

The storm raged and the world tore itself to pieces as Truvius dragged Limpic towards the stern of the ship and the safety of the bubble.

Limpic snarled and spat at the wind and the waves. "How could you? *How could you*!" he wept.

"Look out, Limpic!" cried Truvius pulling him closer.

Dark wings ushered past and then a face appeared right in the eye of the storm.

"Father!" screamed Truvius, wiping rainwater from his eyes.

The face neither looked at him nor acknowledged him from dark and vacant eyes, its mouth hanging open as though caught in a perpetual scream. It swayed this way and that on the wings of the storm before vanishing into the darkness but not before uttering one last baleful cry. "Zarkus!" The voice was not of flesh and blood. It turned the marrow cold.

The clouds around the moon began to smoulder with a silvery light.

"The silver is upon us!" cried Truvius, falling to his knees and cowering beneath his arms. "All is lost!"

At the same time Limpic's flower, which up till now had merely throbbed red, spluttered into life and grew white-hot.

"Ah!" screamed Limpic, flapping the flower to quench the tongues of fire that licked around his chest. An incredible heat swept through his entire body and the more he tried to fight against it, the hotter it became. It was burning even more fiercely than before and throbbing in his hands. Sweat blinded his eyes and he threw his arms up and just let the fire come. Two single darts of flame shot from his fingertips into the silver light building overhead. There was a cry far away and the ominous light went out.

Limpic didn't have time to take it in the gravity of what had just occured. His inner ear was vibrating with hundreds of hissing sounds. "The whisperings!" he moaned. "Make them stop!"

Polestar rocked and groaned until the mainmast and lookout point cracked and crashed into the unrelenting waters.

Arms windmilling thin air, Limpic found himself falling backwards into the bowels of the ship. The hatch had blown open in the tumult. Something tugged at his waist and a flailing shape fell with him. "Oh," he moaned as a bright flash erupted behind his right eye. He had struck the bump on his head again. Groggily he stared through the hatch as the moon appeared, tossed within the fuming sky. Angry, red and swollen out of all proportion.

A dark figure, astride a dark steed, sat within her belly.

Then, nothing.

Chapter 10

"You need to wake up soon," whispered a familiar voice.

"Mum?" Limpic asked.

He tried to open his eyes but the light was too bright and the pain in his head was too intense. A cool hand settled on his brow, like it had done when the fever came.

"Yes, I'm here," said his mother.

"Am I sick again?" replied Limpic. "I've been having such terrible nightmares."

Someone grasped his hand in theirs. "No, son, you're not sick," said another voice.

"Dad?" whispered Limpic.

Again he tried to open his eyes but the light all around him was too great. Through half-closed lids he could just make out two silhouettes.

"You need to stop ignoring your flower," said his mother.

"But it burns," replied Limpic.

"Only when it senses what shouldn't be, and only when you ignore it," said his father. "It knows the difference between right and wrong and for your quest that is all that is needed. Its fire will heal and protect, Limpic. Do not be afraid of it. It will never consume you. Let it guide."

"Get up now, son," said his parents. "You have much to do."

***

Sunlight danced on the ceiling, reflected from puddles of water on the floor. Occasionally particles of dust sifted into the sunbeams, gently falling, falling and intertwining with one another.

Limpic lay staring up, watching the dancing dust, unaware that he was actually awake. Somewhere outside he heard the gentle splurge of water shifting around the keel of a ship, but it could have been a million miles away. He touched the bump on his head and winced. It was enormous. His mind was dull and fuzzy, like a cloud was drifting through it.

He couldn't get a grasp of where he was or why. On a ship, for sure, and there had been a storm, although to look around it was hard to imagine. Things had fared fairly well beneath deck except that the armoury door hung open, sagging sadly on its hinges. Limpic gazed at the weapons all neatly stacked and lashed to various parts of the wall. His bow was there. Brutonia had done an excellent job.

Brutonia!

Limpic sprang up and groaned in despair. The reality of the night before crashed over him as viciously as any wave ever could. He buried his face in his hands and cried sorely.

"I was your captain," he murmured to himself.

"It wasn't your fault, you know," said a voice from behind. Truvius was sitting nearby looking ghastly. His face was almost as swollen and red as the moon had appeared the previous night. "What happened last night wasn't your fault. You saw the moon. The face – it was hideous. Everything is becoming ugly.

That storm was beyond anything anyone could have prepared for. Had it not been for you, your warning, then this ship would have perished."

Limpic licked his cracked lips, which were coated in a fine layer of salt. "I was his captain," he finally croaked. "And I fell asleep."

The two of them were silent.

Details of the storm returned to Limpic. He remembered the awful face of Marah and shuddered. "Something has taken control of your father," he said in a hoarse voice. His throat burned. "And whatever it is has spread to the goblins that attacked us in Tulwood. I knew there was something strange about them. Their eyes were black as tar – as were Marah's." He turned to face Truvius. "What do you know?" he asked accusingly.

Truvius moved painfully, pulling his knees to his chest with a grimace. "It's ... that is, I think it's the Cra," he said dejectedly.

Limpic stiffened. "The Cra? But they're gone. The High Elves banished them to the Shadowlands. My father told me when I was young."

Truvius massaged the bridge of his nose. "That's true, Limpic. And their leader, the fallen elf Sargon, was also exiled. And the High Elves retreated to the Valley of Silence to quell the awful sound of the Great War from their minds. I know the history."

"Then you know the door to the Shadowlands was sealed. No one can open it," insisted Limpic, still trying to clear his head.

"Zarkus opened it," said Truvius glumly. "At least I think so, but I'm not totally sure."

"But ... but how?"

Truvius sighed and rubbed his face. "I told you of our gifts. Zarkus is the most powerful sage we elverns have ever had. His power comes from the moon and the power that holds her in heaven and sustains all life and order. Zarkus wears around his neck our most revered possession – Lunehaert, the heart of the moon. It's how he draws his power. When Marah," Truvius drew in a long deep breath, "when my father became morose, he turned to the darkness. The anti-life – chaos. He began to open doors that should have been left closed and he was banished by King Zenith for his dark arts. After some time Zarkus told me he'd seen Father. Said he'd changed, but he hadn't. It was Zarkus who changed. The ranting and darkness that had seeped into every pore of Father drenched my brother as well. He began to talk about the throne. He said that if Father could just get the throne back, everything would be alright. I told him it was nonsense but he wouldn't believe me. Time spent with Father drove a wedge between us – I couldn't reach Zarkus like I used to." Truvius scratched at a splinter on the deck, then stared at it blankly when it became embedded beneath his nail. He continued.

"The last time I saw Zarkus, before he really changed, he said he'd given Father something. He said he'd got to the heart of the problem, that everything would be alright now, that Father was pleased." Truvius punched his leg. "I should have spoken to the king sooner. I should have done something sooner but I never thought my brother would have a hand in anything so sinister. Then the goblin numbers swelled on our borders and I was off fighting and when I was back I kept an eye on Zarkus without letting anyone know my suspicions. Imagine the sheer trauma if the court heard that Zarkus, second only to the king and queen and beloved by all, was complicit in aiding my father, Marah, the exiled traitor."

Limpic considered this. His head ached trying to make sense of it all. "You think Zarkus gave this Lunehaert to your father?"

"I do," replied Truvius. His face was grave. "At least I think I do. I am in no way a scholar but there lies in our castle a library that holds all our history, and a text on the closing of the door to the Shadowlands with a cryptic verse on its reopening. It says, 'Give what is not yours to give to the shadow behind the door. Give not your heart, but a borrowed heart, and the shadow will rise once more.'"

Truvius's eyes watered and he opened his hands in a helpless gesture. "After that came pages and pages of history but I had found what I needed. Zarkus gave away Lunehaert. A borrowed heart."

Limpic peered at the timber beneath his feet. He followed the grain of the wood until it ran into a dark, twisted knot. His heart and head felt heavy. "So the shadow, the Cra, have the heart of the moon and all her powers," said Limpic flatly. "That would explain the storms and rising and ebbing tides." He looked at Truvius's plain silver ring. "Zarkus and King Zenith have a ring like that."

"We all wear the same ring," replied Truvius. "All of us within the house of Zenith. They were all cast from the same crucible and the same batch of silver."

"Even Marah – your father," said Limpic.

Truvius nodded. "Why?"

"It's just something that's been bothering me," replied Limpic. "The day we met the sea swept you off the Valla Stones. It was like it purposefully went after you but that seemed impossible. How would it know who you were? Now I think your father used your ring to find you and Lunehaert to control the sea."

Truvius paled. "Sh ... should I take it off?" He held up his hand and stared at the ring as though it was an enemy.

"No," replied Limpic. He stroked his flower. Its fires will heal and protect, that's what his parents had said. It had done that twice already. "Keep it on, Truvius. Let them know we're coming. Let the dark know the light is coming."

Truvius nodded. "I suppose the Cra have plenty of willing vessels for their shadow to grow in."

"Like the goblins," said Limpic.

It began to make sense. The goblins were mere fodder; their minds were already dark. They were a means to an end – an army, somewhere the Cra could multiply and grow.

"And that's why goblins are rampaging at the gates of Tulwood. They're possessed by the Cra," said Limpic.

"It would appear so," replied Truvius. "The goblins are controlled by the source of power."

Limpic considered this for a moment. "If we could find the source, the vessel ... if we could find Marah and remove the shadow, eliminate it—"

"The Cra would be destroyed," said Truvius.

Limpic contemplated this again. "There is even more to this than we truly know," he said. "Lunehaert created an opening for the Cra to pass through. The Cra used your father's anger to possess him. Yes, he wanted revenge, but killing the moon – to what end?"

"You never knew my father," hissed Truvius. "To no end – anger, spite, total annihilation." He spat out the last word, and for a moment looked uncannily like his brother.

Limpic was unconvinced but kept his thoughts to himself.

Marah was merely a means for the Cra to sneak back into this world for their own ends. And now they were using Peruvius to drain the moon of her lifeblood and destroy her. But why? If only Limpic had been able to study the book Truvius had found the verse in. He was sure there were more answers in it.

"Do you think," said Limpic carefully, "do you think Zarkus could be following us?"

Truvius looked up in surprise. "Zarkus still has the moon's silver in his blood, so he still has some of her power. I suppose it's possible. Why? Do you think he is?"

Limpic shrugged. "The voice last night. It shouted out Zarkus's name."

"Oh," said Truvius.

"But it's not just that voice," continued Limpic. "I hear whisperings. Every time I've heard them, Zarkus has appeared. In the chamber with the king, in the forest before the attack from the goblins, in the air before the storm. Somewhere out there Zarkus is watching. I just know it."

Truvius gnawed his lip. His face was haggard.

"And I heard the same whispers in the cabin," said Limpic delicately, "during the storm."

Truvius snorted and his eyebrows rose. "But Zarkus wasn't in the cabin," he replied with an air of belligerence.

"I know he wasn't," said Limpic, "but you were."

"Me?" Truvius scowled. "But ... that's preposterous!"

"Listen, Truvius, I don't pretend to understand what you've been through or what you carry in your heart but remember that the Cra seek out pain. They use it to their own end. You must fight it!"

Truvius hung his head. There were dark rings under his eyes. He was deflated. "I know, Limpic, I know," he admitted. "The king always told me that. He often said you become the thoughts you entertain."

"And you carry too many secrets," said Limpic gently. "You should have told me at the very start about the Cra. It wouldn't have changed our course of action but it would have been a burden shared."

Truvius looked up and smiled wryly. "That's the nature of the beast. I'm secretive, Limpic. I always have been. I don't like talking. Talking about things is like crying about things. At the time it might feel cathartic but eventually you have to face the very thing that made you cry in the first place. And if you've talked about it, it means other people know about it and that makes you feel even worse. Besides, why spread the misery?"

"That's quite a conundrum," said Limpic, who kind of understood. "But I do think dwelling on dark thoughts alone is dangerous. They fester."

"I just don't like people knowing my business," continued Truvius, picking at the scar on his cheek until it was red, "and my business is the security of my kingdom, and that relies heavily on secrets."

"Ahem," said Limpic chuckling. "My business is the protection of the Golden Coast and that's not going very well!"

Truvius laughed and then grew pensive. He cleared his throat awkwardly. "Last night, when you were sleeping, your flower was glowing in the dark." Truvius placed one hand on top of the other. "And you were hot to touch. The morning after the silver attacked the Valla Stones, I found you in the same state – hot to the touch and your flower glowing and you murmuring about children and fire."

Limpic pulled his whiskers thoughtfully. "I'm not sure what to say because I don't understand myself." He laughed. "I know that sounds ridiculous but it's the truth. All I know is that when I was younger, I was very ill. So ill, in fact, that it was presumed I would die." Limpic closed his eyes in concentration. "I remember fire, like I was in the middle of it, burning up but never totally consumed. For a long, long time – maybe over a year, fires coming and fires going every couple of weeks. And when they left I always felt sick, or bone achingly tired, or my mouth was full of ulcers so that I could barely eat. And then over time my whiskers dried up like straw and fell out. Once I had the most terrible backache followed by a headache that only disappeared when I lay flat on my back. I'm sure I lay for a whole week just staring up at the ceiling listening to a crow that was trapped in the chimney behind my bed." Limpic paused and peered into thin air. The ship rocked and some dust fell fom the ceiling.

"So what happened?" asked Truvius softly.

Limpic drew in a long breath through his nose. "I had dreams during the fevers. I would pass through an open doorway into a brightly lit south-facing room with green flowery wallpaper. There was a bed and behind it a chimney with the sound of a flapping crow."

"Just like you!" exclaimed Truvius.

Limpic nodded. "In the bed was a strange looking creature, either peering up at the ceiling or rolling about in distress. Every so often he was visited by someone and they addressed him as 'Boy'. I watched Boy go through similar trials to myself. I watched his hair dry up like straw and fall out. I watched him burning with fever as I burned. I watched him laugh in the morning and cry at night as I laughed and cried. I watched him lying, waiting and waiting and waiting as the seasons outside the window changed and the sun rose lower and lower." Limpic sniffed and smiled a half-smile. "The fires subsided and with them my dreams. I was free to come and go as I pleased. My whiskers grew back and life returned to normal."

Limpic frowned and listened for a moment to the sea slapping against the hull of the ship. *Polestar*'s timbers creaked a little as the sun began to wake her up. Eventually he continued, after a long, heavy sigh. His voice was so quiet that Truvius leaned forward to hear. "One night I dreamt again. It was near the end of the year, not long past the winter solstice. I entered the room as before and found the bed empty. Even the crow was gone. For a moment I panicked and then I heard laughter – joyous, happy laughter. The sound of a family at peace. I heard glasses chinking and beautiful music and someone shouting 'A new beginning!' And then more laughter." Limpic stopped speaking and stared into the middle distance.

"What is it?" asked Truvius. "Limpic, why do you look so sad?"

Limpic felt a lump in his throat and a prickly sensation in his nose. The skin around his jaw tightened. "I listened as the music and voices died away and I walked to the window in the room. For the first time I saw the garden outside, and a stone driveway flanked on both sides by huge cherry trees that almost met in the middle. The sun passed by the sky many times and the cherries began to bloom." Limpic stopped and rubbed his eyes. "The sky grew red out to the east, like the sun was rising but the sun was already up. And then I saw flames dripping from the clouds, out there in the east. The cherry trees began to wilt and burn. And then a crow cawed from the chimney ..."

"And then what?" said Truvius, his eyes wide.

"I heard wailing," said Limpic. His eyes streamed and he

rubbed his nose with the back of his hand. "And a voice saying things like, 'no, no it can't be back. I did everything you asked – I went through everything you said.' The flames from outside broke into the room and a shadow fell across the empty bed. The heat was incredible and I had to back-pedal towards the door as the crow cawed and cawed and cawed." Sweat beaded on Limpic's brow and he breathed heavily.

"I tried to wake up but couldn't. Everything was on fire and collapsing in on itself and my body ached like it was ready to burst. I heard someone singing, someone trying to soothe my fears. I felt their cool hand on my brow but … but I thought my bones would turn to dust and I just couldn't breathe. I knew I was feeling what he felt – the boy, I mean. And I had this terrible sense of what lay ahead. There was no curtain of ignorance to shield me. I knew what was coming. The headaches, the ulcers, the lethargy – and the fire, over and over again. Burning everything. My mind splintered and I fell in a heap gnashing my teeth. Just when I thought I couldn't take it anymore there was a sharp stab of pain in my chest and then I was outside the room and the door slammed shut. The paint on the door blistered but contained what was inside and I woke with a start in my own room. Everything looked fresh and clean on a bright winter morning and there was no crow in the chimney."

"And the pain in your chest," said Truvius, "it was your …"

"My flower," said Limpic with a nod. His lips were trembling and his voice was thick. "I woke to find it grafted into my chest and I was well. I don't know what I would have done if it hadn't come, if it hadn't saved me."

"That's, I mean …" Truvius sat back and hugged his knees. His mouth opened and shut a few times as he peered down at the salt-dusted timbers. The ship rocked a little, nudged by an errant swell. "And what about your family?" he finally whispered.

"I found them in the house, waking as I had," said Limpic. "Apparently we'd all slept through the new year. We stumbled bleary-eyed from the house to find a fresh fall of clean white snow. I told them about my dreams and the flower and we all sat down in the snow together and just hugged. Nobody had to speak. We knew a shadow had passed by."

After a moment or two of quiet contemplation Limpic spoke again. "I know my dreams were real. 'A window into reality', as my grandfather once said. I know that Boy is real, and that for a time I walked the same path as him. A child of the fire." Limpic stood and dusted his legs. "About five years later my parents heard the call of the ocean. They took their limpet boat and, like all ullans before them, sailed off into the west. They left me in charge of the Golden Coast. I'm still not sure why – I don't feel strong enough. But I think it has something to do with my flower." Limpic gave a half chuckle. "When I was ill I always expected the call of the ocean. At times I desperately wanted to hear it so that I could be free, but it never came. I just had to keep plodding on, as it were."

Truvius wiped his eyes and looked the other way. "When I'm around you I feel better," he said, his voice thick with emotion. "And your flower has much to do with that. It's good."

Limpic stroked the petals. "I think it is too," he replied. "And I think, I mean I *know* that it stopped the silver that night on the Valla Stones, however incredible that sounds. And last night something was happening again – something that shouldn't have been happening, and my flower stopped it with fire. With a cleansing, healing, protecting fire that knew what shouldn't be there."

"Maybe it's like my immune system," suggested Truvius. "With the silver in my veins I rarely get ill because it fights off infection. It literally rushes to a cut or scratch and closes it before anything can get in."

"Hmm," said Limpic. "That's not a bad analogy. My flower always glows red when danger's near— no, wait," said Limpic thinking back, "it glows red when it thinks I'm in danger. At other times it's pinkish. When things aren't right."

Truvius cleared his throat and patted Limpic awkwardly. "We should get going."

"We're probably badly off course," said Limpic grimly. "We've lost a whole night."

He drew out his compass. The needle pointed to the front of the ship: west.

"Well, we're pointing the right direction, anyway," he said, making for the steps to the top deck. His legs felt leaden and he groaned as he climbed.

He squinted in the bright sunlight and had to steady himself. The air was heavy with the smell of salt that coated the entire deck in a fine dusting of white powder. The sky was as blue as it had ever been; similar to a huge upturned bowl with some flowery cloud-like decorations near its rim. A large, jagged stump protruded from midship: the remains of the mast. Tatters of rope and netting lay in bundles here and there and some even trailed lazily in the waters on either side of the ship. An angry twisted hole was all that was left of the doorway into the main cabin.

"Could've been worse, I suppose," mumbled Truvius, crawling up beside his friend with a grunt. He held his hand above his eyes and surveyed the damage.

"Aye," replied Limpic. "Go up onto the poop deck and check if the bubble is still there. I'll climb onto the forecastle."

They split up, criss-crossing the deck to avoid fallen debris. Limpic clambered onto the shoulders of the forecastle and strained his eyes into the faraway distance. All he could see were the low-hanging clouds. The sea itself was no more than a placid millpond with barely a ripple in any direction.

Limpic turned and called to Truvius. "Well?"

Truvius lifted his hands to his mouth. "Bubble still here. Needs to be tightened."

Limpic pursed his lips and thought for a moment or two. His stomach growled. He withdrew to the main deck and met Truvius. "We should eat something and then give the ship a good checking over. If we find her watertight, we'll sail on."

Truvius nodded slowly and stared far out to sea.

Limpic followed his gaze. "There's nothing we can do for him now. Only complete our quest."

Truvius blinked a few times and gritted his teeth. "I know," he said. "I think there are porridge oats below deck in a bag stored up high. They shouldn't be wet. I'll make a late breakfast while you check over the top deck." He turned on his heel and disappeared through the hatch.

Limpic stood for a moment longer staring at the far blue horizon. He stroked his flower and shook his head. It wouldn't do to dwell on what could not be changed. Brutonia would not have wanted that. Besides, there was work to do and Limpic set about it dutifully and mechanically. Cutting off rope or netting that was too tattered to be of any use and fixing any that could be mended. He drew the bubble tightly to the ship and checked if any of the water barrels were fresh. He found one and drew some water for Truvius. The other barrels were emptied out and set up to catch more rainwater.

"It's ready," called Truvius. They ate their breakfast together in silence by the stump of the mainmast.

"Keel's watertight," said Truvius.

Limpic licked his spoon. "I found my boat hanging over the starboard side. If you could help me drag it in, we'll be on our way."

Truvius rose and followed Limpic and they pulled the little vessel back on board.

"Is it seaworthy?" panted Truvius. Sweat glistened on his forehead.

"Seems to be," said Limpic, running his hands over the rippled shell.

"Maybe we should check the bubble again?" said Truvius, his eyes darting across the horizon.

Limpic put his hand on his arm. "We have to go now."

The sun was high in the sky but it would soon be slipping from its perch on its westward descent.

Truvius nodded glumly and followed Limpic up onto the forecastle. He waited there as Limpic crawled out onto the bowsprit.

Limpic drew in a deep breath and took one long last look around the ship. His lips quivered. "Goodbye, Brutonia," he said, and nudged *Polestar* forward.

Truvius fell on his knees and covered his face with his hands.

Limpic blinked and sniffed as tears streaked his cheeks, blurring the western horizon until the sky and sea became one.

Chapter 11

Limpic woke to a gentle nudging of his shoulder. He sat up quickly and grabbed Truvius's hand.

"What is it?" he gasped. "Another storm?"

"No, I just wanted to let you know the sun is setting," said Truvius, pulling Limpic to his feet.

Limpic stretched and stared at the sinking orb. It was nestling behind a thick belt of cloud that glowed from behind like coals heaped in the fire. He wiped sweat from his forehead. It was definitely getting warmer.

"Good work," he said to Truvius, after his nerves had settled. "I'll take over for a bit and then we can both get something to eat. Maybe you could get a fire started before it gets too dark?"

"Aye, aye, Cap'n," replied Truvius. Immediately his face darkened. Brutonia had been the last to say that. He slunk off into the gathering gloom.

Limpic rubbed his face wearily. He still felt tired. Maybe it was the heat, the closeness in the air. A couple of hours of sleep had done little to dent a leaden lethargy that clung to his bones, and his head felt stuffy and full.

He returned to his perch on the bowsprit and watched as the last of the sunlight bled into the horizon. A few stars were beginning to peek out. The flaming coals were being quenched by the rapid onslaught of the night. Soon a steely darkness shrouded the entire ship and she seemed to be treading in water as black as the pitch between her timbers. Limpic sniffed the air uneasily and his whiskers trembled sensing there was something wrong, or that something was about to go wrong. It had turned *very* dark *very* quickly.

"The fire's lit," called Truvius from the gloom.

Limpic stuck out his bottom lip and made a popping sound. He decided that some food and firelight would settle his suspicious mind. *Polestar* wouldn't drift too far off course with no one at the helm.

"We still have plenty of dried meat," said Truvius sifting through one of their bags. He turned another over and a congealed pile of foodstuffs slopped to the deck. "Most are like this, though – saltwater damage."

"I feel like fish anyway," said Limpic. "We might as well keep our supplies in case we really need them."

So Limpic rooted through the bottom of his boat and found some line and tackle. He attached a small piece of the dried meat as bait and threw the line over the side before checking their bearings. *Polestar* was still sailing due west. He closed his compass with a satisfied click and stirred up the fire. He checked his line: three small fish. He took them to the light of the fire.

"Rainbow trout?" suggested Truvius.

"Em, not quite," said Limpic, studying the fish. "Too small, although the colours are exquisite." He set about preparing the meal.

Soon he and Truvius were licking their fingers. "Excellent," said Truvius with a contented sigh after they were finished. "I could get used to your open-air cooking."

"Thank you," said Limpic inclining his head.

Truvius yawned and stretched his arms high above his head.

"You should get some sleep," said his companion. "I'll take the next watch and call you if I need anything."

Truvius nodded and stifled another yawn. "I might lie in what's left of the cabin," he said. "It feels too dark to lie under the stars."

Truvius took out his Solaar and used it to guide his way to the cabin. After a few minutes the light went out and Limpic was left to the night.

He stirred the fire one last time and went back to his watch, correcting their bearings by a few degrees. He settled himself as best he could and tried to wriggle his clothes into a better fit but they were sticking to him in all the wrong places. Try as he might, he just couldn't get comfortable.

The darkness was oppressive, even with the light of the stars. It was like a weight bearing down on him. And his mind would not settle; it rushed off in different directions searching for something to worry about – a cause for his anxieties. Inevitably it always returned to the darkness.

His flower flushed pink. Something definitely wasn't right. Limpic closed his eyes and massaged his temples. He pinched his nose and felt his inner ear pop. He was about to get up and walk the main deck when he thought he heard something. He halted and held his breath, listening intently. The sound was coming from his inner ear. He tried to open it further but all he could hear were creaks and groans as though he was underwater.

Limpic pinched his nose and swallowed. Something popped inside his ears and warm seawater trickled from them. Left over from the storm, no doubt, and probably why he felt so stuffy.

Familiar vibrations purred inside his ears. Vibrations he hadn't heard for some time – silvery timbres. He stiffened.

"Limpic, I am so very, very ill," said a voice. "I do not think I can rise another night."

The moon!

Limpic strained his eyes in the dark and fear caused his heart to skip a beat. He realised that by now the moon should be well on her way to her zenith but she was nowhere in sight. No wonder it was so dark.

"I'm here," whispered Limpic. He didn't know why he was trying to talk to the moon. "I'm here waiting for you. Come to me, moon, please. You can't give up. I won't let you."

Limpic's mouth went dry and his breath came in short bursts. He closed his eyes tightly and held his breath. Nothing. Not a sound.

"Moon," whispered Limpic. His heart was racing and blood churned around his ears.

"Moon!" he pleaded, "we cannot live without you." His flower blazed red and he knew something had to be done – but what? At his wits' end he stumbled blindly in the dark, somehow navigating to midship or thereabouts where he tripped over the stump of the mast. He lay in a heap staring at the stars. His head spun.

A shadow passed overhead and there was a thud behind him. Limpic rolled over and stood up. His stomach tightened and his scalp crawled. A shape a little darker than the night stood just beyond him. Limpic retreated backwards gagging on his tongue. His flower faded to a dull pink.

"Ge ... get away," he managed to croak.

The dark thing followed.

Something rammed into the back of his legs. "Oomph!" grunted Limpic falling backwards. The back of his head hit a hard surface and his chin was pushed onto his chest. His body had fallen into his boat but his legs still hung over the side. The dark shape appeared by his knees. Limpic's whole body spasmed. He kicked out and fumbled in the dark, trying to release the catch at the bottom of his boat. If only he could find a weapon.

"Tru ..." he stammered, groping blindly in the dark. "Truvius!" His voice was dry and cracked.

His hand fell on something better than a weapon. "Solaar!" gasped Limpic. Relief flooded his body and he turned the shaft of light in the direction of the dark form and it retreated. Buoyed by its reluctance to face the light, Limpic clambered out of the boat and swung the light this way and that.

"Get away!" he yelled, regaining his voice. He shone the Solaar ahead of him and its light brushed over a bundle of clothes lying in a heap near the mast. Was that there before? There was a movement to Limpic's right. He threw the light of the torch in that direction but whatever it was eluded him. Then he heard footsteps, slow and methodical. He spun the torch around again but his light caught nothing.

"You know, on threshing night, when the moon was full, my uncle used to tell me that it was only a reflection of the sun," said a voice close by.

"Zarkus!" said Limpic. His hair bristled. "Zarkus, you must help me."

He felt pressure on his hand, the one holding the Solaar. The pressure pushed the torch upwards so that its light reached out into the heavens.

"My uncle used to say that the moon simply borrowed the

sun's light," said Zarkus in a strange bloodless voice.

Limpic peered at the torch and his eyes widened as he realised the significance of Zarkus's words. "I can give this light to the moon!" he exclaimed.

"And the sooner the better," replied Zarkus, his voice drifting away.

"I'm coming!" Limpic bellowed, suddenly running and using the Solaar to guide his way. He climbed onto the poop deck but caught his toe on the last step, which sent him sprawling across the rough wooden timbers.

"Ow!" he yelped. The Solaar clattered from his hand and spun towards the bulwark where there was an opening for water to drain away. Limpic swallowed and crept gingerly towards it, holding his breath and biting his lip. It was halfway through the gap and shone far out to sea.

"Gotcha!" he gasped after one mad grasp. Then he was up and running to the stern. "I'm coming, Moon, I'm coming! I'll find you!" He raised the torch above his head and pointed it to the east, its light spreading and picking out the curvature of the Earth.

"Come to me, Moon!" he cried.

There was a murmur and a blink on the skyline. A moment of stillness, a moment of quiet contemplation, and then the moon crept over the edge of the horizon, tentative and laboured, ruddy faced and unsure. She stalled, retreated a little and then seemed to steady herself, staggering ungamely until she found her feet. Slowly, ponderously she rallied her legs and strove with growing purpose and poise into the night sky, skirting along the edge of the firmaments sphere. She trailed behind her and ethereal shadow of silver so that her appearance was more like that of a comet arching across the heavens.

Finally, wringing the last drops of light from Limpic's torch, the moon found her empty spot on the western side of the sky. One side of her was shrouded in the shadow of her cycle but her colour was better and silver fingers reached from her face. She kissed Limpic, she kissed the ship and her light settled gently over all the world. The surface of the sea appeared slick and oily and filled with stars.

Limpic sat down wearily. He drew his hand over his eyes and let out a little moan. His torch stuttered one last time and then went out.

"The world will live for another day," he whispered. And then?

"Limpic! Limpic! Come quickly," shouted Truvius, his voice sounding as if on the verge of delirium.

The sense of urgency in Truvius's request sent Limpic's heart back into a panic. He stood up ready to face whatever came at him. He left the poop deck and made to midship, easily navigating by the light of the moon. He found a half-dressed Truvius cradling the bundle of clothes by the stump of the mast.

"Limpic, it's a miracle." He was sobbing.

Limpic stepped closer. He saw an unconscious face within the clothes and his eyes welled up.

"Brutonia?"

Truvius rocked on his heels, giddy with excitement. "He's alive! Our Brutonia is alive! I don't know how."

"Zarkus," said Limpic solemnly.

He turned and stared out to sea. For a moment a lone shadowy figure on a horse stood silhouetted against the skyline.

"Zarkus saved him." He looked to the moon. "Zarkus saved us all."

Chapter 12

Limpic shivered. The day was miserable and humid. A vast curtain of mist rolled across *Polestar*'s bow. Water collected on the end of Limpic's nose and ran in rivulets down his chin. He wiped it away with the back of his hand and sniffed. It was mid-morning and they had been sailing, rather languidly, for a few hours.

They had spent the latter part of the night sitting by Brutonia. Although his breathing was deep and true, he showed no sign of wakening. His face was peaceful and wore a hint of a smile, as though he knew something they didn't but wanted to keep it to himself a little longer. By the first morning light, after dozing for a couple of hours, Limpic had decided to sail on. Truvius was to keep an eye on the sleeping Brutonia.

Limpic stretched his back and rubbed his eyes. His head felt a little woolly staring into the thick mizzle of rain that stuck to every surface of the ship. He thought his eyes were playing tricks on him because every so often he caught a glimpse of a shadowy form to starboard or to port, or he thought he saw eyes that burned with amber fire.

"Here," said Truvius, reaching him a tin cup of hot tea. Limpic took the mug gratefully and cradled it in his hands, the warmth causing him to shiver involuntarily.

"How far do you think we still have to go?" said Truvius quietly. He was staring blankly into the middle distance.

Limpic took a swallow of his tea and it burned its way down into his stomach. He cleared his throat. "I shouldn't think much longer – tonight maybe. If not, tomorrow."

Truvius shrugged and slipped away into the gloom of the forecastle. His shoulders were bowed as though he carried the weight of the world on them.

Limpic took another mouthful of tea and stared at the water droplets running along the surface of the bowsprit, collecting and pooling and running down the side until they became so heavy they fell off into the grey waters beneath.

"Just like Truvius," he whispered to himself.

Ever since the night before and the mention of his brother, Truvius had become disinterested, distracted and distant. It was clear his heart was heavy again, and he was carrying a weight that he wouldn't share. He had taken to avoiding Limpic as much as possible, shying away from any contact. Yet now he had brought tea?

Limpic drained his mug and wiped his mouth. He stood up and stamped some life into his feet. Jagged pins and needles crept from his toes to his calves. The mind was strange – or maybe it was the heart? Surely they should have been ecstatic. Brutonia had been returned to them unharmed and was sleeping safely in the cabin. The moon had risen and set and a new day had dawned. And yet a darkness had fallen across *Polestar*. Limpic could feel it gnawing at his own heart. A melancholy as thick and heavy as the mizzle that cloaked the ship.

He peered into the empty mug and breathed heavily. There was nothing for it. They just had to keep going. They were in

115

too deep and the stakes were too high. "To the ends of the Earth," said Limpic, lifting his empty mug in mock celebration. He stroked the petals of the fire flower. It had burned red when it thought the moon was lost – danger, but had receded to pink when Zarkus came on board. It knew what shouldn't be there, so it knew that Zarkus *needed* to be there? His presence had saved them all.

"Aye, aye, aye." Limpic sighed. The Cra certainly shouldn't be here, that was for sure. They were invaders from outside. And the silver was a threat of their making. Heat rose onto Limpic's face and it wasn't from his flower.

"I'm coming for you," he growled. He dug his heels into the bowsprit. *Polestar* seemed to sense this new steely determination and her timbers shuddered briefly as she leapt forward, cutting almost silently through the gloom. Her prow cast aside both water and mist in equal measure and Limpic contented himself in the knowledge that they were getting closer to their goal.

***

It wasn't until his stomach growled that Limpic realised another few hours had passed, so set had he been in putting some distance behind them. He wanted to look in on Brutonia – not that he was overly worried about him, but his presence would be much appreciated. He had a good, simple heart. He was as steady of mind with the sun on his face or on his back, or with the rain lashing from every direction at once. Some grub, some rest and things to do. That was Brutonia.

Limpic checked his compass and grunted approvingly. They were still on course. He left *Polestar* to guide herself and made his way gingerly across the forecastle, almost slipping on the wet, slimy timbers. He dropped silently onto the main deck and took the deck brush from below the steps that led back up onto the forecastle. Carefully he made to midship. His ears creaked and he opened them fully, hearing the all-too-familiar whispers. He found Truvius slumped against the stump of the mainmast peering sombrely into nothing. He was staring into the void, inviting the darkness into his soul. Limpic's flower fluttered to a dull pink. Truvius was flirting with the Cra.

Limpic thrust the brush head into his stomach.

"Deck needs a good seeing to," he said cheerfully. "Nothing worse for the soul than an idle mind and a healthy body with little to do."

Truvius peered up at him blankly. His pupils became mere pinpricks. He lashed out at the brush, knocking it violently from Limpic's grasp.

Limpic felt his face glow and a surge of heat sweep over him. "Listen here!" he growled, catching Truvius by his lapels and pulling him roughly to his feet. "Get this deck in order right now!"

The flower on his chest throbbed red, but only briefly, and then the anger in Truvius's eyes turned to fear and regret.

"Yes, yes, of course," he spluttered. "Please, please, you're burning me."

Limpic glared at him before his heart softened. He dropped his hands and Truvius scurried off brushing the deck as though his life depended on it. Limpic shook his head and stared at his hands. They pulsed with heat. Truvius's words came back to him: "When I am around you I feel better."

"Hello," said a soft, yet familiar voice.

Limpic turned and the inside of his nose prickled. His flower

117

turned snow-white. Brutonia was standing in the doorway of the cabin with a blanket draped around his shoulders. He looked a little confused and weary but apart from that seemed fine.

"Is the storm over?"

Limpic chuckled. "Two days ago." He ran and hugged his friend tightly, thumping him on the back. "So glad to see you," he croaked through gritted teeth.

"Whoa, steady on!" said Brutonia laughing. He peeled Limpic off. "I'd the strangest dream." He held his stomach and belched. "And I'm so hungry I could eat a horse." He plunged a thick, stumpy finger into his ear and began to rout around vigorously, twitching his mouth like a dog after fleas.

Limpic grinned. "I would give you an army of horses if I could," he said. He laughed and found that his heart wasn't so heavy all of a sudden. The sight of his friend lifted the mood on deck. Even the curtain of rain eased, and somewhere above them a brighter patch began to glow behind the clouds. Soon the sun had managed to burrow its way through and the deck of *Polestar* was bathed in its light.

"I'll fetch us something," said Limpic. "You settle yourself beside the mast here."

Brutonia shuffled over and Limpic went to find food.

***

"Not quite the feast of midwinter," said Brutonia after they had eaten, "but it won't do to complain."

"You certainly stuffed it in," replied Truvius. "Not much chat out of you."

"It's as my father used to say," said Brutonia, "'every bleat a sheep gives it loses a bite'."

118

Limpic and Truvius stared at him then burst out laughing.

"It's good to see you again, Brutonia. It really is," said Truvius, drying his eyes.

"It's the strangest thing," said Brutonia, shaking his head in bemusement.

"What is?" Limpic asked.

"Well," began Brutonia, and he laughed and rubbed his temples before speaking. "The night of the storm I was doing exactly like you asked – keeping my head down. It was awful, water going into my mouth and outta my ears and everything. And then I heard this great crack and saw your boat sliding across the deck. I know how much you love that boat, so I thought if I could just grab hold of it, I could tie it back down again. But as soon as I'd untied myself and stood up, the wind and the waves hit me and I was like a falling tree. I caught your boat alright, or rather it caught me – right behind the knees. Before I knew it, I was in the water." He shuddered at the memory.

"Then all I can remember is being thrown one way and then the other as *Polestar* disappeared from sight. I must have started dreamin' or hallucinatin' or something because ..." Brutonia hung his head sheepishly "... well, I could have sworn I saw Zarkus out in the middle of the storm riding a black horse that had eyes as red as fiery coals." He laughed half-heartedly.

Limpic and Truvius glanced at each other and Limpic remembered the shadowy form he'd seen earlier with the eyes of amber. His throat went dry.

"What happened then?" asked Truvius. His jawline tightened considerably.

"Well," continued Brutonia, "and mind I'd drank a lot of seawater now, won't you. Zarkus comes right up to me on the horse and says: 'Your heart's too big for your head, Brutonia. It always was. You shouldn't have untied yourself from the ship.'" The elvern threw back his head and guffawed. "Well, I just lay right back in the water and giggled like a child. I'd lost myself and now my mind."

Brutonia sat forward and suddenly frowned. "After that I must have passed out because the next thing I remember I was standing in the doorway of the cabin on *Polestar*." He peered at Limpic. "How did I get here? You found me somehow, didn't you?"

Limpic shook his head. "Zarkus found you. He saved you. He's been following us since we left Dalbain."

All of a sudden it seemed very hot and humid.

Brutonia sat back and whistled. "Now there's a thing," he said softly. He grinned a wide toothy grin and the shadow that threatened to fall passed. "Why doesn't he just come aboard? Save that poor horse of his having to tread so much water."

Limpic chuckled and even Truvius snorted in amusement. Then the skin around his eyes puckered and he laughed till tears ran down his face.

"Oh, Bru, it's the way you tell 'em."

Brutonia's smirk soon faded when they filled him in on everything they knew about the Cra returning to Dalbain. Limpic told him what he knew of his flower and everything he'd said to Truvius so that there was nothing hidden from him.

"Secrets," said Brutonia shaking his head at Truvius. "Secrets will be your death, old friend."

Truvius smiled awkwardly. "It is great to see you again, Brutonia. It really is."

Brutonia placed a hand on Limpic's shoulder. "I don't pretend to fully understand everything you've told me about yourself or to really understand what you've been through, but I can say this," Brutonia smiled and patted Limpic's shoulder, "I like flowers." He rose to his feet, dusted crumbs off his huge chest and shook the blanket off his shoulders.

"Are we still on course?" He stretched and ran his thumb along the blade of Dunnehammer.

"We are," said Limpic. "Shouldn't be too much longer until we reach—" he was thrown onto his stomach with a grunt as *Polestar* ground to an abrupt halt.

"What was that?" asked Truvius, gingerly picking himself off Brutonia.

"We've hit something," shouted Limpic over his shoulder as he scurried up onto the forecastle and out onto the bowsprit. He leaned over and strained his neck in the direction of the ship's prow.

"Well?" called Brutonia, climbing up behind him.

Limpic sat up and shook his head. "Nothing. Not as far as I can see anyway."

"Nothing to stern, port or starboard," said Truvius, scrambling up beside Brutonia.

With no warning the ship began to vibrate and creak causing Limpic to lose his footing. He managed to hold on and then gasped as the prow of the ship slowly edged into the water.

"We're sinking!" cried Brutonia. "And I've only just been rescued."

Limpic steadied himself. "We're not sinking," he said breathlessly. "We're being pulled under!"

Truvius lurched forward and clung to the rail that ran around the forecastle. His face was deathly white. "By what?" he stammered.

Limpic pointed. "By that."

Four large fingers made of overlapping black scales curled onto the port side of the forecastle, creeping further and further up. They reached the top and hooked themselves over the bulwarks.

"Look!" cried Truvius pointing in the opposite direction. The same thing was happening to starboard.

"And there!" shouted Limpic, pointing beneath his feet.

Two enormous thumbs, belonging to the eight enormous fingers grasped *Polestar*'s prow. A submerged giant was cupping the front of the ship between its hands.

Brutonia swung Dunnehammer and its blade sparked against the black scales.

"Didn't even dent it!" he exclaimed before being unceremoniously flicked aside where he lay in a dazed stupor.

"We should have run for the bubble!" shouted Truvius. "The vibrations are going to shake the ship to bits before it even sinks." He was trying in vain to jab one of the fingers with his rapier.

Polestar's stern lifted from the water and her prow shuddered beneath the surface. Brutonia and Truvius gave up fighting the giant fingers and clung to the ship's bulwarks.

"Vibrations!" cried Limpic, slapping his forehead. He splashed from the submerged bowsprit and swam to the forecastle bulwarks. Using them like a ladder he climbed to the steps that led to the main deck. The main deck towered above him at a forty-five-degree angle and everything that wasn't tied down came crashing towards him in a chaotic cacophony of rough and tumble.

"My boat!" shouted Limpic. It was wedged near the top of the bedraggled pile of paraphernalia swamping this end of the deck.

He half slid, half fell down the steps and stumbled into the boat. "Aha!" he cried, drawing out the Echo Shell. It was glowing like the colours of the sky as the sun sets – purples and oranges and pinks. It hummed in his hand.

He placed it to his mouth and blew as hard as he could. A sonorous boom lifted from the shell and in the same instance *Polestar* was released and her keel hit the water with a fantastic smack and a great spray of water showered her deck. She rocked backwards and forwards a few times and then sat still.

Brutonia's face appeared from over the forecastle bulwarks, flushed and taut. Truvius appeared beside him.

"What happened?"

"Remember the Echo Shell Amoso told us about – the one Tabitha returned to us in the hallway of the king's castle?"

"When it vibrates we're to summon the Gatekeeper," said Brutonia, thumping Truvius between the shoulder blades.

"Only we kind of forgot that part," said Limpic sheepishly, "and the whole ship began to vibrate."

"No wonder Amoso said to guard it with our lives," said Truvius, rubbing his back.

"And to think I left it in my boat that almost got washed away," said Limpic.

All three laughed, nervously at first and then in full-blown hysteria as it dawned on them how lucky they were to be alive.

"Well, I won't be losing it again," said Limpic. He found some tattered rigging nearby and with his bone knife cut off some lengths and fashioned a cord that he attached to either end of the shell. He looped the whole thing over his shoulders to let it hang snugly by his side. "There," he said, patting the shell.

Limpic climbed up beside his friends, his eyes examining the sky at the front of the ship, which was burning amber behind the mist. "The sun must be setting," he mused.

The mist burned away and the sky became clearer revealing a huge figure seated on a throne of emerald water between *Polestar* and the horizon. His eyes were pure white and stared blankly behind the ship, in the direction they had come.

"Welcome to the Gates of Dusk. I am the Gatekeeper," he thundered.

Chapter 13

They stood, awed, in a huddle at the front of the ship. The Gatekeeper sat on an emerald throne the surface of which moved like seawater. His hands rested on silent waves that arched yet never broke. His robes were of agitated water, restless and moving, held in the form of a man. His hair was silver, like pools of water beneath an overcast sky, always swaying this way and that as though animated by a breeze. His beard was long, swaying back and forth like seaweed waving in a current. And always he stared forward, with eyes as white as snow. The water around his feet steamed and boiled like waters pummelled beneath a huge waterfall. Behind him, seen through his semi-transparent state, reared the Gates of Dusk, and stretching from either side of them were huge walls of emerald rocks cut at different angles. Any one of them could have sunk *Polestar* had she ventured further to her right or left. Indeed, the carcasses of various vessels and floating debris littered the base of the walls.

Limpic felt something dig into his back. He turned and found Brutonia nudging him and nodding.

"Alright," hissed Limpic, "alright, I'll go." He stepped forward and cleared his throat. "We come seeking the Golden

Mile," he said. He was painfully aware of how small and lowly his voice sounded.

"Six others have passed this way seeking the Golden Mile," replied the Gatekeeper.

Limpic licked his lips. "Were there not seven?"

"Seven came but only six passed," replied the Gatekeeper. His voice rose and fell like the swell of the tide but his body remained still. "The seventh floundered and became as silver on the very deck of his ship."

Limpic could feel his companions' eyes boring into his back. *Became as silver.* He must have been turned by the enemy from the west.

Limpic shook away the image in his head. "May we pass?" he asked.

"You sounded the horn," replied the Gatekeeper. "You will catch the flaming serpent and travel to the sun's place of rest."

Limpic opened his mouth to say something and then closed it.

"I think that means we can pass," whispered Truvius.

Limpic turned and glared at him.

Brutonia smiled encouragingly and nodded.

Limpic was about to move when the Gatekeeper continued. "Because you were not responsible for the storm that befell your ship you may retrieve your belongings."

"Our ... our belongings?" stammered Limpic.

The Gatekeeper didn't move. "Your ship is dishevelled – without mast or sail. Its cargo was washed overboard. You may retrieve your belongings."

Limpic fidgeted with his fingers. "It's ... ah, it's not that we don't wish to retrieve our belongings, sir. It's just that the ... the feat seems impossible for us."

"Well said," whispered Brutonia.

"Sshh!" said Limpic scowling.

"Then you may make use of the Critters," said the Gatekeeper.

Before any of them could move or speak or even think, the water before them began to froth as though it was being thrashed by a million fish. A mast and various barrels were taken from the rocks and carried, seemingly magically, onto the ship and the mast was righted and spliced into position.

"Look!" exclaimed Truvius.

They had rushed to the rear of the foredeck and were gaping at the middle of the ship. Tiny eyes with long spindly legs were scurrying all over *Polestar*'s deck like an army of ants. Every surface of the ship crawled and moved like bees around a hive and there was a sound similar to people rubbing their hands together. The Critters worked together as a team, wordlessly passing along barrels and nets, timbers and provisions until the ship was fully restocked. Everything was lashed down as though a storm was about to hit and some of the empty barrels were opened and stuffed with food before being sealed closed.

"There's a quare wheen o' them," said Limpic. Truvius and Brutonia stared at him and Limpic laughed. "What I mean to say is there are quite a lot of them!"

"You're telling me!" exclaimed Brutonia.

With a sound like a flock of birds leaving their nests, the Critters swept back into the sea leaving *Polestar* clean and pristine.

"My hat!" Limpic found it sitting right next to him. He beamed happily and put it on.

"Brr, I don't like creeping things," said Brutonia with a shiver.

"Let's get going," said Truvius, still staring at the mast.

"Agreed," said the other two.

"I presume we just sail towards the gate?" said Brutonia. "Yer boady doesn't seem a talkative type."

Limpic gazed up at the Gatekeeper but he made no sound. He climbed out onto the bowsprit and gently urged *Polestar* forward. They slid softly through the water and passed straight through the Gatekeeper's robes. Water droplets clung heavily to their clothes and the sound of surging water echoed all around the ship.

They came to the gates and paused. They were not really gates at all but rather two enormous stained-glass windows set within an arch beneath a large spire. In the middle of the windows was a huge golden sun that perched on a long winding stalk – an emerald river or the stem of a flower. A silver crescent moon wrapped itself around the left side of the sun. The rest of the glass was made up of purple and pink hues, ambers and different shades of red – all the colours at the end of the day.

Limpic's flower fluttered and shone in cool colours. The window was dotted with fire flowers that blinked and winked as light filtered through them. Instinctively he opened his inner ear and heard music – or voices, he couldn't be quite sure. It flowed around and about him, streaming towards the window, light and airy and yet beguilingly soporific. Limpic stifled a yawn. He had visions of silent empty places where foxes tread and owls keep watch; of moorland heather ruffled by a passing wind, fading into the gloom of an evening as the colours of day melt into oblivion; an empty farmyard in the half-light and a shed where cattle settle into straw and low gently; of firesides and soft comfy beds and dusk light falling across tired, heavy eyes as stories are whispered by candlelight.

"Fire flowers here?" he yawned. His chin settled on his chest.

Polestar glowed in burnished gold and the air was thick with a sweet scent. The huge windows swung open and brightness streamed through the gap, rolling like a cloud as shafts of light dazzled from within. Limpic turned his face away. He gripped the bowsprit with his knees and the ship moved forward without his instruction. For a moment more he was blinded, hiding behind his fingers until *Polestar* stopped and they emerged, blinking, in the light of a setting sun. All the west was aflame. Before them was a golden path, stretching and tapering towards the distant horizon.

The Golden Mile.

Brutonia and Truvius both yawned, lifting their heads lazily from the bulwarks of the foredeck.

"Where do we go from here, Cap'n?" said Truvius, rubbing his eyes. They were red-rimmed and sleepy.

Limpic shielded his eyes from the glow of the sun and pointed to the west. "Right into the heart of the amber eye."

Truvius nodded. "Then let's do it."

Polestar glided off, cutting purposefully through the water with only her lengthening shadow for company. They sailed like this for over an hour, following the near-vertical descent of the sun.

Limpic set his Solaar out to recharge. Brutonia lit the fire and contented himself in preparing an early supper. The three sailors took turns eating and standing watch on the forecastle, ever mindful of the setting sun. Limpic knew that he had to share the burden of guiding the ship. He would not fall asleep so easily this time.

After Limpic had eaten he took over the watch from Truvius.

He sat cross-legged and continually searched the sky at the front of the ship. He couldn't help but feel a thrill of excitement well up from the pit of his stomach as he watched amber fish leap from the waves in front of him. They spread their fins like wings and glided for a moment or two before burrowing back into the golden ocean.

The time came when the sun was no more than a hand span from the horizon and Limpic stirred from his revelry. He called over his shoulder. "Brutonia, Truvius, gather the fire rope and lash it around the bowsprit and forecastle and then anchor it to the base of the mast."

Limpic rose to his feet and tentatively searched the waters as his companions got to work. He retreated to the forecastle and checked the rope was secured, grunting in approval.

"Be ready on every side!" he said. "Who knows what creatures dwell here before they return to the sun. Bring me my bow, Brutonia. I've caught many fish in my time but I've never had to catch a flaming serpent."

The sun had expanded to three times its original size. It was a deep, deep pink but throbbing redder near its base.

"Something stirs in the water to port!" called Truvius.

"Be ready to make for the bubble when I say," replied Limpic. He was tense again, his nerves tingling with adrenaline and his whiskers twitching. The minutes ticked by.

"There's something to starboard!" called Brutonia, returning with the Bow of the Nimue.

Limpic took the bow from him all the while his eyes searching the waters intently, occasionally glancing up to make sure the sun was still right in front of them. It towered above the ship like a crimson tide and was only a fingernail from the horizon, bleeding into the settling gloom of an evening.

Limpic's bow fingers twitched.

"Do you see anything?" he called to Truvius.

"No, the water stills."

"Brutonia?"

Brutonia hastened to starboard and peered down into the golden depths. He shook his head. "I can't see anything ... wait!" He peered closer. "There is something ... I think. I thought I saw something red. Like an eye or ..."

Limpic swallowed and let out a long calming breath. "Keep your wits about you now."

Many minutes passed and finally the sun touched the fabric of the horizon. Immediately the waters began to hiss and snarl, boiling and steaming as she continued to sink.

"Something stirs here!" cried Brutonia. Sweat glistened on his forehead.

"And here!" replied Truvius, his voice excited and nervous and his eyes dancing in his head.

The waters around *Polestar* were relatively calm and serene but the further she drifted towards the boiling sun, the more agitated they became. The air was heavy and thick with steam.

"Steady," insisted Limpic. "All hands steady. That might well be the same something you both see."

He had barely finished speaking when the water on the starboard side erupted startling Brutonia into a yell. A flaming serpent flew out of the ocean and over the mainmast. Water pelted the deck of the ship as the serpent crashed into the waves on the port side causing Truvius to fall backwards in surprise.

"Steady!" cried Limpic. *Polestar* bucked beneath him like a young bull.

The waters began to teem with life. Smaller flaming lizard-like creatures swarmed all around the hull of the ship, letting out ear-piercing screeches. The sea burned with fire and steam as the sun gathered her children from the night. The world's colour was fading.

"Make your way aft, to the poop deck," Limpic told his friends. "Quickly now!" Sweat ran from every part of him and his eyes smarted. It was like standing at the mouth of a vast, open furnace.

No sooner had Brutonia clambered up to stern than a shout came from him. "It's behind us!"

Limpic swung around and stared down the length of the ship. "Get to the bubble!" he shouted. His stomach was in knots. *Polestar* sat between the creature and the sun. It seemed reluctant to move aside the ship. Occasionally it leapt in the air with a snort, sending out steam and fire and a hot wind that dried the sweat on Limpic's face.

"It'll come over the ship," said Limpic. "It *has* to." He tried to swallow but his throat was parched. The waters stilled and Limpic's shoulders drooped a little.

The serpent launched itself over the stern in a sinuous ripple of living flame. Its belly glowed with amber and flicking tongues of fire. With a cry of terror, Limpic drew his bow and an arrow appeared. He coiled the free end of the fire rope around the stem of the arrow and let loose at the creature's gaping mouth. The arrow went right down into the stomach of the beast. Limpic pulled the bow over his head and then lost his footing. He tumbled backwards, clinging to the bowsprit with his fingernails while the sea of serpents snapped at his trailing feet. He groaned and kicked the air.

The great snake roared and disappeared beneath the waves, unfurling a vast length of rope behind it. It appeared then disappeared up ahead, one arching loop after another, heading straight for the sun. The trailing rope finally tightened with a sickening creak and *Polestar* was whisked away at an incredible speed, cutting through the waves like a hot knife through butter. The sun was almost submerged, no more than a glowing dot, and with one last great thrust the serpent leapt into it.

Limpic clambered wearily onto the bowsprit. His heart was thumping against his ribs and his shoulders ached. The air was so thick with steam he could hardly get a good breath. The rope leading from the bowsprit sang with the strain of dragging the ship. If it broke now, it would probably remove Limpic's head from his shoulders. He gulped and ducked down wondering if he should make for the bubble.

With a blink the sun went to her world of rest. Limpic clung to the bowsprit as a limpet clings to a rock. He caught one last look at a star filled sky, then, with great sucking gulps, the ocean swallowed *Polestar* whole and the waves crashed over his shoulders.

Chapter 14

Limpic clung to the front of *Polestar* with all his strength. Never in all his years of exploring the sea had he descended into it at such a pace. The fathoms rushed past and tried to wrench him from his perch, buffeting his face and pressing ever heavier on his chest. It was dark and gloomy but *Polestar* was hurtling through a phosphorescent wake of bubbles and steam, pushing deeper until Limpic thought he was going to burst. He swallowed and swallowed, trying to equalise the pressure building behind his ears and eyes. Fortunately, *Polestar* had spent most of her years in such perilous conditions and she neither flinched nor appeared distressed. From the heights of the heavens to the depths of Earth, nothing could break her.

Limpic was scared of running out of oxygen. I'm at home underwater, he kept telling himself. He swallowed back a sense of panic welling up from his stomach. His eyes were shielded by the thin clear film of his underwater eyelids. His nose pinched closed and he sealed his lips and ears tightly. His lungs ached and his head was beginning to flutter. With every orifice now sealed from the invading waters, he began to breathe through his gills. It only took a matter of seconds for his head to clear and he breathed as easily as if he was on Dalbain's shores.

Far below, in the vast depths of the ocean, great flashes of light silently throbbed. Eventually the velocity of descent began to wane a little and Limpic took the chance to drift back over the ship's hull to check on Truvius and Brutonia. He stopped only to lash his bow to the mainmast and then drifted sternwards. He found the bubble intact, but only half its original size – the result of the huge pressures squeezing it. Limpic gripped underneath it and pushed his head upwards through the viscous membrane. His head popped into the chamber and he was able to see his two friends clearly. The rest of his body trailed limply in the ocean.

"Hello," he said cheerily, opening his eyes and nose fully. "How goes it?"

Truvius and Brutonia were huddled close together peering nervously around their small chamber. It was glowing ever so slightly with an emerald hue. Truvius spoke first, but it was more of a stammer.

"Well, we made it to the bubble alright. But, well, it's kind of cosy."

"What if we run out of air?" Brutonia blurted out. "Or what if the bubble gets punctured or bursts or any other manner of things?"

"Help me in," said Limpic, pushing his arms through.

His two friends grabbed his hands and hauled him in. The membrane sealed itself completely.

"Listen," said Limpic, panting a little. "As long as there is oxygen in the water, there will always be oxygen inside the bubble. It's made from seaweed, remember? And this type of seaweed likes nothing more than to breathe underwater. As far as it bursting, well, my goodness, we would need to touch the core of the world itself. This bubble only gets stronger the more it's compressed. And I don't really know about any other manner of things because it's very hard to worry about things that I don't know about."

Brutonia seemed unconvinced and shifted around uneasily. "Where will we end up?" he asked.

Limpic shrugged.

"So ... what?" said Truvius. "We just sit here and wait to see where we pop out?"

"Please, Truvius, don't use words like 'pop'!" insisted Brutonia, peering around the chamber in alarm. "I think I liked the storm better."

"Hopefully everything is tied down securely," muttered Truvius. "I'd hate to be hit by the same cannonball twice in one adventure."

Limpic laughed and clapped him on the back. "That's the spirit! I passed right over the entire deck and everything seems to be in order. The Critters did a grand job. So now we simply sit back and rest. It's night-time, you know." And then under his breath, "And hopefully I gave the moon enough light to rise again."

"It's always night-time down here," said Brutonia. He groaned and lay back with a grimace as the bubble squeaked.

"We need to try and get some sleep," said Limpic yawning. He watched Brutonia's nervous movements. "We just have to wait it out."

Brutonia grunted and Truvius flinched with every shudder the bubble made.

"Tell you what," said Limpic gently. He remembered a trick he'd learned when he wasn't well. "Lie back and don't sleep. Just stare through half-closed eyes at nothing in particular.

Imagine you're tucked up in bed on a stormy night."

His friends grumbled at first and circled round on all fours like two dogs picking the best spot to lie. Eventually they settled, mumbling under their breaths. Limpic took out his razor shell and began to play gently. He closed his eyes and allowed the music to rise and fall with the movement of the bubble. How long he kept it up he wasn't sure, but when he finally opened his eyes his two companions were sleeping soundly.

Limpic smiled. "Try harder and you can achieve anything," he whispered, "unless, of course, you're trying to sleep."

***

When Limpic woke, all was still. Apparently they had reached their destination. Strangely enough, it was light outside, despite travelling countless fathoms beneath the waves. Limpic roused himself fully then stirred his two companions.

"Wake up. We're here ... wherever that is."

Brutonia groaned and let out a long, steady breath while Truvius rolled over and rubbed his face lethargically.

"I wonder is it still night-time or is it the middle of another day?" he croaked.

"Only one way to find out," said Limpic brightly. "I'll be back soon." The floor of the bubble was spongy underfoot, so Limpic surmised that they were floating on water because the walls were taut.

Tentatively he pushed his head out between the membrane and netting. There was light all around and water beneath him. Limpic struggled out and dropped gently into the water with a splash. It was warm and sweet to taste. He pushed himself away from the bubble and lay on his back to get his bearings. He could see the fire rope hanging limply from the ship's prow. It drifted on the surface of a huge blue spherical lake that *Polestar* floated in. He whistled, trying to take in all that he saw.

He had emerged into an enormous circular cavern the like of which he had never seen before, even in the dwarf cities. The walls stretched upwards until they were swallowed by a mist created by four stupendous waterfalls that thundered into the lake. In these mists sat four rainbows, the end of one touching the beginning of another. They arched around the cavern in crisp, unsullied colours. In the middle of each of these rainbows, where the arch was at its highest, stood an immense golden statue on a large golden pedestal. Between these colossal statues were smaller ones, each holding up empty arms as though waiting to carry something.

That something was a huge blue orb of flickering gas that floated in the middle of the cavern high above all. Slowly it began to descend in the direction of a rainbow, and revealed a restless surface of iridescent colour not unlike the skin of a soap bubble. As the orb drew within reach of the statues, the tallest took it and rolled it left, into the waiting arms of the smaller statue beside it. It in turn passed the orb to the next and then to the next, and the cool blueness of the orb changed to a dull, faded pink.

"The sun!" gasped Limpic as realisation dawned on him. "It's the *sun*." He kicked and stared in awe for a moment and then something occurred to him. The cavern was silent. There should have been the most tempestuous noise coming from the pummelling waters and yet all was quiet. Limpic opened his inner ear and was not surprised to hear voices. Beautiful voices all chattering and bubbling together as waters do. Each had a story to tell; of the places they had seen and come from – of dry arid deserts with shifting sands to lush green pastures where cattle roved, of canyons steeped in mists to fjords packed with snow and ice. And then there was talk of silver lands and the voices became nonsensical babbles before disappearing completely.

Silver lands. It didn't surprise Limpic.

He returned to his friends flushed with excitement. "You'll never believe where we are!" he shouted upon entering the bubble.

"Is there food?" asked Brutonia. His stomach rumbled like a thunderous storm. He blew out his cheeks and burped under his breath. "I could eat a whole seahorse," he complained.

Truvius looked at him in disgust. "Could you not do that, please? The air in here is foul enough."

Brutonia grinned and rubbed his belly. "Not my fault I need me meat."

"Humph," retorted Truvius. His fingers twitched a little and the skin on his forehead tightened. He turned to Limpic. "What took you so long?" he demanded.

Limpic frowned. He'd only been gone a few minutes.

"Why are you angry this time?" Brutonia enquired.

Truvius turned and glared at him. "I'm not angry. I just want to do something. I want to get out of here and get on with our mission. We are wasting time!" He scratched the scar on his face. It was scarlet.

"We'll get food on the ship," said Limpic, ignoring Truvius. "But first you need to see the view. Come on, follow me."

"I wonder," said Brutonia, crawling up beside Limpic to the bubble's wall. "I mean, it's crazy, you know, to be on top of the ocean one day and then down so low another. It's a bit like your moods, Truvius!" Brutonia guffawed and then his stomach growled a second time before he burped again. "Oops, sorry," he quipped, clasping his hands across his mouth.

Truvius gnashed his teeth until the muscles in his jaw stood out like two small eggs. He looked down. His feet where sinking in and out of the bubble floor as though he was wading through marshland. Another grumble from Brutonia's belly soon had him scurrying through the membrane after his friends. They dropped into the lake and Limpic showed Brutonia how to lie on his back and float with relative ease.

"There you are," said Limpic proudly as Brutonia grinned and spluttered around the pool. "You'll be swimming in no time."

"Amazing," gasped Truvius, gazing around their surroundings. His face softened. He caught Limpic's eye and his mouth turned upwards, twitching into a smile.

"The sun," said Limpic, pointing to the glowing orb. "And those statues, see the way they pass the sun from one to another?" Limpic put his head back in the water and dabbled his fingers. "I read many books when I was convalescing – books my grandfather gave me. There was a story of a place such as this where the carriers of day and night reside. Where the sun rests and then continues her journey from west to east by way of the north – the Pillar of the North." Limpic leaned forward and cast his hand around the cavern at each of the large statues.

"When I first looked around, the sun was taken by that statue." He pointed to their left. "That must be the Pillar of the West. It passed the sun to the smaller statues and they have carried it east, by way of the north."

"As my father used to say," said Brutonia, wide-eyed and open-mouthed, "'sometimes there's nothing left to say'."

"Look." He pointed. "Something amazing is about to happen."

The three companions held their breath and lay back in the water staring upwards.

When the sun was passed to the Pillar of the North, it was lifted into the heavens and it throbbed with white light. Then it began to burn with a pale orange flame, like a fire in the hearth only just getting going. By the time the sun reached the Pillar of the East, it was an angry ball of orange and red, flaming like a roaring furnace. It was raised high above the head of the statue and a proclamation thundered around the cavern.

"A new day dawns!"

With that, the sun was flung into the misty ceiling where it disappeared. For a moment the mist receded and the heavens filled the empty void. Stars wheeled and the moon waned. Then the statues bowed their heads and silence and mist reigned once more.

"To have seen such things!" said Brutonia.

They said nothing more for a time but merely floated freely by the hull of *Polestar* until something dark fell through the mist. Limpic felt his jaw tighten. The moon. It collapsed into the arms of the western statue where it was cradled with the utmost care. Without the light of the sun, the moon became the face of the other side. Dark and empty, endlessly staring out into the eternal vacuum of space. Soon it would grow cold all over and its death would be final.

"Why don't the statues help?" asked Truvius in a harsh tone. His anger rushed upon him like the waters of the collapsing falls.

"I think," whispered Limpic, furrowing his brow, "as they are simply the carriers of day and night, they have no power or

141

authority to intervene."

"But what can *we* do?" replied Brutonia in a hopeless tone. "We are but insects compared to things such as these." He threw his hands around the vast cathedral of rock.

"But look where we are," insisted Limpic. "Look how far we've come."

"Pah!" snorted Truvius. "Brutonia is right, we're just insects. Insects who get lost and thrown about." He peered up at the darkness of the moon and his own face darkened. "And we're soon to be extinct."

"Well I'm not about to give up when we're so close," said Limpic, his whiskers twitching fiercely. He stared up at the moon and his eyes glistened. "You asked me to find Peruvius and when I do the moon will live!"

"And of course I'll help," said Brutonia with a huge grin. Limpic almost reached out and hugged him but didn't. Instead he just grinned back.

Truvius closed his eyes and sighed. The darkness passed from his face. "Then let's go," he said quietly.

"Not without our help," thundered a deep voice.

Limpic turned and saw an assembly of merfolk resting upon seahorses. The horses were clothed in armour made of the thickest and hardest shells from the very depths of the sea where the pressure was greatest. The mermen were bare from the waist up and had long hair and some had beards that fell onto their chests. The largest of them wore a crown of twisted seaweed decorated by pearls from oyster shells. His right hand gripped a large spear that reached as high as his crown. There were markings on the shaft of the spear and the point was red like rust. It was he who had spoken.

"I am Managh," he said, "king of the deep." He peered up at

the hopeless moon. His eyes grew hard and his hand turned white on the staff of his spear. "The moon will not rise again." His voice was deep, sonorous. "She will not rise to her zenith and the world will perish. That is the grim reality if you do not complete your quest this day."

"But ... but," stammered Limpic, "surely there is something we can do to give us more time? I gave her the sun's light and I will do it again."

Managh smiled and drew closer. "I know you did, little one, and because of that the world was given another day. But your Solaar will not revive the moon as she makes her northern pilgrimage towards the east. Its light was gathered from the southern sun to be given to a southern moon. Do not be shocked, Limpic. I have my messengers. The rains come from the heavens and end up here. They tell me things. They told me that you saved the moon," he turned to Truvius, "even though you thought you were lost."

Truvius's face coloured and his eyes dropped. "Then we must complete our mission," he insisted. "We must find the pri—" He looked to the waterline.

Still trying to carry secrets. Limpic sighed and looked away. For all Truvius's talk of change, he hadn't changed at all.

Managh smiled. "I believe you wish to find Prince Peruvius," he said. "Well, come now, there is no time to waste. Secrets are of no use to you here. We sit within the Cathedral of the Poles. The waters of Earth surge through here from the mighty Brenn to the lowly Shiman that graces your pool in the forest of Tulwood. The water brings news of everything it has seen and heard." He cupped his hand and the waters surrounding Truvius became animated and surged around him like a giant hand. They gripped him tightly and lifted him from the lake. Truvius's eyes bulged and his mouth fell open.

"It just so happens that I am well acquainted with water because I have been ordained to watch over the kingdoms of the deep," said Managh.

Truvius struggled a little but found he was completely powerless to do anything.

"Please, sir," said Limpic, "We could use all the help we can get. If you could just show us the way, we would certainly go, wherever it took us."

Managh gently placed Truvius back in the water.

"I will do more than show you the way, courteous Limpic," he replied. "I will come with you. Amoso would like me to aid you in any way I can."

"But where must we go?" Brutonia asked.

"Beneath the Pillar of the West, to the pole that can't be found," said Managh gravely.

As he spoke, the great statue cradling the moon began to move. Its legs parted and the folds of its cloak formed an enormous arched doorway.

"I suggest you board the good ship *Polestar*," thundered Managh, "for we are bound for the Western Pole!"

He gathered the waters about him like a living mantle and with a solemn eye cast his hands across the lake. The waters heaved and boiled and then something came twisting and curling from the depths in sinuous coils.

"Fear not!" cried Managh as a leviathan lifted its armoured head above the waterline. "His name is Saurus and he will serve us well."

Limpic, Truvius and Brutonia swam back to the shadow of *Polestar*'s hull where they cowered in a huddle. The enormous beast towered over them and water teemed from its bony brow.

Serve us in doing what? Limpic wondered as the leviathan swept down and stared at each of them with a giant amber eye. It grumbled from deep within its throat and tossed its head with a snort of steam. Limpic was glad when they were all out of the water and on the deck of the ship.

Managh commanded the waters of the lake to lift the company upwards towards the yawning doorway.

He pointed with his spear, crying exuberantly, "To the Western Pole!"

Brutonia cradled his belly and peered despondently at Limpic. "All very exciting but I still haven't had breakfast," he lamented.

Chapter 15

"I promise we'll save you Moon," whispered Limpic as *Polestar* passed beneath the Pillar of the West. He felt a prickle in his nose.

The waters surged forward through the archway with Managh and his legion of followers carried on the crest of a giant wave before the ship. Saurus followed behind like a silent storm momentarily contained within the armour of a wingless dragon. His scales glistened in the low light, sometimes blue, sometimes green and other times grey. He had great bony ridges above each of his amber eyes that gave him a solemn and foreboding presence.

The archway led into a tunnel cut from smooth black stone. The air was stale and hot and rather oppressive. It was hard to make anything out other than Managh's spear which glowed with an emerald light.

"We must make haste," called Managh over his shoulder, "to pass the Bridge of Pardune before sunset. We do not want to be in this tunnel when the sun begins to descend. The final heat of the day is expelled here and sent out into the skies of the west through the whirlpools at the Western Pole. It would be more than any of us could bear."

146

Limpic and his friends looked at one another uneasily and then to Saurus whose neck was arching over the stern of the ship. An acrid burning smell pervaded the darkness. A rumble echoed through the tunnel.

"What's that?" hissed Limpic. His whiskers went rigid.

Brutonia grinned sheepishly and patted his belly. "I need something to eat," he begged.

"Good idea," replied Limpic with a relieved chuckle and the three of them fetched food and water before sitting in a little circle with a tiny fire burning in the grate.

"I needed that," said Brutonia, finishing off a huge platter of cold meat from the barrels sealed by the Critters. His eyes began to emit a low hoary light and he seemed to carry his shoulders a little higher.

Replenished, thought Limpic, thank goodness. He would need Brutonia's strength – of that he had no doubt.

"Who knows where we will end up next," muttered Truvius solemnly, breaking Limpic's train of thought. "I mean, the Western Pole! That's like trying to find the end of a rainbow."

"I think we should retrieve our weapons and armour," said Limpic, not taking his eyes off Truvius. "If King Managh is right, our next destination is our final destination."

Truvius nodded and Limpic wondered what lurked behind his sunken eyes. He seemed to have regressed back into his personal misery, fingering the scar on his cheek and chewing his nails. But he dutifully trooped to the armoury with the other two and they fitted themselves with their weapons – everything they had brought from Tulwood, including their Solaars. They didn't know what sort of world they would be entering next and needed to be prepared for whatever they faced.

Limpic strapped a short sword across his back and retrieved

the Bow of the Nimue from the mast and slung it over his shoulders. He already had his bone knife strapped to his ankle. Brutonia took Dunnehammer, his great double-headed axe and ran his thumb across it affectionately. Truvius strapped two long thin rapiers to his back.

When they were sufficiently weighed down with weapons they went back to the fire and waited. The tunnel walls slid by quietly. There was an occasional cough from one of the soldiers or a whinny from a seahorse. Sometimes Truvius slunk off into the shadows of the ship's recesses only to return a little later, lighter of foot, to take a seat close to Limpic. Brutonia fiddled with his teeth, or occasionally snorted and creased his nose with a sniff. But mostly he just lounged by the fire winking at Limpic when their eyes met or made popping sounds with his mouth.

Limpic stroked his flower and gazed at the fire. He was sure there was nothing to fear from the Cra just now. His inner ear was silent and his flower made no movement; only flushing pinkish as Truvius came and went. His eyes grew heavy and he tried to fight off sleep. The trauma of the storm still lay heavy on his heart but he was no use to anyone tired. He was sure he saw two amber eyes staring from the darkness to port.

"Zarkus," he yawned. But his brain was too tired to worry now and his head began to drop and lift until his chin rested on his chest.

He knew he was dreaming the moment he saw the door. The red paintwork was blistered. He floated towards it and it opened. He was in a bubble, like the one behind *Polestar*, only this one was as clear as crystal water. It was drifting down a dimly lit corridor – or was it the tunnel that led to the Western Pole? There seemed to be twinkling eyes all around him but they turned out to be strange beeping machines beside beds.

A voice startled him. "I've had enough now," it said. In front of him stood a little creature, pink in colour. It was distressed and crying. "I think I've had enough now," it spluttered. It looked like Boy from his earlier dreams, but it wasn't Boy. It was more feminine but with the same bloated moon-face.

"You'll take me to the land behind the Western Pole?" asked the little pink thing. It was staring up at Limpic with large brown eyes brimming with tears. Limpic tried to speak, tried to work his jaws, but his mouth felt full. Then he saw a shadow further along the corridor. It had red eyes and it snorted. It was a horse – a black horse. Its rider had its hood drawn forward. Around his neck hung a great heavy key that caused him to slump in the saddle. *Zarkus*.

Limpic tried to scream and lash out but nothing happened. His head lurched forward with a jar and he woke with a jump. "Ow!" His heart hammered against his chest. He thought he'd gone blind such was the darkness all around. Then he saw the burning embers of the fire. He sat forward and stirred the flames. Brutonia's face appeared, creased from sleep. Truvius emerged from the gloom looking sullen.

"What's wrong?" he asked.

"Zarkus is still following us," said Limpic, struggling to catch his breath. He swallowed and stared into the flames feeling sombre and a little afraid. The spectre of Zarkus had erased most of his dream.

Brutonia peered into the darkness behind the ship. "You mean, Zarkus is actually out there?" He sucked air through his teeth.

"I think so," replied Limpic. "I believe that Zarkus has no more idea of where Marah has gone than we do. My siblings and my people spoke of seeing a rider on a dark horse roaming

149

the waters aimlessly. I think that was Zarkus. He's trying to find Peruvius. I know he was angry that Truvius left Tulwood to find me, but, actually, he helped us – he saved me from the goblins, he told me to find Peruvius, he followed *Polestar* in the storm to see where we were going *and* he saved Brutonia."

"Do you think he believes he can still save Marah?" said Brutonia. "Maybe he thinks he can still save the moon too."

"I think a part of him – the real Zarkus you both knew, wants to reach the Western Pole and make things right," said Limpic.

"But?" said Truvius cautiously.

"But," said Limpic sadly, "the other part is being drawn towards the Cra. I heard their whispers the night of the storm. They are calling him." Limpic pursed his lips. An image appeared in his mind. Of Zarkus with a key around his neck. "Somehow," said Limpic, scratching his chin, "Zarkus is still the key that can lock and unlock the door to the Shadowlands."

"So they want to destroy him so the door can't be locked anymore?" asked Brutonia.

"In a manner of speaking," replied Limpic. "I think they want to control him. A kind of living death."

"And what better way to lure him in than to threaten his home, his moon and his people," said Truvius. "*And* in a weakened state. Zarkus is suffering as much as we all are from the loss of silver. Oh brother, brother, what have you done?" Truvius threw his face in his hands and shuddered.

Brutonia sniffed loudly and wiped his nose. Limpic sat back. The weight of it all was almost too much. His chest ached and his flower blushed pink.

Truvius gathered himself and cleared his throat. "I have been ordered to kill my father." His voice was low and steady. "It was the war council's last command. You were correct, Limpic

– what you said on the ship the morning after the storm. The Cra cannot sustain themselves without a vessel. What is left of my father is still flesh and blood, and flesh and blood can be eliminated." Truvius opened his hands in a helpless gesture.

"So you've finally revealed the last of your secrets," said Brutonia. "*My* father used to say that a man who carries too many secrets carries death."

Truvius didn't move but stared forlornly into the flames.

"And if Zarkus gets in your way, will you kill him too?" continued Brutonia.

"What if the Cra finally break him?" replied Truvius sharply. "Not with the paltry manipulations they use on the goblins. I mean *really* break him and use his powers against us?"

Brutonia sat aghast. His face turned to stone. "What if they break you!" he thundered.

The two rose and faced each other, almost knocking over the fire grate. They wrestled briefly but Brutonia's strength was countered ably by Truvius's nimbleness. They both ended up on their backs panting like two rabid beasts.

"Enough!" Zarkus stepped into their midst. His hood was drawn back and the fire cast shadows across his face, shrouding his eyes in darkness.

"H ... How long have you been here?" said Truvius scrambling to his feet. His face twitched nervously. His scar turned white.

"Long enough," replied Zarkus, inclining his head. "Do not worry, Brother, I am still myself." He drew his fingers down the bridge of his nose in a weary gesture. "When the time comes, I will stand against Father. You have my word."

An uneasy silence followed.

Zarkus turned to face Limpic. One side of his face was now

in darkness, the other lit by the fire's light. "My mind has been clearer since I met you. Since the night I placed my hand upon your arm to direct your light to the moon I have felt … better. You still have a great part to play in this saga, of that I have no doubt. You and you alone will stand at the end. If you succeed, your fires will cleanse. I know that now." He stumbled forward and Limpic grasped him.

"Please," said Zarkus weakly. "Please, remove your hand. I have not the strength for your flames yet. But I will need them." He glanced at Truvius. "We both will."

Brutonia lifted Zarkus to his feet as if he was made of straw. His anger, it seemed, was gone and forgotten. Zarkus settled himself by the fire and sighed heavily before speaking. "Listen carefully and I will fill in as many gaps as I can in this sorry affair. After the Great War, the war between the High Elves, the defeated enemy gathered the armour from the many High Elves who were slain. They took the armour with them upon banishment to the Shadowlands. They knew it would give them form if they were ever to return to our world for they are merely shadows now." Polestar rocked a little then Zarkus continued.

"The High Elves closed and sealed the door to the Shadowlands using the most powerful item in their possession – Solhaert, the heart of the sun. They took Solhaert with them when they retreated to the Valley of Silence knowing that there they would be incorruptible – no one would be enticed to reopen the Shadowlands." Zarkus peered at his hands. "Incorruptible," he murmured. He shook his head and continued. "The Cra knew that Solhaert was beyond their grasp but there was another haert – a lesser one, possessed by those descended from the High Elves."

"Lunehaert," whispered Limpic.

"Lunehaert," replied Zarkus with a nod.

"The Cra needed a foothold – a way back to our world to gather intelligence. With Lunehaert they could create a temporary opening to allow the Cra to return to our world safe within the body of the one who summoned them – Marah. Father." Zarkus hung his head and spoke through gritted teeth. "I gave them that opening and now they are proceeding with their ultimate goal – to open a great rift between our world and the Shadowlands."

Brutonia wrung his hands. "But that's impossible! How could they even do that? You said yourself that Lunehaert is not powerful enough to open the door permanently."

Zarkus clasped his hand to his brow and a strangled, almost hysterical, laugh fell from his lips. "Watch now the skies with fear and dread, watch heaven's fall to Earth. The death of one so highly born would ring destruction's birth."

"Wh … what does that mean," stammered Truvius. His face was gaunt.

"It means the Cra are going to kill the moon," said Zarkus. "The death of one born of the heavens would release such cataclysmic energy that it would literally tear a seam in the very fabric of the sky. Especially if that energy was controlled and directed solely for this purpose by Lunehaert."

Brutonia's mouth fell open and his shoulders sagged. "But … but." There was nothing else to say.

"And now we know," said Limpic after a long deathly silence. "They used the anger of Marah and the …" he peered sheepishly at Zarkus "… and Lunehaert to cross over."

Truvius lifted his head. "And now they are using the gift of Peruvius to drain the moon of her silver and her life. Her death will open the rift."

"And once opened, the Cra can move across in power and numbers, safe within their fallen armour," continued Limpic.

"And with the High Elves still in the Valley of Silence," said Brutonia, "nothing will stand in their way."

"We must find Peruvius and take back Lunehaert," said Limpic.

"And if we are too late," said Truvius, "if the rift is opened, can it be closed?"

Zarkus pursed his lips and stared sadly into the firelight. The skin on his forehead puckered into a frown and his eyes glazed over. He stroked his fingers and his face relaxed and he smiled as though resolving some inner conflict. "There is a way," he conceded, "but none that any of you can help with."

Limpic's stomach turned over and he looked away from the firelight. Somehow Zarkus was still the key. However heavy that burden would be.

Zarkus rose to his feet and dusted his knees. "The stage has been set," he said flatly. "Only we can alter its ending." Then, gathering himself, as if preparing for the battle ahead, he drew back his shoulders and lifted his head. "When we find Father, he will be dressed in the armour of his lineage. The blood of the High Elves runs in the veins of the elverns – we are their descendants. The armour we craft has some of their power, so destroying him and retrieving Lunehaert may be more difficult than we imagine."

He glanced at Limpic and his eyes moved to the flower on his chest. Limpic understood: the Cra were as safe within elvern armour as they were in the armour of the High Elves.

A call from the darkness startled them.

"We must keep our eyes and ears open now at all cost," called Managh, appearing by *Polestar*'s starboard bulwark. He glanced questioningly at Zarkus. "We are nearing Pardune. Who knows what darkness lurks in a world so far from the light of the sun."

If possible, it seemed to be growing steadily darker, and even Managh's spear and the meagre light of the fire soaked into the grim curtain all around. Saurus grumbled overhead.

"King Managh," said one of the soldiers, returning to *Polestar*'s side, his face dappled by shadow. He rode on a magnificent seahorse and had an oyster-shell shield strapped to his back. A broadsword hung down the side of his seahorse's neck.

"The scouts say Pardune is almost upon us. All is quiet and calm. There's no sign of any adversaries."

Managh stroked his beard thoughtfully and knitted his eyebrows together. "That worries me, Magnus. Have the soldiers in starfish formation with the strongest at the tips. *Polestar* will sail in the centre."

Magnus bowed. "As you wish, Your Majesty."

He quickly gave his orders and the legion of soldiers efficiently surrounded *Polestar*. She was encircled by a well-equipped and battle-hardened regiment. Behind this came Saurus. Only his plated chest showed in the light but an ominous rumble descended from the throat that was veiled in darkness. It even caused Managh's steely stallion to whinny like a young colt.

Limpic's flower sputtered and glowed red: danger. Warmth ran down his arms. He returned to the prow and stood on the forecastle. He shone his torch ahead and its light sent the darkness scurrying for cover. He opened his inner ear. There was nothing to be heard above the normal spectrum of sound but his flower trembled in his chest. Some remnant of the Cra were near.

Up ahead was another archway. Around its lip was chiselled PARDUNE. Upon passing through they emerged onto a vast stone bridge that spanned a chasm of unfathomable width. It was similar to an aqueduct, with many arches supporting its weight. The towers of these arches grew thicker as they descended into the bowels of the Earth where they were simply swallowed up by the vast emptiness. Water could be heard frothing from some unseen source and the air became cool and damp. Limpic shivered.

They moved on cautiously, their eyes straining into the thick shadows beyond the light of Limpic's Solaar. Every creak from the ship caused the entire regiment to flinch. Every crumble of rock and they flicked their gaze this way and that. The tunnel had been easier to sail through because the walls could be seen and nothing could creep out on them unexpectedly. This capacious cavern was different; it was exposed. Every dark recess or ridge seemed to contain a pair of eyes. They were being watched. Truvius and Brutonia both shook their torches and their light took away some of the fear of the Bridge of Pardune.

"I hate being stared at!" hissed Brutonia.

Saurus's presence behind them was comforting, though. It would take a brave or foolish adversary to engage with such a beast.

Managh's spear was glowing especially vibrant.

"At least we can see better now," Brutonia called to him. "Your light is as good as all of ours together."

Managh shook his head grimly. "I am not causing it to shine. It senses something evil lurking nearby. It is a warning."

Yes, a warning. Limpic's flower glowed a little more.

The sensation of being observed only heightened with this revelation and Limpic felt the skin on his scalp crawl.

"Keep your eyes peeled," muttered Managh, but the vastness of the cavern carried his words in an ever-increasing echo.

When it finally died away and everyone caught their breath, another sound snuck in from the shadows. It took them a while to figure out what it was: laughter. But it wasn't the beautiful sound that sparkles between friends; it was callous and cold-hearted. It was derisive and demeaning. Some of the seahorses whinnied.

"Steady," said Managh.

"I hate being laughed at more than I hate being stared at!" fumed Brutonia.

A few nervous chuckles sounded from Managh's legion.

The hideous laughter faded away and was replaced by animal-like calls, the makers of which eluded the light of the torches.

"I think I preferred being laughed at," mumbled Truvius.

Limpic held the Bow of the Nimue in readiness, sweeping his gaze backwards and forwards in an arc as he followed the aggressive noises. He had his torch strapped to his shoulder so that it shone where he turned. Something dark darted from the confines of the shadows with a moan. Limpic didn't wait to find out what it was but drew his bow string. His hands throbbed with heat and the arrow that appeared on the bowstring burned at its tip.

"That's new," said Limpic before releasing the arrow. It sang and hissed through the shadowy cloak that screeched and fell back. Limpic felt the air move to his left. He turned and a goblin lurched at him. It was dazzled by the Solaar and grabbed at its eyes. Limpic loosed another flaming arrow and the creature

157

vaporised. His blood was thoroughly pumping now. He stopped to catch his breath and turned to midship. His light picked out Brutonia battling by the mast.

"Take that, and that, and that, and that!" roared Brutonia sweeping goblins to their deaths with his trusty axe as though they were standing corn.

Limpic ducked. An arrow zipped over his head making a *pfft* sound as it passed. Something groaned behind him and a goblin fell against him with an arrow in its chest. Its black vacant eyes rolled backwards and then it simply burst into a smoking residue that rose into the cavern ceiling.

Steadying his legs and wiping sweat from his eyes, Limpic shone his torch aft and caught sight of Saurus being swarmed by goblins. The great serpent roared and thrashed beneath the water. *Polestar* twisted to starboard and thumped into the side of the stone bridge with a loud crash. Limpic fell heavily onto his side and his teeth rattled together. Every light in the cavern went out.

Limpic groped in the dark for his bow. From near the tiller a light went on. It was Truvius. Another light went on in the middle of the deck. That was Brutonia. Limpic turned his own light on and pointed it upwards.

His whiskers bristled. All around the ship were thousands of wailing goblins and hobgoblins writhing over one another like a swarm of rats. It was hard to make out one particular form but it appeared that their noses were so long and their chins were so curled upwards that they almost touched. And between this were their mouths – thin black lips drawn back to reveal large blunt teeth. There was a palpable intake of breath from the entire regiment of soldiers before a bright flash lit up the entire cavern and hung for a moment, ebbing slowly away.

"There!" cried a voice.

Limpic turned and yelped in surprise. "Zarkus!"

Zarkus sat astride a black horse, floating in mid-air on the far side of the cavern. His steed's eyes burned like fiery coals and wreaths of smoke seethed from its flared nostrils. Beneath it churned a black restless cloud that sparked with lightning as the creature pawed impatiently.

"Your time runs short," called Zarkus from beneath his hood. His voice echoed through the cavern. He turned towards Limpic and pointed at him. "By your fire we live or die." He raised his right hand and it began to glow in a ball of light. He flung the light into the cavern. Goblins screamed and fell from their rocky perches to their deaths. With a violent kick of his horse, Zarkus galloped through the air and disappeared in a clap of thunder.

"No, Zarkus, wait!" yelled Truvius. "Stay with us!"

There was little time to process his outburst as the enemy quickly galvanised itself in a panic, snapping at one another violently as though suddenly fearful.

Saurus sensed this too and put the crown of his head to the bubble at the back of *Polestar* and shunted it forwards with a great flick of his tail. The surge of energy broke the ship free of Managh and his soldiers and Limpic found himself pressed against the railings of the forecastle.

Managh raised the waters of the bridge and swept after the huge leviathan as a cool wind rushed into their faces, sucking goblins into the mouth of the tunnel they had just left.

"The sun sets!" bellowed Managh. "The tongues of fire will soon be upon us!"

There was an almighty blast of wind, as though some giant had just released an enormous lungful of air, and then a flame licked out of the tunnel from behind. Any and all remaining goblins were instantly turned to ash.

"We'll never make it!" screamed Truvius.

Chapter 16

The entire company rushed towards the other side of the chasm with the sound of wailing goblins filling the air. The cool wind increased to a violent squall and then, as quickly as it had risen, it stopped and the air was still and calm.

"Is it over?" gasped Limpic. The mouth of the tunnel was pitch-black but the stones around the edge glowed amber.

"Quickly! Quickly!" urged Managh. "The calm before the storm befalls us. We haven't much time!"

Saurus was pushing with all his strength and speed so that the prow of *Polestar* was in danger of lifting from the water. The entrance out of the chasm suddenly appeared from the receding blackness as a bright flash lit up the archway at the other side of Pardune.

A wall of heat swept over Limpic and he instinctively covered his eyes. When he was finally able to see again everything was blurry and shivering like the air above a hot slate roof.

"I can hardly breathe!" he gasped. The air in his lungs burned like a hot furnace and his mouth was dry.

"Keep going!" shouted Managh. "We're almost there!"

With one last great effort, Saurus shunted *Polestar* through the arch and immediately plunged beneath the surface of a large lake that was deep and cool. The regiment of mermen followed him to the very depths. King Managh stayed by the side of *Polestar* and caused the waters to pin her to the rocks just inside the doorway. He then lifted a great wall of water to cloak himself and those on board the ship.

With an ear-piercing screech like metal grinding over metal, the energy from the sun roared over the Bridge of Pardune and through the large chamber Limpic and his friends were hiding in. Managh held firm and raised more water to replace that being vaporised by the overwhelming heat. Great tongues of hungry fire swept past, devouring anything and anyone that stood in its way. A few sorry goblins ignited like straw before disappearing in a flash of wiry cinders.

When the sun's energy was finally expelled, the chamber fell quiet smelling acrid and charred. Only after several minutes did Managh allow the waters to recede. Sweat poured off his face and chest. He increased the light of his spear as Saurus's face broke the surface of the lake.

"That was a close call," said Truvius puffing out his cheeks. His face was blackened and his eyes were red-rimmed as though he'd been shovelling coal into the dwarves' ironworks.

"Is everyone still here?" asked Managh, shining his spear around the chamber.

Clouds of steam made it hard to see but his emerald light picked out dozens of eyes. It appeared that his entire regiment was accounted for. Saurus's eyes blazed far above their heads, scanning all around. He was moving restlessly. Further above his head was a huge domed ceiling with figures cut into the rock. Limpic and his crew pointed their torches upwards, dispelling the blackness. They could see that the figures were entwined together and flowing towards the centre of the ceiling with outstretched arms and hands. They were reaching up from the darkness of the night to embrace a sun carved from solid gold. Apparently darkness had not always reigned so completely here.

"We must travel quickly now," said Managh. "Everyone into position. Soldiers, front and rear. Limpic return to your position on *Polestar* and guide her. Truvius and Brutonia, get to the bubble and hold on tight. Our journey will end at a whirlpool that springs up on one side of the Western Pole."

Limpic followed his friends to the poop deck and made sure that the bubble was drawn tight. King Managh's warning about a whirlpool felt particularly dire.

"Are we ready?" called the king.

"Just a moment," answered Limpic as he gave the bubble one last pull. Saurus had been watching him silently, but he turned hastily and peered back over his vast body.

"What is it?" Limpic enquired. His flower flushed pink. He shone his torch to where Saurus was looking. His pulse quickened. The water had begun to spill upwards into a fountain.

Saurus turned to look at Limpic and threw his armoured head in the direction of King Managh with a disgruntled flick. It was clear he wished everyone to leave. And quickly.

The spewing water suddenly rose to very nearly the same height as Saurus's head. As the water fell away it revealed an enormous worm-like creature with bulbous lifeless eyes. It was almost translucent, with a gaping mouth full of black teeth and a pink hairy tongue that seemed to sniff the air.

"Let's get out of here!" cried Limpic, rushing to the prow of the ship. His skin was crawling. With one last frantic look over

163

his shoulder, Limpic saw the two creatures crashing together and Saurus's body coiling over and over until both disappeared. The waters thrashed into a foaming tempest as *Polestar* and Managh's regiment fled from the chamber. At first they dropped downwards into a vast trough and then sped through a black tunnel. Limpic wasn't sure what was up and what was down and had a very real fear that his head might leave his neck at any moment. He didn't even know if he was facing the right way. His head was thrust down into his shoulders as the ship lurched upwards once more and then the blackness broke and all was light and blue and he was facing forward hurtling through a clear tunnel that must have been holding back fathoms of seawater. Just in front of him rode Managh and his regiment, riding upon the crest of an eternal wave. Their horses bucked and snorted beneath them as they tossed their foaming manes back over their shoulders. Drops of water pelted Limpic's face.

Their path suddenly changed and they ascended, spinning around and around a huge whirlpool. Limpic's head spun and his stomach heaved somewhere between fear and sickness. He gripped the bowsprit with his legs knowing that he no longer controlled *Polestar*. She was at the will of the whirlpool.

"Can't hold on much longer!" he gasped through gritted teeth and then there was a violent bone-jarring shudder and the ship spun a few more times before settling into a gentle bobbing motion.

"Oh, I'm gonna be sick," groaned Limpic. His tongue hung from his mouth. Between the whirlpool, visions of a hairy pink tongue and the rocking of the ship, his stomach was churning.

When he eventually came round, he was aware of being wet all over and he listened to the sound of crashing water. Limpic wiped his eyes. As soon as he could see clearly his breath caught in the back of his throat and every hair on his body stood on end. What he was witnessing seemed impossible: *Polestar* was bobbing along the lip of what appeared to be an enormous cauldron filled with mist and swirling cloud and flashes of phosphorescent light. On either side of the cauldron were two vast whirlpools, one of which *Polestar* had just ascended. Water constantly frothed up from their gaping mouths. The sides of the cauldron were made from walls of water that defied gravity and bubbled upwards, spilling over the lip. It was this upward surging of water that held *Polestar* back.

"Where are we now?" groaned Brutonia. He was standing on the forecastle, dishevelled and rather green about the gills. His cheek was bruised. "I feel like butter in a churn."

"Don't even mention food," moaned Truvius, looking no better. His red headband had dropped over one eye. The other eye was still rolling around of its own volition.

"But ... this can't be!" shouted King Managh over the roar of water. His face was taut and his eyes were wide.

"What is it?" Limpic shouted back. The wonder of the spectacle soon turning to fear.

"The Western Pole should be here," cried Managh.

"Where?" bellowed Truvius as he fixed his headband.

Managh pointed to the vast mist-filled abyss and his shoulders slumped.

"Then where is it?" called Brutonia.

Limpic wiped some water from his face and swallowed. "It must be down there," he said. "At the bottom of that." He looked to each of his friends and flicked the remaining water from his whiskers. "And that's where we have to go."

Brutonia craned forward to look over the edge and his face

paled. It was his turn to swallow.

Limpic thought for a moment. Mist puffed from the cauldron in a steady stream like smoke from a pipe. It drifted far before falling and rolling along the surface of the grey restless sea that stretched for miles in every direction. Warm air lifted Limpic's hair from his forehead and he began to formulate a plan – an extremely silly, foolhardy plan at that.

"King Managh," he called, "have you ever seen smoke rise from a chimney?" The king frowned and then grinned. His pearly teeth sparkled within his beard.

"No chimney, lad," he boomed, "but I have seen thermal water spouts rise from fissures in the seabed." He rubbed the whiskers of his chin. "If I can draw water from the side of this chasm and create a cushion beneath us, we might just have a chance. We might just have a chance indeed!" Limpic smiled at him and nodded.

The king slapped the side of the ship and barked orders. "Magnus! Get these soldiers and seahorses tethered to *Polestar* this instant." There was a clamour of activity and the sound of seahorses whinnying and soldiers moving as one.

A nervous laugh came from behind. "Ah, Limpic," said Truvius, "you're not thinking of doing what I think you're thinking of doing?"

Limpic turned and grinned but his eyes were steely. "That's exactly what I'm thinking of doing."

Truvius's nervous smile vanished and his face blanched. "Grab hold of something, Brutonia," he stammered. Two big, burly arms were thrown around him with a whimper.

"Not me, you big tree!" growled Truvius, fighting off his friend. "Grab hold of the ship and don't look down!"

"Here we go," said Limpic firmly. He stood up, grabbed the

line above his head with one hand, glanced at Managh, nodded and then leaned forward. *Polestar* trembled as though protesting at what she was being asked to do. She stilled then crested the lip of the cauldron. At the same time King Managh's spear throbbed with light and a tongue of water slid beneath the ship's keel with the sound of a swelling tide. *Polestar* hurtled down into the misty depths.

"Mother!" cried Brutonia.

Limpic opened his mouth to scream. His body was tight and coiled, awaiting the ferocity of a long drop. But the drop never came, nor did the scream. The prow of *Polestar* lifted and she levelled out and fluttered downwards like an autumn leaf falling from a tree.

"Ha ha!" cried Managh, riding to starboard. He had one hand on the bulwark of the ship and his face was split into a wide grin. "You were right, Limpic. It seems the water rising upwards is causing an enormous updraught of air. We are no more than particles of dust to these forces. If I can keep my water cushion tethered to the side of this unholy cauldron, we might just make it. At least I can guide us down a bit." He slapped the side of the ship. "Ho ho, lads, hear that?" he growled. "We might not die after all."

"Yo ho!" roared the king's soldiers in one voice. And they struck the side of the ship in unison while their mounts whinnied and bucked.

Limpic sighed and at once the tightness in his body fled and he sagged to his knees. His heart was beating so fast he thought it would burst from his chest. He started to laugh and Brutonia and Truvius followed suit.

"You're crazy, Limpic," said Brutonia, wiping away tears from his eyes.

167

"I think the term they use on the Golden Coast is 'an eejit'," said Truvius.

Limpic grinned and rubbed his face then ran his fingers through his hair. "An eejit," he mused. "A quare big eejit. And I've lost my hat again."

But his musings didn't last long. Something emerged from the mist, striking up towards the keel of *Polestar*. Something silver and tall, very tall.

"The Western Pole," said Managh in a hushed voice.

Limpic stood up and held onto the line above his head, watching the pole intently.

The first thing he saw was an enormous 'W' sitting atop a huge shaft of metal. A small podium encircled the shaft a little way up from its base and a ladder led down to a large circular platform with ornate railings. Four turrets jutted up from the railings. This platform sat on top of an almighty spire and was reached by a stairwell that looped around the spire itself. Beneath this was a tower with a diameter at least ten times the length of *Polestar*. But as the ship fell further, it soon became clear that this tower simply sat on top of another column that was wider again.

"The Tower of Glorian," said Managh with a nod towards the smaller of the columns. "The seat of the Western Pole."

Polestar fell a little quicker until she was in the shadow of the main column. It seemed to taper slightly, growing wider near its base.

"The other poles have towers like these," continued Managh, "although it is said that the North Pole eclipses the three others for might and wonder."

"It's silver," said Limpic. He rubbed his face against the side of his arm, shivering as he thought of his own home.

It had grown silent, eerily silent, except for the drip, drip, dripping of condensation sliding off smooth surfaces.

"I suspect the entire city is," said Managh. "The weight of metal has caused it to sink."

Sure enough, other towers that encircled the pole began to emerge from the gloom, each one of them encased in a cold shroud of silver.

Eventually *Polestar* dropped through the mist and the rest of the city was revealed. It fell in tiers away from the foot of the Western Pole in ever-increasing circles; uniform circles with terraces that led downwards onto lower levels. Limpic could see its streets, empty and smooth. Vast circular roadways the likes of which he had never seen before. The city was divided into segments by other roads, like the slices of a cake, with the Western Pole at the very centre. Indeed, the entire city looked like a giant tiered cake, covered in silver icing with towers for candles.

But unlike other cities, this one was silent and lifeless.

"Behold the great city of Meridian," said Managh with a rueful cast of his hand. "Hold steady, we must retreat to the flooded outskirts." His spear throbbed and the water beneath *Polestar* hissed and withdrew like a wave receding back into the ocean. *Polestar* was pulled further and further away from the pole until she reached a vast wall with many arches that encircled Meridian. With a gentle splash her hull settled into calm waters surrounding the city.

"Look," said Truvius, pointing at another ship close by.

"It's an elvern ship," said Brutonia. "It's *our* elvern ship." She was slimlined and built from overlapping riveted timbers. Her symmetrical bow and stern curled gracefully into the air. Apart from a cabin at the stern, her deck stood open and was

169

lined with shields and oars. By her empty mast stood a lone figure captured in silver.

"It's Titus," said Truvius. "Second in command of the elvern's small fleet."

"We should make our way into the city, don't you think?" said Limpic, trying to ignore the blank stare of the elvern statue. He felt a cold shiver run down his spine and settle in his bones. We are getting close, maybe too close. What if the silver takes us now? But his flower fluttered and the coldness in his bones fled and warmth bubbled up. He knew somehow, as it had done before, that his flower would protect them.

"I'm sorry," murmured King Managh with a shake of his head, "but my regiment and I can go no further with you. We must wait here for you to complete your mission. We have been given dominion and power over the waters only. Any foray into other kingdoms would have disastrous consequences. But let me advise you to head straight for the Western Pole. It holds the source of your quest, of that I am certain."

Brutonia swallowed hard and looked firstly to Truvius whose eyes were downcast, and then to Limpic who nodded bleakly and filled his chest. Once more the three of them were to go on alone.

Limpic turned to Managh and bowed graciously. "Your Majesty, it has been a pleasure and an honour to serve with you."

King Managh smiled. "The waters are right to revere you, Limpic of the Golden Coast. You are indeed a remarkable creature. It has been *my* pleasure to have served with you, and we will do so again. I am sure of it. You were well chosen to lead this expedition." He turned to the other two. "You have done well to come so far and to have overcome many terrors.

Be sure now that your wits will be sorely tested. The water will start to rise as the moon attempts to move on, though I fear her attempts will be futile." He handed Brutonia and Truvius two shells that could be placed between their lips. "Hopefully you will be out before you need these but there is enough concentrated air in them to give you one hour of steady breath underwater. I'm afraid we don't have any more. We ocean dwellers have little need of breathers."

Appropriately equipped, Brutonia and Truvius threw the rope ladder over the side of the ship and climbed down to the harbour. The mist, which had swirled restlessly high overhead, fell in lazy trailing tendrils that clotted here and there. The city was soon shrouded from view and buildings and walls became no more than dark, shapeless masses.

Before Limpic left he hugged *Polestar*. "Thank you. I hope we live to see your decks again." With that he clambered over the side and joined his friends, vanishing into the gloom.

Chapter 17

Inside the first wall was a large courtyard. At the far side of it was another wall – higher and with many arches. Through one of these was a vast flight of terraced steps, but it was hard to see any further because the mist only lifted sporadically, like a set of drapes in the wind. In the middle of the first courtyard were many strange and wonderful shapes, all clothed in the solid mantle of silver. They would have been beautiful but for their origin.

"It's the city's inhabitants," whispered Brutonia.

"And the city's trees," added Truvius.

"Come on," insisted Limpic, "we can't do anything for them here."

They kept low and moved on silently, allowing the mist to cloak them almost completely from view. They had little need of their torches because the city gave off a pale white light. Limpic took the lead as his eyes were the keenest of the group, adapted as they were to searching the sunless depths.

They reached the first of the vast terrace steps and made their way to the top before Limpic stopped abruptly. His flower was pink.

"Back!" he hissed, slipping on the smooth metal step. He

dropped to his belly and Truvius and Brutonia followed suit.

"What is it?" whispered Truvius. "I can't see anything."

"The other side of this courtyard," replied Limpic, his eyes straining into the gloom. "Goblins. Maybe twenty."

There was a cracking sound. "Let me at them," growled Brutonia, flexing his knuckles.

"It appears we don't have to," replied Limpic. "They seem to be squabbling with each other. Like ... they're afraid."

"Pah!" snorted Truvius. "They don't feel anything."

"Shush! They're coming this way," whispered Limpic. His breathing was short and shallow. If the goblins found them now, surely all would be lost.

It was their stench that revealed them first, and then their dark shapes appeared from the gloom, huddled together and grumbling in low voices. They walked right past, moving briskly and away in the direction of the city outskirts. Their stench moved with them.

"Phew!" said Limpic, breathing out slowly.

"Ah, should've let me at them," lamented Brutonia. "Even their smell is repulsive."

"We didn't come to fight an army," said Truvius, rising to his feet. "Stealth and surprise are our only weapons."

"The way seems clear now," said Limpic, scanning all around. "Let's go." He threw one last glance in the direction of the goblins. Rats leaving a sinking ship, maybe? Then he moved off, trailed closely by his companions.

They continued like this for some time, stealthily manoeuvring through each tier of the city. Always heading towards the centre. There were no more goblins to be seen, or smelt, and eventually they reached the final tier that led them to the base of the Western Pole. All three were breathing hard and sweating.

"Well?" whispered Truvius.

Limpic blew lightly through his lips. "Seems clear," he said. "Only one way to find out."

He crept forward. Truvius and Brutonia followed him but stopped shy of the doorway into the tower. They knelt, instead, by a group of figures who had been turned to silver.

"They're goblins," said Brutonia a little too loudly. "Truvius, they're goblins."

"Not all of them," replied Truvius grimly.

He was standing in the middle of the statues peering at a figure in the centre of the group. Not misshapen or hunched like the goblins all around him, he was slim and fine, on his knees peering lifelessly up into the sky, one hand open in supplication, the other grasping the leg of a goblin.

"Tabias!" said Truvius.

"Who?" stuttered Limpic, his whiskers twitching.

Truvius swallowed and rubbed his mouth. His eyes were glassy.

"It's Tabias," he replied meekly. "Another of the seven."

"What happened here?" said Brutonia. His voice was trembling. "Did the goblins do it?"

Truvius was on his knees. His face was deathly white. "No," he replied, "he was just getting too close. Look what's in the goblin's hand."

"A boot? A silver boot."

"Not just any boot," said Truvius. "It belongs to Tabitha. Remember she appeared in the castle with the Echo Shell? She had one boot missing."

"Yes, yes, I remember," said Brutonia. "So a fight must have broken out here. Tabitha used her Starstone to escape with the

Echo Shell, recognising its importance. The goblin caught her boot but was held back by Tabias—"

"And they were all turned to silver," continued Limpic. "That seems to be the way of it."

"This is crazy," moaned Brutonia. He wrung his giant hands.

There was a cry from the doorway and a figure with a large curling chin and nose sprang at them.

"Brutonia!" hissed Limpic.

The big elvern immediately launched himself at the fleeing goblin and pinned it to the smooth silver ground. It was spitting and grunting in a language Limpic found both alien and repulsive.

Suddenly Brutonia sat back and the goblin spat out another rambling tirade of nonsensical babble before fleeing.

"What is it?" Limpic asked, placing his hand on Brutonia's shoulder. "What did it say?"

"The Living Death." Truvius had moved to Brutonia's side, ready to fight if needed. "The Living Death is madness," said Truvius, his face drawn.

Limpic gulped. The Cra. The Cra are here. He licked his lips and peered into the yawning doorway that led to the base of the Western Pole. He was suddenly afraid and very tired. He would have liked nothing better than to lie down and sleep away his troubles.

"Look!" gasped Brutonia, pointing in the direction they had come from. Some semblance of a silvery light had begun to fall across Meridian, diffusing through the clouds above. The city, for a brief second free of mist, was spread out beneath their feet all the way back to *Polestar* and the mermen. The ground beneath them throbbed with dull vibrations.

"The water!" said Truvius. "It is rising. The outer wall is

175

already breached."

The spectacle roused Limpic from his stupor and he sprang to life. "The moon!" he cried. "The moon must be trying to rise. She is pulling at the water around the city. Let's go. If the moon can struggle on, so can we."

He didn't wait for a response but darted straight into the tower and sprinted across a long gloomy hallway. When he reached the end, he stopped suddenly and his arms windmilled backwards. Truvius and Brutonia were travelling at a similar rate and almost stumbled into the back of him.

"What is it?" hissed Truvius. "Let's keep going before we drown."

"Can't," panted Limpic. "Look, there's no stairs up or down." He shone his torch ahead and a huge circular chasm opened out beneath him, swallowing up the cone of sunlight. The trio were standing on a balcony that jutted out from the wall.

"Now what do we do?" said Brutonia, struggling after their sprint. He was weighed down rather heavily with his armour and Dunnehammer.

"I don't know," admitted Limpic, tugging his whiskers. "I suppose we could—wait, what's that?"

Something flashed past the light of his torch. He moved his wrist to track the object and when he found it he gaped in astonishment.

"A flight of stairs," muttered Brutonia in disbelief. "Look! There, at the edge of the light, they're floating. Clockwise, I think. But they seem to be leading down."

The stairs brushed past the rim of the balcony but only just. They were pointing towards the middle of the cavern.

"Do we go down?" asked Truvius.

Limpic looked back along the hallway to the city outside. The water would be rising. But his flower strained forward and downward. It had protected him so far. Now it seemed to be guiding. Limpic chewed his lip but a flush of reassuring warmth permeated his entire body.

"We go down," he said. He was absolutely sure.

Limpic drew himself up and bent his knees a little. "The next time it passes we jump," he whispered.

Brutonia gulped but Truvius poised himself eagerly.

"Get ready!" murmured Limpic. "Here it comes." His whiskers were tingling.

Just as the stairs approached the edge of the balcony, Limpic dropped out into open space, anticipating their arrival. He timed it perfectly and landed deftly on the third step down. Truvius jumped a little later and would have stumbled off had Limpic not grabbed him.

"That was close!" Truvius whispered through his teeth as the stairwell continued on its circular path.

Brutonia was still crouched in the hallway they had just leapt from.

"Jump!" hissed Truvius as the stairwell came back round again. "We'll catch you."

Brutonia rocked backwards and forwards and at the last minute slipped onto his knees and almost tumbled into oblivion.

"Next time!" called Limpic as the stairwell disappeared into darkness again. He flicked on his torch so that Brutonia could see better.

"We'll have to grab him when we pass," said Truvius.

Limpic nodded.

"Stretch out your hands to balance yourself," he said as the hallway approached once more.

Brutonia dutifully did as he was told and as the stairwell passed, Truvius and Limpic grabbed his outstretched arms.

"Help!" cried Brutonia in shock as he tumbled onto the stairs and ended up hanging over the other side with both his friends pulling hard to bring him to safety.

"Next time just let me fall," he groaned. "I think my arms are three inches longer."

Limpic and Truvius grinned at each other before picking Brutonia up and descending ten steps. When they reached the bottom, the great gulf of the chasm rose to meet them again. Within seconds, another set of stairs, lower than the first, came sweeping past in the opposite direction. This time they had to step onto a narrow landing just when the two sets of stairs were in line. Once on, they turned, descended another ten steps, and were met by another lower flight of stairs that circled the cavern in the original clockwise position.

After repeating this process a few times, they reached the chasm floor and moved to the middle to work out where to go next. The stairs continued to glide silently around the perimeter of the room, flashing in the light of the Solaars. The surrounding walls were full of doors, most of which were closed. Limpic shone his torch around and the light glinted off the cool silent shroud of silver. It covered everything – even the doors, but his light picked out a corridor that stood open.

"Well?" whispered Truvius, shuffling over beside him. They had little time to decide other than to make the obvious choice because footfalls could be heard from above. There was another sound too: the drip dripping of water. The ocean had already reached the internal keep and was now flowing into the bowels of the city.

"Come on," said Limpic, disappearing into the open

doorway. The tunnel was low with an arched ceiling, and, like the tower, there were doors all along it. And, like the tower, silver was the dominant colour. They came to a crossroads.

"Which way?" wondered Brutonia. "Not that it will matter much – we can't open a door that's sealed in silver."

Before Limpic could answer Truvius butted in. "You take right and I'll take left." He disappeared down the corridor.

"I'll go straight ahead then," said Limpic to himself as Brutonia shuffled right. He moved cautiously but found every door encased. He was just beginning to doubt his decision to climb down into the depths of the city when the flower on his chest began to flutter as if by some other-worldly breeze and its veins glowed purple.

"I wonder," said Limpic, feeling his heart flutter a little as well. "It's never done that before." He was standing beside a red door, blistered by fire and marked '22'. It was the only door he'd seen that wasn't silver and he recognised it instantly: the door from his dreams when he'd been ill. Limpic licked his lips. He touched the blistered paintwork. It was warm beneath his fingers and some of it crumbled away. His fingers hovered near the handle but his flower tugged closer. He turned it and felt the door click open. Limpic took a quick glance right and left but Brutonia and Truvius were nowhere to be seen. In fact, a quietness had fallen all around as though time itself had ceased. Even the incessant dripping of water had stopped.

The answer to his flower lay behind this door, he was sure. Limpic eased it open and stepped inside.

Chapter 18

He blinked and found himself in another dimly lit corridor. It had a clean, clinical smell. He heard strange whirrs and beeps and an occasional groan. On either side of him were rooms filled with beds. On each of the beds lay small pinkish creatures, most of whom seemed to be sleeping. By every one of their beds stood a strange device and it was from these devices that the steady beeping was coming. He moved further in, his feet making squeaking sounds on the floor. The room to the left drew his eye. It was not so dim as all the rest. In fact, it looked sunlit. Limpic's whiskers twitched and he moved closer and laid his fingers against the cool glass.

"Oh, my," he mumbled. His stomach flipped and his body tightened. Opposite him was a south-facing window that looked out onto a stone driveway flanked on either side by cherry trees in full bloom. The room itself was bright and its walls were covered in flowery wallpaper. In the centre of the room was a bed, empty with neatly folded linen. The head of the bed stood against a chimney breast.

"The room from my dreams," whispered Limpic. He looked at the chimney breast and listened – no sound, no crows trapped, no Boy in the bed. His body relaxed. Tiny teardrops of blue flame fell from his flower. Limpic knew no danger lurked nearby but a slight sadness whelmed up in him.

"You don't have to come back here Limpic," said a voice vaguely familiar.

Limpic jumped and looked behind him.

"Who … how do you know my name?" he managed to mumble. The figure was mottled in shadow and indistinguishable from the surroundings, although he was taller than Limpic.

"You know me," said the figure. "We walked the same path for a time." Limpic inhaled quickly.

"Boy," he whispered.

The shadow's head inclined. "It's as you say."

A million questions swirled around Limpic's head. His flower reached towards Boy, its petals glittering in the low light.

"Who are you, really?" asked Limpic. He felt a lump in his throat.

"No one in particular," said Boy. "But you. You're the important one."

Limpic stood still. He heard his breath coming to and fro. He heard machines beeping and a low moan from one of the beds. Somewhere in the distance footsteps slapped against the smooth floor and then faded away.

"I thought," said Boy, "that since you have arrived here by way of the Western Pole we might meet briefly."

"But where *is* here?" said Limpic.

"It's where the children of the fire come," replied Boy.

Limpic contemplated this. "Are you a child of the fire?" he asked.

"Aye," was all Boy said.

"Am I?" asked Limpic.

"In a manner of speaking," said Boy. "You exist because this place exists."

"I don't understand," said Limpic. He began to fidget with his whiskers. "I used to dream about you when the fires came and then somehow, we parted."

"We parted because of your flower," said Boy. "It led to another way. A brighter way. I continued on my own path, darker though it was. Along with the others."

"Others," murmured Limpic. He closed his eyes and pressed his fingers into them. He remembered his dream on *Polestar* just before they sailed over the bridge of Pardune. He had seen a place like this. "I dreamt about someone else. Someone who looked a little like you but wasn't you. They wanted me to take them away from all this. To the land behind the Western Pole."

"Abigail," said Boy. "That's her name. She's a little girl."

"Are there many of you?" asked Limpic.

"There are very many," said Boy. Another groan from nearby and Boy's head turned. Still looking away, he continued. "We are all children when the fire comes. From young to old." Silence returned, punctuated only by heavy breaths and the odd grunt or a beep from one of the blinking machines. Boy breathed deeply and his voice quivered. "But some are so much younger and their light has barely flickered."

"Abigail," said Limpic. "And you."

Boy cleared his throat. "Look behind you Limpic. Look back into the room."

Limpic turned and gazed through the glass. His stomach somersaulted. The room had changed completely. The walls were white and windowless, although to his left was a glass panelled door that led into another room. Facing Limpic was a bed with two chairs on one side and a high table on the other. On the table stood a framed picture with three people smiling and hugging. In front of them was a black and white dog with lolling tongue. A family picture. The family were huddled together now. Mummy and daddy holding the hand of a small girl in the bed.

"Abigail," whispered Limpic. His throat constricted and his flower dripped tear drops.

Someone in a white tunic came through the glass door. They wore an apron. Limpic heard muffled voices and observed tired smiles. The figure in white cleaned the room methodically. They finished by wiping the framed picture, winked at Abigail and then left.

Limpic peered closer, comparing the face in the picture with the one in the bed. They could not have been more different. The face in the picture was healthy and plump with bright eyes and curly blond locks. But the girl in the bed. Her cheeks were unusually swollen and red; her brown eyes, which should have sparkled with youthful innocence, were tired and grim; her lips were cracked and dry from ugly sores. She ran her hand over her pale bare scalp, criss-crossed with tiny blue veins, and then she dropped her chin onto her chest and began to cry.

Limpic tensed and slapped his palm to the glass. "No," he whispered. "Can't I take her away. I'll take her away from it all." His eyes blurred over.

"There's nowhere else to go Limpic," said Boy. "She's where she needs to be right now."

"What's wrong with her? Is the fire a disease?" Limpic asked, remembering how it had almost consumed him. He shuddered.

"Do you see by her bed. The strange beeping machine," said

Boy.

Limpic nodded.

"Do you see the tube that runs beneath her pyjamas. Do you see what it's attached to?"

"Aye," said Limpic. "A clear bag with red liquid."

"Liquid fire," said Boy.

"Liquid fire?!" blurted Limpic. "Wait. What? I thought the fire was a disease?"

"No Limpic, it's the cure."

Limpic sagged back. His voice stuck in his throat. "It's the ... what?" His hands instinctively ran over his stomach, his lips, his hair and finally tugged at his whiskers.

"It does what it's supposed to Limpic. It does it very well. Only ..."

"It burns," replied Limpic.

"It burns," said Boy. "Indiscriminately. It doesn't know where the bad ends and the good begins. It can be a dark path to travel."

The door to the left opened and someone walked in. Dressed casually, they stood by Abigail's side speaking in low inaudible tones.

"The doctor," said Boy. "Pick that up and put it to your ear. It's a phone." He pointed to a shiny curved thing that hung by the glass window. Limpic did as he was told. The phone was about the size of the Echo Shell although completely smooth and black. As soon as Limpic placed it to his ear the voices in the room became clear, if a little tinny and faraway.

"So, you'll be very pleased to know that Mr Bear is completely clean," said the doctor, handing a small stuffed animal to Abigail. She took it gleefully and crushed it to her cheeks. "And," continued the doctor, "Mr Bear and I have had a very serious discussion. A *very* serious discussion indeed." The doctor looked at the stuffed bear. "Would you like to tell Abigail the good news, or shall I?" The bear stared back impassively and Abigail giggled.

"Heh," chuckled Boy.

Limpic grinned and wiped his nose.

"We won't be using this nasty stuff anymore," said the doctor, removing part of the tube and pushing the beeping machine away. "We have something better. Much better. Something tailored just for you Abi. And Mr Bear of course."

Abigail pulled Mr Bear close to her cheeks and smiled coyly.

"A few wise heads have discovered a better way of fighting back," continued the doctor. "We're going to use your own immune system, Abi. To finish off what we've started. It'll be just like that time you had a bad cold and your own body got rid of it. What do you think of that Mr Bear?"

Abigail made Mr Bear's head nod and then she laughed. The doctor ruffled Mr Bears ears and then lightly tapped Abigail's nose. "I just want to have a few words with your mummy and daddy in the other room. I think Mr Bear is too tired to listen to any more boring talk so maybe the two to you could have a little nap. Eh?"

Abigail nodded and settled back in her pillow with Mr Bear on her chest. For a moment Limpic could have sworn she looked right at him and then her eyes grew heavy and she drifted off to sleep. The room began to fade away and then went dark.

Limpic put the phone down and swallowed. Something tailored just for you, he thought. Something that would know what was good and what was bad? He tugged at his flower.

"But what has all this got to do with me?" he asked quietly. "You said I was important. That I exist because all this exists."

185

Limpic leaned his forehead against the glass.

"Imagine a seed of an idea," said Boy. A small round ball appeared in the gloom of the dark room. It merely blinked with a tiny white light. "Imagine that seed born not in the sunlit lands or well-watered pastures, but born of flame and bitterness. Born in arid lands. Lonely lands. Shadow lands. In hardship and pain. An idea lying, waiting in the dark. Waiting in desperation, for inspirational water." The tiny ball grew larger and then flattened like it had been stood on and was now a disc lying flat. Limpic placed both hands on the window and pressed his nose against the glass. His breath caused tiny clouds of condensation to form and recede. The disc stood on its side. It was back lit and revealed an image in silhouette. A sickle moon and a face within it, peering up.

"That's me!" gasped Limpic. His heart swelled.

"But imagine more," said Boy. "Imagine even more than this. What if he carried something? A symbol of life. A symbol of hope of better things to come. Something that rises out of the fire but could only be realised *by* the fire. What if that something needed somewhere good to grow?"

The entire room became engulfed in flame. It licked against the window causing Limpic to step back. Sweat dripped down his back, but Boy seemed unperturbed.

"Imagine all that fire, all that energy tailored to fight against what should not be. Devouring *only* what should not be. The bad. And leaving all that is good. Like Abigail's own immune system fighting back. Wouldn't that be a better path to travel?"

As Boy spoke, the flames began to swirl around and around like a whirlpool receding into something in the middle of the room.

"Oh!" gasped Limpic.

A flower hung suspended in the dark, lit from within by its own light. It had five petals with purple veins and it drank in the last remnants of the uncontrollable flames.

"Imagine a fire flower Limpic," whispered Boy. "And it can be so."

Limpic slumped against the window. A violent sob wracked his body and he pressed his eyes tight together. When he opened them the flower was gone. The room was as it was before. Bright and its walls covered in flowery wallpaper. In the centre of the room was a bed, empty with neatly folded linen. The head of the bed stood against a chimney breast. Opposite him was a south-facing window that looked out onto a stone driveway flanked on either side by cherry trees. A crisp blanket of snow covered everything and it looked as though spring had returned and the trees were blooming with white petals instead of pink.

And all was clean and new.

"You have your flower Limpic. Go and do good things with it," said Boy.

Limpic plucked his flower and pondered. It knew what was good and what was bad. It knew what shouldn't be. It had shown again and again that it would stop the Cra. And his parents had said to let it guide.

"Aye, aye, aye," he whispered.

Echoing footsteps were coming in his direction. Limpic flattened himself against the glass and stiffened.

Chapter 19

"It's pointless, Limpic," said Truvius. He puffed, out of breath. "I went as far as I dared but all the doors are locked behind silver." He drummed his knuckles against the door Limpic leaned against. "This one's silver too, I see."

Limpic came back to his senses. He stepped back. The door was indistinct from all the others. Silver.

"No joy," said Brutonia, striding up the corridor. "Hey, Limpic, your flower's glowing."

Limpic peered down and smiled. "So it is," he said.

Truvius and Brutonia glanced at each other.

"But that still doesn't help us find Peruvius," said Truvius.

"I'm sure he's around here somewhere," said Limpic, turning on his heels and striding up the corridor. The thought of Abigail suddenly lightened his mood. Her eyes were brighter after they had parted. A spark had returned. Something tailored just for her. He began to whistle and gave a little jump and a kick, just for the sake of it. His companions trotted up beside him.

Brutonia's face was grave. "You know, my father used to say that stress can do things to a person's mind."

Limpic stopped and patted Brutonia on the cheek. Grinning,

he said, "Don't worry, Bru, you aren't acting any more peculiar than usual, but I'll keep an extra special eye on you."

Brutonia's mouth fell open. "But I meant—"

"What about Peruvius?" said Truvius sharply. "He could be behind any one of these doors, if he's here at all."

Limpic drew still. He was standing with his back to his friends. "Well, flower," he whispered, "you've protected me from the silver that comes from the Cra. You've led me down here. Will you help me? It would be *very* good if you did."

"Limpic!" snapped Truvius, stepping in front of him. "Do you know where Peruvius is?"

Limpic ignored him. He let the sensation of warmth from his chest permeate his entire body. He felt peaceful and his mind was clear. He let his flower guide all his actions. It fluttered and its head quivered and strained towards Truvius.

"I don't," said Limpic, "but it seems you do."

Truvius stepped back "What are you talking about?"

Limpic gripped Truvius's shoulder. "Where is your cousin Peruvius? You seek him. He is of your blood. And you both wear the ring of your lineage. You will know which door he lies behind but you must let go of all other thoughts."

"I … I don't," stammered Truvius. "Please, Limpic, your hand is hot. I don't …" Truvius's eyes fluttered rapidly and his shoulders sagged. The warmth in Limpic's body had passed down his arm and settled where his fingers gripped his friend's shoulder. He opened his inner ear.

Thump Thump. He heard the vibrations of Truvius's heart. And then, further away and fainter, another heartbeat.

Thump Thump. Limpic adjusted the muscle in his ear to better hear the lesser vibrations.

THUMP THUMP

"Peruvius!" gasped Truvius. "I can hear his heart – he's here! This way!" He walked further along the corridor, bypassing identical doors. Limpic held his shoulder all the while and walked behind. Brutonia followed, shuffling his feet to be as close to Limpic as possible. The heartbeat grew louder.

"There," said Truvius, after they had walked several hundred paces. He pointed to a silver door that swelled outwards. Despite its mantle of metal, the grains in the silver coating signalled that it had once been a heavy wooden door.

"How do you know?" said Brutonia, furrowing his brow.

Limpic released Truvius, who blinked. "Know what?" he replied, yawning as though emerging from sleep. Then his face cleared and he pounded the door. "Peruvius!" he shouted. "Peruvius, we're here." The pounding only thudded dully against the metal. "I know he's in there. I heard his heart!" insisted Truvius and he slumped against the frame.

"But that door is solid silver. How on earth are we going to open it even if Peruvius *is* on the other side?" said Brutonia.

Limpic's flower glowed bright white and stretched towards the handle. "Step back," he replied resolutely. The warmth in his body throbbed even more intensely and once more his hand reached forward.

"Look!" cried Brutonia.

Truvius stepped back and gasped. The silver on the handle retreated at Limpic's touch. It began to flow away in every direction, in tiny beads of metal, like water running over an oily surface. The entire door was revealed showing the knots and grains in the wood beneath. The wall surrounding the frame also cleared uncovering bricks that had been painted white. A cobweb in the corner of the doorframe quivered as a spider scurried for safety.

Limpic steadied himself and leaned against the wood. It gave way with an ominous groan. The other side was darker than anything he had experienced. It immediately gripped his outstretched arm like an iron fist and he struggled to catch his breath. It was as if his arm had been severed from the rest of his body. The air was stale and dusty, like a windowless room left to rot. "Come on!" he winced. "We have to go on. Hold my shoulder."

Truvius and Brutonia obeyed, trudging into the unlit world blindly with one hand on the shoulder of the person in front. There was nothing else to see or feel except dust beneath their feet. Their eyes might well have been floating worlds of their own because the rest of their bodies had been eaten up by the utter blackness.

"Can you light one of the torches?" whispered Limpic. Sudden dread gnawed at his heart and his fire flower went out. He remembered King Managh's ominous warning before they had left *Polestar*: "Be sure now that your wits will be sorely tested."

They stopped momentarily while Brutonia, who was in the middle, groped blindly to retrieve his torch. When he flicked it on, its light was feeble and frugal, barely denting the darkness at all.

"Has it run out?" enquired Truvius.

Brutonia grunted. "It was fully charged before we left and I've barely used it. It should still give enough light for another few days at least."

Truvius tried his but the effect was the same: the light was dull and sickly, more like a fruitless trickle from a dying sun.

"Ohh!" moaned Brutonia. "I feel awful. How long have we been here? It seems like days."

"Weeks," said Truvius. His voice was dull and hollow. "We've been here weeks."

"No, we've only just got here," replied Limpic. Then he stopped and frowned. "At least I think so." He hung his head. It was hard to think. How long had it been dark? And cold?

"It's so quiet," grumbled Brutonia.

Limpic stumbled on before stopping when something moved past his shoulder. He was sure of it. His blood ran cold. The Cra – are they here? His scalp crawled. Old fears crept into his head of fevers and sickness, of burning up in the darkness and loneliness of the night. And yet he felt cold, especially his feet. Like they were falling asleep and no longer part of him.

"This is hopeless," grumbled Truvius. "I can't see, feel or *hear* anything. What are we supposed to be doing? I knew I shouldn't have come. Oof!" He stumbled and fell to his knees. "Something tripped me!"

Limpic felt his way back to where Truvius lay. The coldness in his feet was spreading up his legs and they were now stiff and heavy like lead. He groped about in the dark and worked his fingers over the object that had tripped Truvius. There were actually two things – both smooth and cold and about a hand's breadth apart. They moved upwards like young saplings and then came together as one broad trunk. Limpic's whiskers tingled and he swallowed back bile rising in his throat. He felt Brutonia breathing heavily over his shoulder. The warmth of his breath juxtaposed with the coldness beneath his fingers caused Limpic to shiver. He struggled upright. He could barely drag his legs beneath him. He had something oval cupped between his hands.

"Brutonia, shine your light here," he whispered hoarsely.

The big elvern obeyed. He shook his Solaar in an attempt to

wring the last drops of energy from it. Its frugal light picked out a face. A silver face.

"Oh, my goodness!" he exclaimed, dropping his torch.

"One of the seven," said Limpic. His fingers trembled on the solid cheeks.

"Oh, Limpic!" moaned Truvius. "I am sorry. I am truly sorry. I should never have brought you to this terrible place. We are going to die, Limpic. We will be turned to silver! I am sorry!"

"Pull yourself together!" snapped Limpic. He reached for Truvius and shook him. "I didn't come all this way to fail. At least you remember why we're here now – the seven have made sure of that, so their lives were not wasted. Now we must go on."

"You are right, Limpic," stuttered Truvius, gripping his hand. "You are always right, my good friend. You are the best of us all, truly you are."

Limpic loosened his grip on Truvius's shoulder, although his fingers, like his legs, had become stiff and cold. He stumbled and Truvius leaned in to support him.

"What is it?" asked Truvius.

"I ... I don't know," panted Limpic. "Can you taste that?"

"What?" said Truvius. His voice was tinged with concern.

"It's like ... like metal," answered Limpic. He clung to Truvius like a dead weight.

"When did you get so heavy!" grunted Truvius.

Brutonia's voice sounded nearby, small and timid. "I've found something," he said. He waved his Solaar so they could at least see what direction to go.

"Come on, Limpic," insisted Truvius, dragging him across the dusty ground.

193

They found the big elvern cradling something in his arms.

"Peruvius!" exclaimed Truvius. He lowered Limpic to the ground and then fell to his knees beside the prostrate figure. His lower half was encased in solid silver and fused to the ground like he was growing out of it. Truvius moved his fingers up until they touched the edge of a golden sheet that covered his face. He removed it quickly.

"Peruvius, I knew it was you. I could feel it was you!"

The elvern groaned and shook his head weakly. "You shouldn't have come here," he whispered pathetically. "I don't know how you made it so far but they'll turn you to silver. Can't you hear it, the whispers, the maddening whispers. Oh, Mother, Mother, I am sorry!" Peruvius wept pitifully.

"Where are we?" Limpic asked. He dragged himself closer. His body was so heavy and clumsy.

Peruvius coughed and drew in a long, deep breath. "The unlit world," he croaked. "The far side of the moon."

Chapter 20

Limpic sat back, too stunned to speak. He grabbed fistfuls of dust and ground them in his hands. *The far side of the moon*. He shook his head. His breath caught in his throat. He groaned. All this time and Peruvius had been in plain sight, languishing on the other side of the very moon he was killing. The very moon the trio had been chasing these many days.

"Limpic," whispered Brutonia. "What do we do?"

Limpic shuddered. "What do we do?" he mumbled. "What do we do?" He gasped for air, panting like a dog that is too hot. His very bones ached and at any moment his body felt like it would collapse under its own weight.

The far side of the moon.

Limpic fell back and lay staring, unsure whether his eyes were open or shut. Blood was thundering around his temple. The darkness was oppressive.

"Limpic," whispered Brutonia, concern in his voice. "Limpic, what do we do?"

Limpic didn't answer. He didn't care anymore. Why did he have to make all the decisions? Why was everyone so desperate that he should know all the answers? He was only one little ullan. One little ullan whose home was forever lost to silver. It was his job to look after the Golden Coast and he had utterly failed. The cliffs and coves, beaches and harbours were gone. Instead they waited, silver as far as the eye could see. Silently brooding over the ullan who had abandoned them. He'd failed his parents. Couldn't they see he wasn't strong enough? Brona, of the clan of the Grey Whiskers was stronger by far. He allowed Brutonia's voice to fade away until all was quiet.

All except a strange clicking at the back of his nose. His inner ear was vibrating. He tried to swallow it away but the clicking only got worse. He opened his ear and the clicking stopped. Silence. But then he heard another sound: a crow cawing. His heart thumped.

Cold fear crept over Limpic's chest and pressed down hard. He struggled to breathe. It felt like someone was sitting on him.

"Caw! Caw!"

What if the fire flower never came? he thought suddenly, and his heart skipped a beat.

"No, no!" moaned Limpic, rocking his head from side to side. "Not that, please, no, not that!" He had a vision of a room on fire, of an empty chimney with a trapped crow cawing and scrabbling behind brickwork, and in the middle of the room a bed and in the bed Boy. Limpic's stomach churned. His throat ached and ulcers broke out on his gums and lips. And his whiskers, his beautiful whiskers, began to dry up like straw.

"I don't want to see this!" cried Limpic. "I don't want to *feel* this again."

He had memories of fevers and burning up in the darkness and loneliness of the night. Of walking aimlessly through the quiet empty house from one room to the next hoping someone would hear, hoping someone would come and bring comfort but finding only silence and the long, dark watches of the night.

"Please!" he moaned. "Please, I don't want to be sick." His body ached – a bone-aching throb of incessant pain. His stomach burned with fire. "Please, I just want to go home!" cried Limpic. Huge tears welled in his eyes and flowed unimpeded down his cheeks. Limpic hadn't the strength to wipe them away. He didn't even know if it was his body that ached any more or whether it was Boy's.

Two red eyes glared down at him.

"Zarkus?" he croaked. The eyes just stared and Limpic heard whisperings. Not like before, though. Not mindless hissings that swept this way and that and all about. These were directed right into Limpic's heart. Right into his very fears.

"Look," they insisted.

"No," replied Limpic, trying to turn his face away.

"Look," they said.

Limpic tried to fight but it was no use; his face wouldn't be turned away and his eyes couldn't be closed.

"No," he groaned.

"Yes," whispered the Cra. "Everything burns. Look, see for yourself. The boy is alone. You are alone."

Limpic tried to look away but the image was seared into his brain. He grew cold all over and just when he thought it was the end a voice spoke in the darkness.

"Why are you back here Limpic?"

"Boy?" asked Limpic.

"Aye," replied Boy.

"I'm scared," said Limpic. "Can't you take me away from all of this? I just want to go home."

"You *can* go home," said Boy. "Just not yet. There's something dark standing in your way and you have to pass through it."

197

"I don't know if I'm strong enough," whispered Limpic.

"But if the only way home was to travel into the dark, would you go?" asked Boy. "Even if you knew what was coming?"

Limpic tried to swallow but his mouth was so dry. "Aye," he croaked. "Yes, I want to go home. I want to see the sea. I want to hear it and swim in it. I want to go home to the Golden Coast. I want that more than anything."

"Then you have your flower," said Boy. "It will never burn or consume you. Always it will try to protect you, even from yourself. You will know when to use it." The voice faltered and then began again, thick with emotion and at times almost breaking. "But if the whispers do come, and you are tempted to remember the past and see only darkness and hopelessness, then look closer. We children of the fire were not alone."

Limpic looked. His heart fluttered. A corridor floated past his eyes. With beds and beeping machines and squeaky floors. Where the children of the fire gathered. And by their beds, sitting patiently, those they loved and who loved them back.

"We always had our families, always," whispered the voice.

Limpic remembered Abigail's parents, sitting beside her holding her hand.

There was someone else – two people, no, three people, no … too many to count. Some in white tunics and others in blue bending over the beds, smiling, cleaning, bringing toast, checking heartbeats.

Listening.

And always bringing hope.

"A means to an end," one of them said. "Just a means to an end."

"Not alone," said the voice, trailing away. "Not when *they* were there. The kindness of strangers. Who took us in and gathered up the broken pieces of our lives. We drew hope from them as one draws life from the sun."

Limpic wiped his eyes and sniffed, only now realising he'd been crying. The vision fled. So too did Limpic's pain and sickness. It was like his body ceased to be. He was turning to silver and had been all the while he lay there in the dust clothed in his clumsy, heavy body, wrestling with the darkness.

"This cannot be the end," he cried. "There must have been a reason I was here."

"None," replied the Cra as the silver reached Limpic's chest and trickled towards his jaw.

He shuddered. "Then why was I sent for – why was I chosen for this quest? Why do I have to wear this flower – can't you see it burns?" cried Limpic. "Can't you see it hurts!" He blinked as silver trickled into his eyes.

You have your flower. It will never burn or consume you. Go and do good things with it.

Boy was right – his flower had come. It had come for a time such as this. His flower was here right now. Through the numbness and coldness Limpic felt a spark of warmth ignite in his chest. His body began to tingle all over, like it had pins and needles and was coming back to life. The stiffness and coldness lifted and Limpic could feel his warm blood pumping around his warm body. His fingers and toes ached and itched as though he had just come in from the cold and doused them in hot water. But especially he felt his fire flower and the weight of silver on his chest lifted.

"What are you?" rasped a cold, bloodless voice. Limpic sat up and saw Peruvius staring at him blankly. His eyes were black as pitch and something dark fanned out behind his head like a snake curling back ready to bite.

"I am … hope," replied Limpic, peering at his hands, "of better things to come. And I will not be constrained." Truvius and Brutonia were both in their original positions but motionless, with faces twisted in fear and eyes wide and vacant. Facing their own internal nightmares, no doubt. Silver was beginning to flow up their legs.

Limpic's flower glowed red. "Back!" he commanded.

Peruvius bared his teeth and hissed a cold breath of silver but it fell like flakes of snow before Limpic's feet. He tried to breathe on Truvius, who was beginning to move his head and work his jaws.

"Don't touch him!" growled Limpic, lifting his finger and stabbing the air.

Peruvius's face contorted in pain and then twisted into a hideous, tooth-filled smile. "Silver is too good for him anyway. Besides we have what we need." With that Peruvius's body convulsed and the shadow fled.

"Aye, aye, aye," sighed Limpic. Such heartless hatred. He lay back and closed his eyes. Just for a moment he needed to remember something pure and good. He imagined, not a sea of solid silver but a living, breathing, happy sea that would forever roll to shore. He remembered his promise to the moon. He pictured the sky at night; the great and glorious blanket peppered by a billion tiny lights. A billion tiny stars so far away that it was a wonder they could shine at all. And yet they did. Even though they were surrounded by eons of darkness they still shone and they still lit up the night sky. Only when the clouds swept in were they hidden. Hidden but never gone. But there were no clouds on the moon – not even on the far side. There was only …

Limpic opened his eyes and gasped. "I can see eternity," he

whispered.

"What?" replied Brutonia, who had been pawing at his side.

Starlight danced and crackled in Limpic's eyes like the sun glinting off restless waters.

"Limpic!" shouted Brutonia in glee. "Your eyes, they're glowing!"

"It's only a reflection of what comes from above," whispered Limpic. "Look up, Brutonia, and see for yourself."

The big elvern blinked and raised his chin towards the sky. He began to laugh and then to cry, and then to laugh again. "I can see the stars. You're right, Limpic, I can see for miles and miles. It looks like ... forever."

Suddenly it wasn't so dark all around. It was only here, at the edge of the world, when all other lights went out, that the very shores of eternity shone the brightest.

"Yes, yes," murmured Peruvius. "The sky is so full of light, now that you mention it. I can see it too." His own eyes flickered a little and a faint hoary light shone from them.

"If someone could help me stand," said Peruvius, smiling weakly. "As you can see, I am somewhat incapacitated." He rapped his knuckles on his silver legs but at least he was no longer fused to the moon. Limpic and Truvius peered at each other and each grabbed the prince beneath an arm and hauled him to a standing position.

"What is that sensation?" gasped Peruvius, leaning heavily on Limpic's shoulder. "There is warmth in you. You've set me free. Ah, my mind clears. You have burned off the last mists of winter." He pushed both Limpic and Truvius clear. "Stand back," he urged. "I am myself again." Peruvius closed his eyes and breathed out slowly. He let out a soft moan from the back of his throat and then breathed deeply through his nose. The silver on his legs throbbed with light and began to seep inwards and upwards causing the veins on Peruvius's neck to bulge and glow beneath the skin. His entire head emitted a ghostly pallor. His eyes flashed open, like two full moons suddenly appearing from behind dark clouds. "I am well," he said and his eyes continued to shine.

"What in the name of all that is normal and decent and wholesome and … and good is going on!" blurted out Brutonia. "I have a blinding headache and a serious case of the hoobie-joobies!"

"I think it's heebie-jeebies," said Limpic.

"And I have those as well," replied Brutonia.

"Bru, it is you!" laughed Peruvius, hugging the giant elvern before growing sombre. "I have turned the world to silver, that is what happened. And whatever silver was left in the moon is now embedded in Meridian, causing her to sink. It was the whispers. They went right into the heart of my fears. I could no longer think for myself. And every thought, and every image in my head, became silver." His voice broke. "The last thing I remember was my mother reaching for me, and then she too was gone. The dread of that memory imprisoned me here and I have been fighting it ever since. But the silver was taking me – as you saw yourself. I would not have survived much longer if you hadn't arrived. I do not know how you made it so far."

He looked at Limpic and his flower and recognition shone on his face. "I saw you, just now, and on the Valla Stones. The Cra wanted me to destroy the Golden Coast. They feared it – or, rather, they feared someone who would come from it, something that burns them." Peruvius held his hand to his brow. "Yes, yes, I remember. A silver hand – I sent a silver hand to the Golden Coast and you stopped it. That same warmth I felt just now as you lifted me I felt then. And even … yes, even on board a ship, during a storm. I tried to turn the ship to silver but there was a terrible heat and I was driven back." Peruvius smiled and his eyes sparkled. "After that you could not be found. It was as though you were being hidden or protected. Now I know things will be put right because *you* are here. The Cra were right to fear you."

It was only now in the light that Limpic could see Peruvius's features. His build was somewhere between that of Brutonia and Truvius: he was neither heavy nor light. His shoulders would have stood reasonably square were it not for the roundedness set in them by distress and fatigue. He wore white armour that was stained grey by dust and dirt. Thrown off his shoulders was a tattered red robe attached by two large silver brooches cast in the image of the moon.

His face was warm and friendly, his eyes large and round, his lips full and red and his nose quite broad. All in all, his was a friendly countenance, devoid of sharp edges. He swept his fair hair back off his forehead where it fell in curtains just above his eyes.

"Come," he said, his voice as pleasant as his features despite his long captivity, "we must not tarry here any longer. We will follow your footsteps back to the door." Peruvius strode off.

"How do we fix this?" said Truvius, grunting in his efforts to fall in step with his cousin. "What can we do?"

"I must get to Glorian," replied Peruvius, "the seat of the Western Pole. On my own I am too small and weak to release the amount of silver that has sunk this city and even now covers much of the world, but using the Tower of Glorian as a conductor, I can draw the silver through her."

"Is that why you were taken here?" asked Brutonia, skipping

203

to catch up.

"Yes," replied Peruvius. "The tower was used in reverse to absorb silver from the moon. That and the fact that the Western Pole is almost impossible to find." He drew back his lips and sighed through his teeth. "The tower was also used as a weapon. Silver that was stored here could be sent anywhere across the globe when the moon was up. By manipulating my mind during the quickening, when the silver flowed, it could be sent back to the moon. It then fell on whatever I was instructed to let it fall on – Tulwood, the Golden Coast, Mother." Peruvius wiped his eyes.

"Then it's time it was set free," said Limpic.

"Agreed," said Peruvius. "But first we must get back to Meridian." He kept up his pace.

Truvius fell back a bit and kept close to Limpic. He seemed to stumble and trip as though his vision was darker than the rest. Limpic said nothing but reached back and took Truvius by the hand to help him keep up. His flower had returned to a faint pinkish hue. They passed the silver statue they had come across earlier and found three other sets of footprints heading off in different directions.

"At the end of each set of footprints stands the rest of the seven," said Peruvius, stopping briefly. "Truly they were brave souls to have made it so far, but everybody fears something and eventually the Cra find that fear. And once found and broken, silver can flow unimpeded."

"What can we do for them?" Brutonia asked.

"There is nothing we can do yet," replied Peruvius. "Not until I reach Glorian and set the silver free." He turned on his heel and his cloak swooshed behind him.

They trudged on until Brutonia called out in surprise. "My

feet are soaked!"

Limpic bent down and felt the ground and found the dust had turned into a quagmire. Not far ahead stood the doorway to Meridian and there was water seeping from behind the cracks in the frame. In fact, water was running down the door from the very top, which meant only one thing: the entire corridor was flooded.

Chapter 21

"What is it?" Peruvius asked.

"Water," replied Limpic. "We're too late. The sea has flooded the lower levels of the citadel. Unless—"

"Unless what?"

"Well," continued Limpic, "unless I can ask King Managh for help. He should still be outside the city."

"But how can you ask him if you are in here?" said Peruvius.

"I might be able to get the water to help us – the vibrations, I mean.

"Vibrations?" questioned Peruvius, obviously perplexed.

"Or I suppose," muttered Limpic, thinking back to everything they had come across already. His hand fell on the Echo Shell dangling by his side. He hadn't been apart from it since almost losing it on *Polestar*. "That's it!" he cried.

"What's it?" replied Peruvius frowning.

Ignoring the looks of bewilderment, Limpic knelt by the door where the water was gushing. He took a deep breath, placed the Echo Shell to his lips and blew until bright dots appeared in front of his eyes and he keeled over.

"Limpic, Limpic! Are you alright?" his friends shouted,

drawing him up and splashing water over his face.

"I'm fine," he said, sitting up weakly. "If the Echo Shell can call *Polestar* and the Gatekeeper, surely it can call the king of the deep?" A wry smile crossed his lips and Brutonia thumped him on the shoulder with a cackle.

"Now what?" enquired Peruvius as soon as Limpic was able to stand.

"Now we wait," replied Limpic, pushing the heels of his hands into his eye sockets. His head felt woolly from the exertion.

"You are certainly a curious creature," said Peruvius. "I will have to hear more of how you came to be part of this desperate mission but that can wait for another time." He winced and stumbled forward. Brutonia grabbed him.

"My muscles aren't used to moving after so long as a prisoner," he said panting. "Regardless, I must get to the tower quickly!"

"If your message doesn't reach the king, what do we do?" Truvius asked Limpic.

"We open the door and I swim as hard as I can while towing Peruvius," said Limpic grimly. "He'll have to wear one of the breathers."

"You would never beat the floodwaters," said Truvius doubtfully.

Limpic shrugged and held out his hands helplessly. "I have no other ideas. Do any of you?"

Silence echoed back and all eyes were downcast. Peruvius looked worried, clasping and unclasping his hands.

After what seemed like an age there was a booming sound from the other side of the door and the water stopped pouring in. Limpic put his ear to the timber and listened.

"Well?" said Peruvius, hanging onto Brutonia's arm.

"Stand back," replied Limpic. "The door'll be opening."

"But won't the water pour in?" exclaimed Truvius. "We'll be washed away!"

He had little time to worry because the door cracked then creaked open, slowly at first and then with great purpose. The water behind stood like a wall of clear glass with an emerald mist swirling within its depths. The swirling mist spun around and around as though it was drilling towards them. When it reached the surface of the glass wall, it opened to reveal a tunnel. Inside sat a merman on his grand sea stallion. His shield was no longer strapped to his back, nor was his broadsword sheathed. He appeared dishevelled but managed to smile weakly.

"I am Magnus," he said breathlessly. "King Managh sent me. He thought he heard a whale down here and sent me after its song. Something too strange to ignore."

"I remember you from the Bridge of Pardune," said Limpic. "I'm the whale, well, sort of."

Magnus bowed. "Very clever of you. You have found the captive, then?" He gestured to Peruvius.

Limpic nodded.

"You are at war?" said Truvius, inclining his head towards Magnus's unsheathed sword.

The soldier nodded. "We were attacked shortly after you left, when the waters rose higher than the city walls. I only just managed to slip away unnoticed." He sheathed his sword.

Truvius was obviously troubled. "Who leads the enemy?" he enquired.

Magnus shrugged. "I'm inclined to say no one at present, although, just before the battle began, two figures did appear briefly on top of Glorian."

Truvius looked to Limpic and Brutonia and shrugged awkwardly.

Peruvius moaned. "We must hurry," he said weakly, "or it won't matter who's fighting what because all will be lost."

"I thought you couldn't leave the ocean?" said Brutonia grunting as he half-carried, half-dragged Peruvius into the tunnel. Everyone else followed.

Magnus grinned. "Technically I haven't left it – I just followed it in here." He winced as a splash of water fell from the roof of his tunnel. A bracelet on his right arm flickered with an emerald light.

"The bracelet draws its power from King Managh's spear," said Magnus as the group gazed at its colour. "And the king's power comes from the sea." He grunted as the light flickered and then re-established itself. "As you can see, that power has become unstable. I can no longer guarantee the integrity of this tunnel all the way to the surface. You must choose who will accompany the prince and take the breathers in case my air pocket collapses."

Truvius stepped forward and placed a breather in Peruvius's mouth. "Take him, Brutonia."

"No, Tru—" Brutonia tried to protest but Peruvius choked and Brutonia had to hold the breather for him.

"He needs your strength. Get him to the surface. That's an order!" insisted Truvius. He stepped back onto the moon and the door began to close. Limpic's flower strained towards him. Blue tears fell from it and Limpic threw himself through the door and crashed into his friend. The two of them went sprawling into the wet dust as the door closed with an ominous thud.

"Limpic!" shouted Truvius. "That was silly of you. You can breathe under water, remember?"

"I know," said Limpic, sitting up and drawing his legs to his chest. His flower was beginning to glow red. "But I couldn't think of you here alone and I just wanted to be with you."

"I am glad I came to find you," said Truvius. "You've been the leader on this whole expedition while all I did was sulk and pass snide remarks. I've been pretty hopeless, actually. I'm sorry."

"Listen—"

"You know what darkness really is?" Truvius said.

Limpic didn't speak. He could hear the whispers coming for his friend.

"It is the absence of light," said Truvius. He fingered the scar on his cheek. "I know that – I have always known that. And anger, bitterness … that living death you spoke of, it's just the absence of hope. Funny," said Truvius with a smile, "I have been so wrapped up in guarding the realm and defending it against dark forces that I've forgotten what it is I most love about it. Simple things like the way the sky changes on a thundery day, or when sunlight falls through the trees and finds a little pool to lie in – and friends, good friends. You know what I mean?"

Limpic nodded and then shivered as the air crackled like ice underfoot. His flower burned.

"Ah, isn't this poignant," said a voice close by.

"Zarkus!" exclaimed Truvius, staring wide-eyed at the cloaked figure by his side.

"Hello, Brother," hissed the shadowy form.

Chapter 22

Limpic's mouth fell open and he sagged backwards. Zarkus was a shadow of his former self. Blackness hung around him like an aura, like he was peering at them from the mouth of a cave.

"Zarkus," pleaded Truvius, rising to his knees, "it's a trap. The Cra plan to consume you!"

"Sit down!" hissed Zarkus.

A dark claw struck Truvius across the face and he tumbled backwards. Blood oozed from his lip.

"I see you still bear a scar on your cheek from the night you tried to save Peruvius. Do you know it was I who gave you that scar?" Zarkus seemed to float rather than walk towards him. His breath steamed from his mouth in freezing vapours.

"And it was I who gave you yours," countered Truvius.

Zarkus flinched and touched the scar above his right eye. A dark smile curled his lips. "You couldn't save Peruvius then and you can't save him now. Legions are waiting at the very entrance to Glorian. Peruvius will never reach the Western Pole. And to think you are to die here and give up your life for nothing!" Zarkus cackled ghoulishly. His voice had lost all remnants of a living, breathing entity. It was dark, flat and soulless.

He drew closer, holding his hand out in front of him as if examining it. He threw back his hood. His eyes looked heavy, like he was falling asleep. His nose was small sitting above a thin mouth. His lips were a deep red, almost black. His hair was almost gone and his skin was grey and dry, like old parchment – like he was ready to shed it.

Truvius shrank back in disgust. He rubbed his lip with the back of his hand. "Oh, Brother, Brother, what have they done to you?"

Zarkus cocked his head to one side. His features changed – almost like a mask had slipped away, and his eyes came alive. "Run, Brother! Run and don't look back," he suddenly cried.

Then just as suddenly the mask reappeared. The animation in his face fell away. "Or stay," whispered another voice, the flat voice, "stay. Join us."

"Zarkus, you have to fight it," said Limpic. "You saved me. You saved Brutonia. You can still save your people."

Zarkus turned quickly to look at Limpic, as if he had forgotten he was there. His voice came alive again. "I couldn't save Father. I thought I could." He grimaced as though a spasm of pain wracked his body and his countenance fell. He turned back to Truvius, lifted a long bony finger and pointed at him. "We're the same, you and I, brother. Give up this flesh and I can save you from this prison. I know what you've been thinking – that it's your fault, all of this. That Father went mad because of you, because Mother died giving birth to you. You replay the past in your head over and over and over."

Truvius rubbed his face. He rose slowly and met Zarkus's gaze. His eyes blinked and he took two steps backwards. Limpic heard the whispers loudly. He felt pressure rising behind his eyes and wondered when his flower would come alive. It was merely glinting red in the starlight.

"My fault," said Truvius. "Yes, yes, it was all my fault." His eyes became sleepy. "I'm tired of fighting it."

"Tired, of course," replied Zarkus in a silky voice. "Don't fight it." He drew closer.

"Truvius," shouted Limpic, stepping between him and Zarkus. "Truvius, look at me. None of this is your fault. Your father chose his own destiny. He chose his path – him alone. He invited this misery upon us all."

The blackness of Truvius's pupils swelled until the whites disappeared completely. "Tired of fighting the anger," he said flatly.

Limpic began to panic. "The Cra are the enemy," he pleaded. "They are the deceivers. They know where your weaknesses lie. They probe them and use them. Your father's was the past, the elvern throne, apparent injustice. Zarkus thinks he failed to save his father. And you, you think your life is worthless because of your mother's death. Don't you see? You're dwelling on the past the way your father did. Looking back on what is done and cannot be undone. King Zenith warned you – warned Marah. The past cannot be changed but it *can* destroy the future. We live here, now, in this time, in this moment. Only this!" His flower began to stir.

Truvius moaned.

"What are you?" snarled Zarkus, stepping up to Limpic. "How did you get this far? Why didn't the silver consume you?"

"Because of this," said Limpic, slapping his chest. His flower inflated and then burst into flames. Limpic knew the time was at hand. He reached out and grabbed Zarkus by his scrawny wrist.

213

"Let go! Let go!" screamed Zarkus. "You're burning me!"

Limpic felt the flames rising in his chest and running down his arms into his hands. He held them back as much as he could. "You said the time would come when you would both need my fire," said Limpic, his eyes ablaze. "Do you think this is the time? I will not force it on you."

"Do it!" cried Zarkus as the shadowy mask slipped.

"Do it, Limpic," pleaded Truvius, throwing his arms around his friend. Limpic let loose his flames and they hunted down the shadow of the Cra in an all-consuming wave of fire. He felt warm all over and then, as quickly as it had begun, it was over and the flames subsided. His flower turned crimson, then orange then back to white.

Truvius lay to his right looking healthier than he had ever looked. To his left lay Zarkus, no more than a bag of bones, his skin dry and parched with sores spreading from his chapped lips onto his cheeks.

"Thank you, Limpic," he whispered hoarsely. "You have set me free." He licked his dry lips and coughed. Spittle flecked his mouth and his breath was harsh. "But now you must go – back to the surface as quickly as you can. The Cra have many goblins guarding the way to Glorian but your fire can destroy them. Recover Lunehaert from Father. I will hold back the floodwaters until you are through the door. Then you must swim as though your life depends on it – because it does."

Before Limpic could reply the doorway to Meridian opened again. Water sagged through but held. Limpic glanced at Truvius.

"Go!" gasped Zarkus. His hand was raised to the water. "Just as the moon can push and pull water, so can I, but my strength fails me. GO!"

Limpic nodded and dived into the water, sealing his eyes, nose and mouth. Immediately the sea pressed in around him, causing his head to creak and squeak. The water was bitterly cold and gnawed and numbed Limpic's brain so that he struggled to remember what he was doing. A current gripped him and he was thrown end over end through the narrow tunnel bouncing ungainly off walls and ceilings. His head span and his stomach lurched even after the current subsided and he was suspended in a large open space. A faint light swirled far overhead.

"Oh", groaned Limpic, blowing underwater bubbles. He realised the light above wasn't swirling at all – it was just his head. It wasn't until something hard clipped his shoulder that he registered where he was – hanging among the floating stairs. The realisation sobered him and he sought safety.

Bam!

He was pinned against the side of the large stone structure. The force rattled his teeth together and crushed the air from his lungs. His shoulder ached from the impact but the cold water numbed it. Limpic jostled further up the side of the stairs until he reached the top. He gathered his strength and pushed off. For a moment it seemed like he was not going to be free of the twisting current caused by the stairs' circular movement but then, release. He kicked hard and soared up through the waters, gathering speed as he went. Then another stone stairwell lurched from the darkness and caught Limpic's toe and he was sent spinning sideways into the wall.

"Oomph!" he grunted as bubbles streamed from his lips. The same shoulder took the full impact and for a moment his arm hung limply by his side. I need to get to the centre of the cavern, thought Limpic, flexing his hand gingerly. Feeling in his arm returned and he propelled himself from the wall and hung in empty space. Around him the stairs, dark and cumbersome, circled. He steadied his positon and swam upwards, gaining speed and confidence knowing he was in the middle of the cavern, far from the circling stairs. An explosion beneath sent vibrations tearing through his skull and he was buffeted by a surge of water. There was nothing he could do to control his ascent. He yelped in pain as his foot struck something extremely hard. Had he passed through an opening?

His ears popped and his head became light and dizzy but he had little time to dwell on his discomfort because his flower throbbed red and then an arrow grazed his right shoulder. It fizzed through the water and disappeared. Limpic convulsed. A face had appeared in front of him – eyes wide and dark, large blunt teeth sawing together as a stream of bubbles seethed from its mouth. A goblin, in the last violent throes of drowning. Limpic shuddered and screamed silently, throwing out his fist instinctively. The creature's face stilled and floated off into the gloom, a shadow moving from it.

Limpic was left wrestling with a heart that was beating far too fast to sustain underwater breathing. Slow, he told himself. Breathe slowly.

Without warning he breached the surface of the water.

"Ah, my ears!" groaned Limpic as he fought to stay afloat. High above his head the ceiling curved towards an enormous circular opening from which floodwaters were spewing at an alarming rate. The noise was deafening and Limpic had to steer away from the centre of the room so as not to be crushed by the deluge.

"Limpic!" shouted a voice close by.

Limpic blinked as his numbed brain sought to decipher the

huge silhouette peering down at him from an armoured sea stallion.

"Magnus! Where am I?"

"In the lower levels of the Western Pole!" shouted Magnus above the wild roar. "Obsidian Hewn will descend from that opening above your head. Brutonia has already passed through. You'll only get one chance to reach it before we are overcome!"

Limpic frowned. "Overcome?" he yelled.

Magnus nodded around the room and gripped his shield and broadsword tightly. Blood oozed from a wound in his shoulder.

Limpic gasped and wiped water from his eyes. He saw the face he had seen in the water. In fact, he saw hundreds of them, all peering down from the silver rafters and walls of the great circular room: goblins possessed by the spirit of the Cra.

One of the creatures threw itself from the rafters and Magnus clipped it with his sword. It screeched like a rat and the body of the goblin fell into the water. Just like before, a shadow left the dead vessel, moving like smoke from a fire. Swirling upwards it entered the body of another goblin.

"The more we kill the stronger they become," shouted Magnus.

"The shadow within them is becoming more concentrated," replied Limpic, ducking behind Magnus as another volley of arrows fizzed past. "Their strength and tenacity will only increase as we near the source."

The roar of water stopped as the opening overhead was plugged momentarily. As the plug continued its descent it managed to wash some of the goblins from the ceiling.

"Obsidian Hewn," called Magnus. "It begins at the summit of the Western Pole and descends as far down as the floating stairs. Once it touches the water you must climb on!" He lifted his shield quickly to stop another volley of arrows. "I cannot go any further than the water allows me but I will rise with the tide and try to stop them following you!"

There was a commotion near the ceiling and then something large fell into the water beside Limpic. He reached out and grabbed it.

"Brutonia!" Limpic shouted.

"Limpic!"

"Where's Peruvius?" yelled Magnus, raising his shield to deflect yet another volley of arrows.

"Up ... above ..." stammered Brutonia, struggling to stay afloat. "He's trying to reach Glorian. So ... many ... goblins!"

Limpic lay on his back floating behind Magnus. He was shivering with adrenaline now but the cold had left his bones and he felt warm.

"I'm glad ... you taught ... me to float," panted Brutonia.

"Me too," Limpic joked, cradling the giant elvern on his chest.

"Da said I could swim like a brick!" croaked Brutonia. His teeth were chattering and his lips were blue. There was little silver left in his eyes. "How come you feel so warm?" said Brutonia.

"It's not me," replied Limpic. "It's my flower. Do you still have your breather?"

Brutonia nodded.

"Put it in," replied Limpic.

"Why?" said Brutonia. "I can flo—"

There was an enormous splash as the silver disc hit the water sucking Limpic and Brutonia under with the immense force of its descent. Down and down they pressed tumbling over and over in the bubbling cauldron. Limpic could only hope Brutonia had done what he asked.

Once he felt the solid footing of Obsidian Hewn beneath his feet he knew the disc was in the ascent once more. Wearily he held onto Brutonia as the disc emerged back into the room where Magnus still fought, this time firing off arrows from a huge bow. The water was higher than before – they were definitely closer to the ceiling, but there was no respite because Limpic and Brutonia were directly beneath the water pummelling down from the room above. Limpic turned himself over so that he was on top of his friend. He allowed the avalanche of water to break over his back and shoulders, but the force was so great that his arms began to buckle. The silver surface was so slippery.

"Can't … hold … on," he spluttered.

His grip faltered. He slid and grappled with the edge. His throat was on fire and his lungs were burning. His heart was leaping from his chest.

Then he slipped.

Chapter 23

"I've got you, Limpic!" shouted Brutonia, grasping onto his arm. "I've got you." His face was contorted in pain.

Limpic peered into his eyes. They were beginning to glow silver. Through sheer stubborn resilience his friend was drawing on reserves he didn't even have. Brutonia pulled Limpic back onto the disc. He placed himself over Limpic's battered body and broke the full force of the cascading waterfall across his broad shoulders.

"This is the second time I've done this!" he bellowed, grinning broadly. "I needed a shower anyway!"

"Hold on," Limpic kept saying. "Another second, another second."

Just when it looked like even Brutonia's massive strength was about to fail, the pressure disappeared and the constant pummelling subsided. Brutonia groaned and rolled sideways onto his back. They had entered the Tower of Glorian and risen above the floods. Outside Limpic could hear the terrible sound of battle and the walls of the tower trembled and the windows were lit by flashes of light.

Obsidian Hewn continued to climb towards the pinnacle of the tower. Overhead Limpic could see another opening, just like the one they had passed through from the room below. A little light peeked through the hole but it was hard to see what was on the other side. When the disc finally slipped through the barrier, Limpic's skin flushed and the hairs on the back of his neck stood on end. Goblins and hobgoblins were everywhere, huddled around the entire room like crows perched in the silver rafters of the curving ceiling. As soon as the disc appeared they scrambled over one another and called out in a strange tongue. Brutonia had been crouching on his knees beside Limpic but he drew himself up to his full height and pumped his chest full of air.

"ARE YOU STARING AT ME?" he snarled.

The room went silent.

Limpic grasped Brutonia's ankle. "Aye, Brutonia," he whispered weakly. "They're *all* staring at you."

The enormous elvern clenched his fists until each knuckle cracked and then he shrugged his left shoulder and the shield on his back appeared on his arm. With a shrug of the right shoulder, his great axe flickered in the low light. His right eyelid twitched up and down and his face twisted into an awful scowl.

"I HATE BEING STARED AT!" he thundered, shaking the very ceiling. "Come on, then, what are you waiting for!"

The creatures held back briefly, almost unsure of what to do with the monstrosity before them. They cocked their heads to one side then opened their mouths in a silent scream and swept in upon the disc. There, they were duly sent to their miserable end – if not crushed by the awesome power of Brutonia's shield, they were scythed in two by Dunnehammer.

"Is that it?" roared Brutonia, foaming at the mouth. "Is that all you've got? I come all this way and I find a nest of pathetic rats to contend with!"

The disc finally reached the summit, halting momentarily within a circular room where it fitted perfectly within the floor. A narrow pathway encircled it. Limpic crawled off and Brutonia stepped back, sweat dripping from his brow.

"You must go," insisted Brutonia. "I'll wait here and hold back the hordes, as Magnus is doing on the lower levels. Whatever strength you have left must be conserved for Peruvius."

"Aye," muttered Limpic and he crawled for a small doorway that led onto a smooth landing overhanging and encircling Glorian. The spire of Glorian towered above him and a set of twisting stairs led from where he stood to the mist shrouded summit.

Limpic rested for a moment. He was bone-weary and exhausted to the point that his legs and arms trembled. He could hear Brutonia shouting at any creature that attempted to enter the chamber. The air bit at his warm skin and his breath sent out puffs of steam. All around was the noise of flooding water and the cries and shrieks of battle. Limpic steadied himself, drew a hand across his eyes to wipe away droplets of water and then mounted the stairs, trudging heavily towards the invisible sky.

The battle was raging beneath him. He could see Managh and his soldiers being driven back time and again by a rolling mantle of darkness. It was not going in their favour. Flashes of orange light plumed from the dark cloud, revealing ships teeming with goblins and hobgoblins as their cannons roared and spat death. Something stirred in the waters between Managh and the dark tide. A huge head surged out of the water. Limpic stumbled and checked his balance. Saurus! And he was breathing tongues of fire. He watched as the giant lizard fell on enemy lines with the company of Managh streaming behind him. Their cries throbbed up to meet him and pricked his spirit into action.

"Move!" Limpic shouted to himself as the water levels rose further and further until all of Meridian disappeared. The moon was still labouring to rise and pulling the sea with her. Limpic gritted his teeth and ran with renewed vigour. "Must keep going," he muttered. "Have to reach Peruvius. Have to help the moon. Have to give her back what is hers!" Suddenly the stairs opened out and Limpic spilled onto the prodigious platform that stood on the very pinnacle of Glorian. In the middle of this was another, higher platform from which rose the great 'W' of the Western Pole.

"You won't make it, my prince!" screeched a voice – Marah, or the creature his spirit had become. Dressed for combat, his black armour seemed to consume whatever meagre light there was. Limpic could only see him from behind and the once glorious cloak of the house of Zenith lay tattered across his shoulders. The insignia of the phases of the moon were barely decipherable and the cloak ended threadbare above the knee, torn at a ragged angle. At his feet lay Peruvius, scrambling backwards and thrusting with his sword.

"Back! Back!" Peruvius screamed, kicking himself free and throwing his sword at his enemy.

Marah turned away as the sword pinged off his shoulder. Peruvius wriggled onto his belly and tried to crawl away as best he could but Marah quickly recovered and pinned him to the ground with his foot – a foot encased within layers of overlapping black metal plates that tapered into a long, vicious toe.

"Ah!" screamed Peruvius, squirming in agony as the armoured foot was driven deep into the small of his back as

223

though he were an insect to be squashed.

"Leave him alone!" shouted Limpic, throwing himself on top of the horrible form.

With a violent thrust Limpic was unseated and landed painfully on his back, knocking the wind from his lungs.

"Aw," he groaned, arching his back and trying to catch his breath. He rolled onto his side and tried to sit up but something forced him back down. He found the same foot that had squashed Peruvius now firmly planted on his chest.

"I ... I can't breathe," panted Limpic. The foot was crushing his lungs.

"What are you?" The vicious toe jabbed Limpic beneath the chin, driving his head backwards. "Gills?" said the voice in surprise. "And to think we actually feared you! Weakling!" The toe pushed harder, right against Limpic's Adam's apple.

"Gah, gah," he choked, trying to swallow away the pressure.

Limpic's hands raked about of their own accord. His right hand brushed against something – the hilt of his sword. He grabbed it firmly and thrust across his chest with all his strength. The blade crashed against hard metal and went spinning into the night. There was a cackle.

"Aw!" grunted Limpic. His arm went numb.

The foot was removed and an armoured hand reached down and caught him by the scruff of the neck. He was lifted as easily as if he were made of straw. For a moment Limpic thought he was staring into the face of a black owl but he soon realised that the helmet of Marah's armour had been fashioned into the likeness of the night predator. Large black wings swept backwards and upwards from the sides of the helmet and the nose plate curled downwards in imitation of the bird's beak.

Protecting the neck was a skirt of metal beaten into the form of the owl's tail feathers. Only Marah's chin and bloodless bottom lip could be seen beneath the helmet, visible from behind two huge talons that served as a chin piece.

"How did you make it here without being turned to silver?" said Marah.

Limpic fell under the steady glare of two blood-red eyes that burned unblinking from behind the helm. His flower throbbed red but did not flame.

The armour must protect the Cra from my fire, Limpic concluded as Marah's grip grew tighter. It was just as Zarkus had predicted aboard *Polestar*. He turned from the dark lord's gaze and glanced over his shoulder. Peruvius was trying to get up.

"Run!" screamed Limpic, "Peruvius, run!" Limpic kicked out but his feet simply thrashed against thin air.

"Filth!" screeched Marah. "Filth! Your world is doomed!"

Limpic didn't see the blow or the hand that dealt it. Just stars flashing across his eyes and then the warm metallic taste of blood in his mouth. The hand that gripped his throat tightened.

"Brutonia!" croaked Limpic. "Brutonia, to me!"

He kicked and thrashed but couldn't shake himself free of the relentless grip. The world began to close in around him, his blood thundered around his temples and his vision narrowed to a tiny dot. He knew his legs were still kicking, but they might well have been someone else's. Life was being squeezed right out of him.

Then there was freedom. Peace. He was looking down on it all and no longer part of it. Free from the burden of existence. Like he was in a bubble. He saw his crumpled body lying at the feet of the dark lord. He saw Brutonia running up the stairs, screaming, flailing at Marah with a fury full of grief and despair, Dunnehammer flashing savagely and sparking at every direct hit. He saw the dark lord stumble backwards under the blows from the embittered elvern. He watched Peruvius climbing slowly to the summit of Glorian.

But it was hopeless. The moon was falling. Limpic watched it. And as it fell it tore a seam in the fabric of the sky, opening a portal to the Shadowlands. Limpic stared through the portal into a dusty blood-red world. Legions upon legions of dark-armoured warriors waited on the other side ready to surge into this world and take ownership. Behind them, hundreds of miles deep into the Shadowlands, stood an ominous black pyramid. From its peak came two shafts of red light cutting the seam into Limpic's world using the chaos of a dying moon. And from the bottom of the seam sprouted a dark rainbow. It arched downwards until it touched the waters around Glorian: a bridge between the two worlds. And as the moon continued to fall, silver spread over everything that had not yet been turned. Even Brutonia struggled vainly to throw off its cold hand but eventually he stiffened and Dunnehammer shuddered to a stop just as its blade touched Marah's neck.

Polestar broke the surface of the sea and stuck fast at a strange angle as silver crept over her foredeck and towards her prow. Limpic caught sight of someone crouched near the front. Truvius! He sprang nimbly from the ship just as the silver touched the very tip of the bowsprit. Limpic could see Truvius's back. He saw that the silver was already trying to climb up over his ankles. He tried to shout out – tried to warn him, but his mouth wouldn't move.

"Back! Back from where you came!" screamed Truvius, slashing wildly at the armoured form of Marah.

"You have no power over us!" cackled Marah, parrying

226

Truvius's blows with brute force. "Look, the silver is upon you as it will be upon the whole world. The moon's silver shall be the world's silver and we shall march through unimpeded. Our world shall be your world!"

"Not if I can help it," said another voice. Zarkus!

"YOU!" screeched Marah. "What can *you* do?" But there was doubt in his voice.

"You forget yourselves!" cried Zarkus, "I am still the key!"

Marah fell back under this renewed assault as the two brothers fought side by side against the father who had betrayed them both. A bright flash of light from Zarkus's fingers caused Marah to clutch his face. The distraction allowed Truvius to drive his sword, unhindered, into the joint where the chest plate met the arm. For a moment victory seemed assured. The blade was buried to the hilt, angled down into the chest where the heart lies. Marah began to shudder and he collapsed. His armour crashed and clattered into all its individual parts. But no sooner had the last piece stopped ringing than the armour came back together, held only by the power of the shadow that dwelt within.

Goblins poured from the mouth of Glorian to aid their dark lord.

"Not me, you fools!" he screeched, sweeping his sword to the scrambling form of Peruvius. "Destroy him before he releases the silver!"

The goblins swarmed around the Western Pole, tripping over one another in their eagerness to do their masters bidding.

And silver continued to flow. Already it had reached Truvius's waist and he was rooted to the spot. Even Zarkus began to wane under its influence and one of his feet became as stone.

227

"This is our world!" screeched Marah and a vicious biting wind ripped his cloak from his shoulders and sent it swirling into the air. It snagged across the huge 'W' of the Western Pole where it unfurled with a snap. For a brief moment it revealed the faded insignia of the house of Zenith, the phases of the moon.

Something stirred deep in Limpic's chest. My world. Limpic pondered that. It would be easy now to float away – he felt drowsy. He could just go to sleep and it would all be over. He would wake on the shores of eternity and be with his parents. How many dark paths must I tread before I can go home? To go back would mean pain. Pain. Limpic felt his chest burn. Part of him just wanted it to be over. Surely he had done everything in his power to survive and succeed? Just like he had when he was younger and death had stalked so closely. But just like then Limpic knew it wasn't his time. He had not heard the call of the ocean.

What are you? Marah had demanded.

"I'm the guardian of the Golden Coast," whispered Limpic. The burning in his chest grew more intense. "I am the guardian of the children of the fire." Limpic felt his nose prickle. To go back would mean pain. "I'll go back!" shouted Limpic.

He began to fall and as he fell, he began to feel. And as he felt he began to scream. The bubble was bursting and reality crashed about his ears like floodwater. His head hurt from where his boat had struck it. His jaw hurt from where Marah had hit him. His throat burned from where Marah had crushed it. Even his ankle ached from an injury he had sustained as a child. And all these things came back at once but nothing compared to the fire that was flaming in his chest.

"Ah!" Limpic sat up with a cry of surprise. His legs were

still unsteady but his mind was crystal clear. He took the Bow of the Nimue and fired volley after volley of flaming arrows upon the goblins who were trying to reach Peruvius. His arrows flamed like long spears and the goblins fell back.

Limpic's body ached from utter exhaustion, not to mention being throttled half to death. His flower seemed to sense this and it stilled, merely throbbing red in the half-light. *It will never consume you. Always it will try to protect you, even from yourself.*

Limpic knew that to defeat what was left of Marah would take whatever strength he had. Unlike Truvius and Zarkus, Marah would not invite the fire upon himself.

Limpic rested and tried to massage life back into his legs. "I am strong enough," he muttered weakly.

The turrets of Glorian began to glow and a silvery trail reached from them towards a crouching figure. It was Peruvius. He was on his knees peering upwards. He spread his arms out wide and looked straight up into the moon. She seemed to nestle on the very tip of his nose. Then, whatever was bubbling within the turrets finally erupted and a stream of silver light entered Peruvius's fingers and hands, ran along his arms and into his neck and then pulsed from his eyes straight into the very heart of the moon. She started to fill out. The darkness across her face began to flee. She rose, slowly at first and then faster and faster.

Limpic thought the sky was falling on top of him and then he realised that he was rising towards it, or at least Meridian was. It was rising with the moon. He felt a strange vibration deep within his chest. It spread rapidly throughout his entire body bringing his legs back to life.

"Please," he begged his flower. "I can do this. I *am* strong enough. Just give me one more try!" He knew what he had to do: He remembered the snake-like image of the Cra when it fanned out behind Peruvius's head on the moon. And there was one sure way to kill a snake; remove the head. His flower burst into life and Limpic rose with a shout as fire fell from his hands. He charged through the assembled goblins, casting them right and left. Any arrow they fired ignited like straw and fell harmlessly to the ground. Limpic skipped around the prow of *Polestar* as her mantle of silver loosened and she sank back into a living, rolling and receding sea.

Limpic saw his sword glittering in the low light and scooped it up with one hand, never missing a step. He leapt at Marah, bringing the flame-drenched blade down in a vicious arch. "I am Limpic and this is my world!"

The blow drove Marah to his knees and sent his helmet skidding into the darkness. Limpic's sword shattered into a million fiery pieces and he cast the useless hilt away in disgust. He buried his hands deep into the smoking remnants of the creature's head.

"You want to know why I wasn't turned to silver?" he screamed, shaking the armour like a mad thing. "Because nothing bad can touch me! And you *dared* to touch me!"

Cold throbbing pain shot up Limpic's arms as his fire fought with the darkness; a darkness that revelled in its own night and hated the light. For a moment Limpic's fire was held. He gritted his teeth and leant on his arms trying to drive deeper.

"I *am* strong enough!" he shouted.

The darkness tried to twist away. It tried to retreat and seek refuge. Somewhere gloomy where it could wait and brood and then return with a vengeance. But Limpic's fires were all-consuming. And they were good. Every sinew in his limbs strained as the flames grew white-hot. It felt as though the sun itself was streaming through every pore in his body; as though lightning bolts were coursing through his veins and seeking out every place the darkness hid. Fire raged from Limpic's hands, mouth and eyes, licking Glorian clean of the filth of the Cra. Then, with one last great throbbing flash of white light, it went out.

Limpic slumped to his knees. Wind buffeted his face. His body sagged forward and he panted with exertion. Amid the wreckage of armour something caught his eye.

"Lunehaert," he croaked. He scooped up the jewel and it throbbed in his hand. *Thud-thud, thud-thud.* It was warm to the touch. Living.

"Zarkus!" cried Limpic, forcing himself to stumble and crawl towards the elvern. He fell heavily into Zarkus's arms. For a moment the wind stilled and everything was quiet.

"It's alright, Limpic," said Zarkus cradling him to the floor. "Rest now. I'll finish this."

His face was gaunt but gentle and his eyes were kind. He placed Lunehaert around his neck and immediately glowed with the pallor of a harvest moon. His cheeks filled out, his hair grew back and the angular bony ridges in his face disappeared. "I am myself again," he said with a smile. "Thank you, Limpic, where the flower grows." With that he turned and marched defiantly towards the awful dark rainbow, his cloak billowing out behind him.

Limpic was crying and he wiped his eyes and nose. Brutonia roused him.

"What's happening, Limpic?" he said weakly. My face is tingling."

"It's alright, Brutonia, it's alright!" replied Limpic, echoing the words of Zarkus from moments ago. "Your face is coming alive just like everything else."

The wind blew once more and mist and shadows and swirls of light all wrestled for existence. Limpic closed his eyes and clung to his friend as the wind tugged at his clothes and the waves of a sea that was once more alive erupted with pounding ferocity and sent dull echoes through the Tower of Glorian.

Limpic stole a glance at the sky. The mists rolled back and revealed the full moon, at first phantom-like but swelling and burning brighter as she drank in her lifeblood. He heard the silver singing and flowing beneath him. He heard water pouring from every opening in the city, crashing down to meet the rising ocean. Meridian rose from her silvery death, hissing and groaning as the pit she once sat in began to heal.

"Let go!" cried Zarkus. He was trying to destroy the dark bridge that arched from the portal in the sky. Already several legions of the Cra were gathering at the top, ready to descend. "Back to the Shadowlands!" he screamed sending out bolts of lightning from his fingertips and smashing the Cra with great hulking waves of water. His power was both awesome and terrible to behold.

The bridge of darkness began to warp. Its middle bulged out of shape until it gave way and was sucked through the rift. The rest of it fought back, like a congealed mass desperately sticking to whatever it could. But the pull was too great. The darkness began to lift, peeling from the waters around Glorian. More and more of it was sucked through the doorway and yet Zarkus held back from destroying it completely. He dropped his hands and turned his back on the great rift in the sky. He took off Lunehaert and kissed it. His eyes skirted around and finally rested on Limpic's flower. He smiled.

A cold voice echoed from the Shadowlands. "You cannot

keep us back forever!" it snarled. "Darkness! Darkness lies in the heart of all! Sargon grows stronger. The elves will hear the sound of war again. Silence cannot endure!"

The last remnants of the bridge lashed out one final time, like a whip, grasping around Zarkus's ankle and pulling him into the air.

"No!" cried Truvius. He threw himself at his brother and gripped his hands, the pull lifting him off his feet.

Limpic followed and caught Truvius by the ankles, but he too began to lift off the ground. "Brutonia!" cried Limpic. "Help!"

He felt tugging at his legs and, peering down through half-closed eyes, he saw that Brutonia held him by one ankle and Peruvius by the other. Their eyes glowed bright silver and they had their legs wrapped around the 'W' of the pole.

"Truvius!" screamed Limpic. He could barely get enough air into his lungs to shout. "Truvius ... I ... can't ... hold ... on. Please—"

"I won't let go!" cried Truvius. "I won't let go."

"You have to," said Zarkus. His voice was calm; full and thick, warm and kind. Beautiful.

"No, Brother, I won't," wept Truvius. "There has to be some other way."

"This is the way," replied Zarkus. "I am the key. I will shut this door. I will make everything right, just as I made everything wrong."

"But I can save you," said Truvius.

Zarkus smiled. "Look at me, Brother. I am myself again. I am already saved. Now let me go. Let me go, Truvius."

Limpic ground his teeth. He could feel the sinews in his arms creaking. His fingers began to lose their grip on his friend's

233

ankles. "TRUUUVIUS," he pleaded.

Truvius's hands shook. He hung his head and began to cry. "I love you, Brother," he whispered between clenched teeth.

Then he let go.

Chapter 24

The citadel was empty of its stolen bounty and the sea was all but in place again. It flowed around the Western Pole like an excited child, rushing this way and that, exploring coves and bays long forgotten. The shadow of the night had fled. The sun stood high in the sky, drawing colour from every meadow, flower and tree. It washed over the citadel and its walls turned snow-white and its towers were burnished gold. With the sun came a breath of wind. With the colours of the day came the scents of a world that had newly awakened. Limpic and his friends lay in a crumpled heap on the large platform, drinking in these colours and filling their lungs with the dewy air.

Down by the shores *Polestar* floated idly on a serene sea. By her side was the legion of Managh, and he was at the front speaking to the great serpent Saurus. On either side of the city, on what could be classed as the northern and southern sides (if they even exist in a pole that is fixed completely west) were two swirling whirlpools, the northern one spinning anti-clockwise, the southern spinning clockwise.

"Well," said Limpic, "I guess it's finished then." He thought of his siblings, his home and his fellow ullans. Free at last. He could hardly believe it.

"Yes, I believe so," replied Peruvius solemnly. "'And when darkness has all but covered the Earth, let he who betrayed give all that is his, and the world shall know rebirth.' The forced sacrifice of the moon opened the portal to the Shadowlands, but the self-sacrifice of Zarkus closed it again."

"Zarkus knew what he had to do to save us," said Limpic. "He had made up his mind on *Polestar* long before my fires ever freed his soul."

"To Zarkus," said Brutonia lifting Dunnehammer.

"Zarkus!" replied the others.

With a sigh Peruvius rose to his feet and stood over Truvius. "How do you feel?" he asked.

Truvius looked up, squinting in the sunlight. He sniffed hard and smiled and the scar on his cheek that had so often throbbed crimson began to fade away. "Like I've just been awakened, *really* awakened," he replied.

"I know exactly how you feel," said Brutonia. "There's nothing like turning to silver and then back again to make you appreciate being alive." He fidgeted with his chain mail. "When we get home, I might ask Sophia to marry me."

"Well about time," replied Truvius.

"It's as my father used to say," replied Brutonia, "'a handsome young buck can't run forever'."

"Well, you're neither handsome nor young," said Truvius chuckling. "You should think yourself lucky anyone is interested in you at all!"

Brutonia grinned and pulled Truvius to his feet. He hugged him tightly and the two shared a tear over their friend and brother.

"It's alright, Bru," said Truvius. "Zarkus is whole again." He lowered his head and his eyes fixed on something in his hands.

"Here," he said handing it over to Peruvius, "Lunehaert. Zarkus gave it to me just before ... well, it's yours now."

Peruvius smiled and shook his head. "No, cousin," he replied, "the fact that you find yourself unworthy to wear Lunehaert tells me you are indeed worthy. You have come through great testing and proven yourself." He pressed Lunehaert into Truvius's hand and put his forehead against his cousin's. "And besides, Zarkus chose you," he whispered.

Truvius wiped his eyes and cleared his throat before placing Lunehaert around his neck. It glinted in the sunlight and looked very much like two small cupped hands that had been clasped together as one. It was made from some kind of crystal and liquid silver swirled within its depths as the jewel flexed and pulsed. Truvius's face flushed and his mouth dropped open.

"I can feel the moon," he gasped, "throbbing through my veins!"

Peruvius laughed and patted his back. "I should think so. You wear her heart and I gave her back her blood. Come, we must return home." With that he began to descend the spiral stairs, trailed by Truvius and Brutonia.

"Aren't you coming?" called Brutonia over his shoulder.

"Soon," replied Limpic. Brutonia nodded and followed his friends.

Limpic climbed, heavy-footed, to the pinnacle of Glorian, just beneath the enormous 'W'. His inner ear was creaking and his flower was swaying like it had never done before. Its colour was changing and shifting like the colours of the day. It almost looked like it was dancing. His gaze followed the long shadow cast by the Western Pole. He opened his inner ear and then began to laugh. No wonder his flower was dancing. Music flowed from everywhere and from everything. Even from the lands beyond the west. *And then all creation sang. The stones, the sea, the sky, even the light. All that was rejoiced and their voices could not be quelled.*

And, like a leaf caught in the playful mood of the wind, so too was Limpic's spirit pricked and lifted and moved and held. His face flushed with blood and tremulous waves rose up from his feet and spilled across his entire body. He both laughed and cried at the sheer beauty of it. And, in this raptness of soul some veil lifted and he saw a glimpse of a land of light and a citadel whose towers dwarfed even Meridian's. And a river flowed through it, milky in colour and curling between green hillocks and flowering glades. Trees stood by the river, drinking deeply from its waters. Their branches stooped low, laden with fruit of all colours, shapes and sizes. The fruit bulged and ripened in the blinking of an eye, tumbling into the water where it jostled together, bobbing and winking under a golden light. Playfully it slid towards the citadel among a chattering chorus of cathartic song.

In front of all this, in front of the citadel and the meadows and the trees, separating that land from this were swathes upon swathes of fire flowers. They spilled right to the edge of Meridian and sent out sweet draughts of air so heady and honeyed, that Limpic's soul ached to be there and also to see the Golden Coast again. His eyes blinked rapidly as the vision left and there was only the shadow of the tower of the Western Pole stretching across an eternal sea of azure blue. But Limpic felt refreshed and lighter of foot.

"Come," said Limpic to his flower. "Our other paradise awaits." He made his way into the tower and descended on Obsidian Hewn. The disc was smooth and black with a subtle shade of emerald green. Tiny air bubbles appeared at its edges where light caught from passing windows. Down it descended through rooms filled with books and others filled with strange whirring machines and past windows looking out onto the ocean in every direction. Limpic's ears popped and he could hear the wind sighing outside, full of nature's many songs that had lain silent for so long. And then there was the eternal echoing of the sea. Limpic couldn't wait to get into the fragrant summer air and dip his feet into an ocean that was no longer so troubled. He longed to see his limpets.

Outside the sky arched overhead in the deepest blue and gulls circled the towers of the city. Other birds, in all the colours of the rainbow, swooped together in vast aerial formations, chirping ebulliently.

The streets of the citadel were paved with white slabs cut from marble and they echoed with the sound of dancing feet. Those feet belonged to creatures of many kinds, who had stood for so long in silver poses, and they danced and sang until they drowned out all other noises. Their happiness only increased when Limpic stepped from the tunnel at the base of the Western Pole and was reunited with his friends.

The collected creatures rose up with tumultuous applause and cast ticker tape and confetti from on high. Somewhere deep within the surrounding towers, bells began to peal with joy. The city of Meridian was alive. The four elverns who had languished on the moon were alive again too. They stumbled, rather bewildered, from the tower, blinking under the glorious sun. Peruvius took them under his care. He also took charge of Tabias, the elvern who had helped Tabitha escape back to Tulwood with the Echo Shell.

A host of city dwellers stood in a circle around a group of befuddled goblins – the same goblins that had been encased in silver at the entrance to the tower.

"Don't worry about this lot," said one of the group, catching Limpic's eye. "We'll take care of them and any more we find skulking about. This item is rather intriguing, though." He handed Limpic a boot.

Limpic smiled. "I can take care of this. It belongs to Tabitha, an elvern who escaped just before she was turned to silver. I'll return it to her."

The two shook hands and Limpic moved on.

"Thank you, thank you!" cried a strange creature, shuffling towards them and shaking each of their hands.

He wore a medallion around his neck. His face was clean and pleasant, dominated by a bulbous nose and wide blue eyes. He was obviously the mayor or the keeper of the city.

"My name is Triphaith, and on behalf of the people of Meridian let me just say that this is—"

He couldn't finish his sentence as a great cry of joy burst from his lungs and his arms and legs sprang outwards like coiled springs. He performed several of the largest star jumps Limpic had ever seen. The creatures lining the streets did exactly the same thing. When they all jumped at the same time it seemed that the city was filled with spindly giants.

Eventually Triphaith gathered himself and thanked everyone profusely and shook everybody's hand a second time.

"Is there anything we can do for you – anything at all?" Triphaith insisted.

"Yes, yes," roared the crowd. "Anything at all."

"We could carve your names into our city's walls," said Triphaith enthusiastically.

"Yes, yes, carve their names," approved the crowd.

"We could write your stories into the annals of our city's

history."

"Yes, yes, make them history!"

"We could paint your portraits and hang them in our halls."

"Yes, yes, hang them, hang them!" roared the crowd, getting quite carried away.

Triphaith nibbled at his fingers, deep in thought and then his eyes suddenly lit up. "I know!" he exclaimed. "We could sculpt you into statues and place you at the city gates!"

"No, thank you!" cried all the adventurers at once.

Limpic grinned. "We've had quite enough of statues for a while!"

"Very well, then," said Triphaith. "What would you have us do?"

Peruvius put his arm around the mayor. "We don't want you to do anything except have a long and well-earned celebration."

"You mean ... a party?"

"Yes, if that's what you want to call it."

The mayor stroked his chin thoughtfully before turning to his people, a wide grin on his face.

"PARTY!" he roared, and the crowd went wild.

There were arms and legs and heads flying everywhere and from everywhere. There were creatures doing somersaults and others doing backflips and still others dancing and singing. Limpic and his friends were lifted up and whisked right out of the city. The springing creatures ran with actual springs in their steps so each time they took what appeared to be a small pace it turned into a great stretching stride.

They quickly passed over a large swathe of green meadow and huge fields of flowers, through a forest with a bubbling brook and then out the other side and downwards, sweeping gently to the shore where *Polestar* sat anchored just beyond a sandy white beach. The elvern ship sat further along the shore and from her starboard side a figure clambered down. He stumbled through the surf and sat wide-eyed on the white sand.

"You should attend to Titus," Peruvius said to one of the seven. "Tell him he finally found me."

The elvern grinned, saluted and jogged off to help his bewildered friend.

Tents and pavilions were erected, music and cooking began, wild celebrations broke out and the sounds of bells from the city rolled down to greet them. The sun pressed onwards but seemed to tarry a little longer than usual for the mood was so bright. King Managh and his guard came as close as they could and passed their blessing upon the ten friends. Brutonia waded out to thank Magnus for everything he had done for him and Peruvius. Managh bade them goodbye and wished them all a pleasant journey home. Evening was drawing on and it was clear that Peruvius was desperate to leave before the moon came up, but it was hard to escape from the thankful, joyful populace.

"But how are we to get home?" Brutonia asked. "We were many days reaching the Western Pole and I don't even know how we could find our way back."

"We only have two Starstones between us," said Truvius.

"Urggh!" said Brutonia, sticking out his tongue and screwing up his face.

"We will take *Polestar*," said Peruvius, "and be home before dusk. We are, after all, at the end of a rainbow. And I just happen to know a thing or two about rainbows." His eyes sparkled.

"But, begging your pardon," said one of the seven, looking around at the pale blue sky, "there aren't any rainbows in the sky today."

"Ah, that is where you are wrong," said Peruvius mysteriously. "Rainbows are always there and that's a promise. You just need water to colour them in."

He moved further down the beach to where the sea was lapping gently onto the sand. The crowd followed along behind.

"Limpic," said Peruvius, "much has been asked of you already, but there is one more thing I would like you to do for me."

Peruvius drew close to him and whispered into his ear.

Limpic smiled. "I've never asked it to *do* anything before, only listened to it, but I'll try my best."

He marched into the surf and the sea played around his ankles making a great fuss of him. He cupped his hands and took some water and placed his mouth into it. Drawing air through his gills he began to make a thrumming sound at the back of his throat until the frequency of the vibrations were too high for anyone but him to hear.

"Rainbow," he whispered, "rainbow."

The sea called to him in the same manner, in wails and pitches like the song of the whales. A song that only Limpic could hear and only Limpic could understand.

"Rainbow, rainbow …"

"Well?" said Peruvius after Limpic had let the water fall.

Limpic grinned. "You should hear what I hear. The sea is … happy. It's so alive! I think it will help."

Sure enough the waters around Limpic's ankles swirled and he chuckled gleefully. A fine mist rose up and kept rising, arching further out to sea. Where the mist travelled, the rainbow followed, appearing from the air like magic. The city's inhabitants murmured in astonishment as the rainbow disappeared far into the horizon. Its end could have been

243

anywhere.

"It's time to go home," said Peruvius. "If the residents of Meridian don't mind, we will leave the elvern ship here. Call it a parting gift."

There were small boats on the sand that the revellers had been using to race one another. The ten adventurers climbed in and were rowed to *Polestar*'s hull. She rocked a little as they embarked and then she sailed forward, right into the base of the rainbow. Immediately she was lifted from the water and her prow turned until she had her stern to the city. Limpic and his friends ran to the poop deck and leaned out over the tiller, waving goodbye to the land of the Western Pole and the city of Meridian. The people cheered and sang about elverns and an ullan until their voices dwindled into the distance. The sun fell lower and lower and the city of Meridian and her towers suddenly disappeared from view, taking with her the shadow that she cast across the sea.

"There are only two ways to find the Western Pole," said Peruvius as *Polestar* sailed through the seven colours of light. He was peering back towards Meridian. "The end of a rainbow, which is the easiest when you know how, or the way you came, which is much more difficult."

"I'm glad we're in the sky," said Truvius. "It is so beautiful at this time of the evening. Though I'm glad we came the other way – it makes everything so much *more* beautiful."

Peruvius looked surprised but Truvius smiled.

"I've learned a lot these past days," he said with a shrug.

Brutonia put his arm around him and squeezed him tight.

"I'm glad you're alive, Truvius, and that you don't seem as grumpy as usual, and if that means I get a pay rise, then so be it. But most of all I'm just very, very glad, really." He pushed

Truvius out to arm's length and looked at him strangely. "How did you make it off the moon?"

Truvius grinned and stroked the side of *Polestar*'s hull. "It was all thanks to this old girl. And Zarkus." Truvius's grin faded to a half-smile. "He was able to contain us within a pocket of air long enough to reach the floating stairs. And then we reached the tunnel out of the tower and were swept out with the current. Suddenly *Polestar* sailed into view all on her own and Zarkus shoved me into the bubble." Truvius continued to stroke the timber of the ship affectionately, even bending down to give her a kiss.

Peruvius raised his eyebrows and shrugged at Brutonia.

"Are you sure you weren't in the water too long, Truvius? I mean, it can leave you feeling a bit peculiar, what with the lack of air and everything."

Truvius laughed and threw a quick glance at Limpic. "Oh, I'm fine," he said. "In fact, I've never felt better."

"Well, it's amazing what everyone has learned on this trip," said Brutonia. "Truvius, you've learned not to be an intolerable grump all the time. Limpic, judging by the way he despatched the Cra, has learned something more about his flower. And me, well, I learned to float – or at least I learned to stay afloat long enough for someone to rescue me!"

"And let's not forget you said you'll ask Sophia to marry you," said Truvius.

"Hmmm," said Brutonia scratching the side of his nose. "I said I *might* ask her to marry me."

"Heh, heh, so you learned nothing really," said Limpic.

"Didn't you just hear what I said?" replied Brutonia affably. "I learned to float!"

They passed the highest point of the rainbow and were

quickly sailing down the other side. It was a beautifully clear summer's evening and the air was fresh and fragrant. The sky was beginning to change, turning a deep shade of blue. Soon stars would prick the fabric of the firmament and the moon would rise. Limpic felt a tingle of excitement pass through his chest and prickle the end of his nose. He was very much looking forward to seeing the moon ascend in all her silvery glory. As for the ground beneath them, it was hard to tell where it began and ended because peering through the depths of a rainbow is very much like peering through a stained-glass window. It was clear, however, that they were dropping down into a forest. The width of the rainbow began to narrow, allowing the greenness of the trees to rush in from both sides. With no more than a gentle sigh *Polestar* settled in a clearing beneath a leafy patch of trees and nestled a little to port.

"It's raining ships!" cried some elverns, who had been sitting nearby. They rose and fled.

The glade was not far from the castle and Peruvius wasted no time clambering down from the ship and making his way inside.

News of his unexpected appearance travelled faster than he did and he was met in the grand entrance hall by his father.

"My son," whispered King Zenith drawing a hand to his mouth. "Is it really you?"

Peruvius stepped forward and embraced him.

"Yes, Father, it is I."

"My son," wept the king, holding him close.

"The moon is rising, Father," said Peruvius. "I think you will want to see her."

"She is well again?"

"Yes, she is most well," replied Peruvius.

"Your mother, she is ..." the king wept. "She is still imprisoned."

Tears welled in Peruvius's eyes. "Do not worry, Father," he said smiling. "It is nearly time. I wanted to be here myself to set her free. I am sorry for causing you further distress but I could not endure Mother waking without me. The look on her face when she was turned to silver haunts me even now."

King Zenith nodded. "I have missed her counsel and her love so very much."

"As have I, Father, as have I," replied Peruvius. He turned to his friends. "Will you help me carry her to the clearing? And you, Tabitha, I have been told of the part you played in the freeing of Meridian. Will you help?"

"Of course," said Tabitha, bowing and trying to hide her bootless foot.

As Peruvius, Limpic, Brutonia, Truvius and the seven cradled the silver statue of the queen, the castle fell silent and the people hung their heads. They marched solemnly through the archway as the moon began to rise above the treetops. Peruvius did not look up until he was standing in the middle of the clearing, just to the right of *Polestar*. Already the galleon's hull was beginning to shimmer with a bluish hue from the moon's light.

"Stand back, please," whispered Peruvius.

The gathering obeyed and stepped backwards, forming a large sombre ring that encircled the prince and his mother's silver form. Peruvius cradled his mother's face in his hands but his eyes were tightly shut. Not till the full moon had risen to her zenith and the whole world shimmered in her cool light did he look up.

The statue was just another in the middle of a ring of statues, standing in a forest of statues with leaves of silver all caught under the breath of the moon.

"Peruvius," whispered a soft voice that had not been heard for so long.

"Mother," replied the prince, clasping the queen's hands.

There had been none of the spectacle of the freeing of Meridian. The seas did not roar, nor did the mountains quake, but the queen took breath again in the land of the living and there was much rejoicing to be had.

Chapter 25

Limpic knew the queen was watching him. She had drawn him aside and now they were alone by the Pool of Reflections. The pool was contained within a stone basin that sat on a pedestal in the middle of a little round tower also built of stone. The tower was nestled among moss-covered rocks and old decaying leaves, high up on the banks of the River Shiman. Small openings looked down onto the river and tree branches were visible, stooping low and skimming the surface of the water. Foam gathered around the tips of the branches for here the river lay languidly, deep and cool and mottled with shadows.

Limpic looked up from his feet and met the queen's cool grey eyes. A shiver of wonder swept down his spine. Her fair hair was held back off her high forehead by an intricate crown. A filigree of silver. It spilled either side of her cheeks and lightly touched her fine bare shoulders. Her face was heart-shaped with high regal cheekbones blushed with pink. Her slim nose twitched when she smiled and her slender red lips parted a little to reveal teeth as white and gleaming as any oyster pearl.

Limpic looked back to his feet and fidgeted with his compass. He had always associated beauty with nature but this queen was something else entirely. Truly a descendant of the High Elves.

The queen leaned forward. "There is something, or should I say some things, on your mind."

Limpic took a last look at his compass, relieved to see the needle pointing due north. He put it away and cleared his throat. "I was wondering if it was possible for me to see the little girl again."

The queen smiled and touched the surface of the pool with a long slender finger. "I can can show you what was and what is."

Concentric circles moved away from the queen's fingers and the dark pool began to lighten. Limpic leaned forward as a scene began to play out from the centre of the water. A young woman walked through a forest carrying a child in her arms. A man was with her and the two of them laughed as the child made faces.

Limpic's heart sank. "But that is not her," he said sadly. "The little girl I met had brown eyes, not blue."

The queen smiled knowingly. "Do not look at the child, dear one, look at her mother."

Limpic frowned and then studied the young woman, trying to catch sight of her face and, hopefully, her eyes. She stopped walking and handed the child to her husband. Then she turned and stared straight into Limpic's eyes and smiled as though she knew he was watching. She cast curly blond locks back from her forehead. Her cheeks were blushed pink with the cool forest air. Her lips were red and full. And her brown eyes sparkled and dazzled, full of life and hope for her future.

"It is her!" exclaimed Limpic, drawing a hand to his mouth. "She is well. She is older. She is a mother!" Tears spilled down his cheeks, blurring the vision of the girl who was now a woman.

"Yes," said the queen laughing as the image began to recede. "She is all of those things. Time passes quickly in worlds unseen."

Limpic sniffed and tried to swallow the lump in his throat. He wiped his eyes with the back of his hand and began to fidget with the flower on his chest. "She kept plodding on." His voice was thick with emotion.

"Wisdom allowed her to fight back using her own immune system," said the queen. "Thus, what was good survived and what was bad did not. Just like your flower."

Limpic rubbed both sides of his face. His lips were trembling. "What about my flower?" he implored.

"Elohas," said the queen. "That is the name of your flower, or one of its names. It means 'Knowledge' or 'Wisdom'. Your flower knows the difference between what is good and what is evil. You witnessed this yourself many times on your quest."

Limpic chewed his bottom lip and drummed his fingers in his lap. "Your voice, Your Majesty. The night I received this flower I remembered a cool hand on my brow and the voice of a stranger – a beautiful voice. It was yours. You were there the night my flower came."

The queen smoothed her dress around her knees. Her face reddened a little. "That *was* my voice and you make me blush to call it beautiful. Yes, I was there the night you received your flower. Word had reached me of your illness and I travelled north to give what aid I could. I had never seen such an affliction. I gave you something to alleviate the fever and cool your brow. I found singing seemed to help, so I sang." The queen looked away. The skin around her neck tightened. When she looked back her eyes were red. "I was given something from the High Elves. Many, many moons ago. It was a seed. A tiny, insignificant seed. Taken from a flower that grows beyond the Western Pole. I was given instructions. I was told that this seed was to be added to water from the river Shiman just before it was given to a child of the fire. I would know this child by their affliction. The resulting flower would protect them. And the child would protect all."

Limpic listened. He barely breathed. All the while his fingers played with the petals of his flower.

"I had wondered for years how I would know this child of the fire," continued the queen. Her face grew solemn. "I gave you the tonic as soon as I saw you. But days passed with little change. I was preparing to leave to seek council with the High Elves when your condition deteriorated. I could no longer control your temperature and then I saw flames begin to creep all over your body and I was driven from the room by their intensity." The queen furrowed her brow and her eyes glazed over. Then they flickered and she came back to her senses. Her eyes fell on Limpic's flower as she continued her discourse. "It was as though reality blinked. One moment all was hot and laboured and the next … all was well. All was cool, calm and peaceful, and that's how I found you lying on your bed no longer tossing and turning. No longer burning and sweating under a heavy burden. I found you in perfect repose. Peaceful. Sleeping with gentle breaths in a room that was brighter – whiter even. And with your flower. I watched it swallow the last tongues of that uncontrollable fire."

The queen's mouth twitched and she cupped her face in her hands. "I'm sorry, Limpic," she whispered. Her voice was tremulous. "It's just, I have never seen such a transformation, and I have never felt such a feeling as I did in that room. It was beyond anything this world has to offer. When I looked out through the window, I saw the first snow of winter gently settling and I knew you were well."

Limpic stared into nothing simply contemplating all that he had heard. "I had a feeling like that," he finally whispered, "on the Tower of Glorian. I looked into the land beyond the west and ... well, I had that feeling. And I saw my flower – the fire flower, Elohas. Wisdom." The two sat quietly for a time. The river gurgled. A brief sigh of wind caused the trees to moan. An errant leaf fluttered past the window.

"It took time for the seed to germinate," said Limpic, breaking the silence.

"Pardon?" replied the queen.

"The seed you gave me. It took some time for it to germinate," said Limpic. "Like an idea, desperately searching for inspirational waters and a place to grow. Somewhere good."

The queen frowned. "I suppose so," she said.

Limpic grinned and looked into the forest. Thinking about seeds and flowers reminded him of Horas and his potions. And all the things the forest provided.

"Isn't it strange how we find many antidotes against evil hidden within the fabric of our own world," said the queen as though discerning Limpic's thoughts. "Hidden in nature just waiting to be found. Is it wisdom that discovers these secrets or is it wisdom that anticipates their discovery? Or is it wisdom that puts them there in the first place?"

She smiled at Limpic and he smiled back. They sat in silence content to listen to the world waking from slumber. The trees strained and stretched as a breeze returned with renewed vigour. A bird called from the forest, then another and another until the air was alive with their chatter.

"Look," said the queen, "the sun is rising and so must we."

She took Limpic's hands in hers. "May I?" she asked.

Limpic nodded and the queen kissed them.

Then she placed her hands either side of his face and kissed his forehead. "Dear, sweet, good Limpic," she said with a smile. "Where the flower grows."

Chapter 26

The night was nearing its end when *Polestar* finally sailed to the tip of the Devil's Toe on the Golden Coast. The bubble had been removed and her decks were cleared and cleaned. She was free to return to her slumber having given so much.

The forest elverns revered her and, under Limpic's tutelage, agreed that she was indeed a 'quare vessel'. They paid even greater homage to Limpic, making him a knight of the realm and a defender of the weak. Everyone loved him as their own brother and son and shook his hand and patted him on the back and did everything to demonstrate just how much he meant to them, the little ullan from the Golden Coast. And, of course, Limpic just blushed and said he hadn't really done all that much and so it went on.

Brutonia didn't get around to asking for Sophia's hand in marriage but they did go for a rather long walk in the forest.

Tabitha, the elvern who had returned the Echo Shell to Tulwood, was reunited with her boot and she answered one last mystery that had perplexed Limpic: how she had come to land in Tulwood during the day as silver overtook her.

"It was the night before," she said. "I knew the silver was

upon us and I sought to return to Tulwood with the Echo Shell, but the silver followed me and I lost my train of thought. I must have travelled all around the world until my Starstone began to sputter and die and silver chilled my marrow. I felt something warm drawing me and I saw Tulwood in my mind's eye, and a flower – your flower actually." And Limpic remembered how his flower had glowed yellow just before Tabitha had returned. It had guided her home.

So the mystery was solved and everyone gathered for one last celebratory banquet filled with laughter, dancing, singing and eating. Brutonia and Sophia arrived a little later than everybody else and they seemed rather pleased with themselves.

"I'm sure we'll meet again soon," Limpic had called as *Polestar* set sail down the River Shiman that flowed from Tulwood to the eastern shores of Dalbain. With Brutonia's strength, half a dozen horses and some of Tulwood's best engineers, they had devised a method of rolling the ship to the deepest part of the river.

From there, Limpic had perched once more on the bowsprit as *Polestar* cut through the night, his legs dangling either side. He sang one of his little songs to the moon and she sang back and the two renewed their love for each other.

Finally, he stood once more on the shores of Dalbain, on a balmy moonlit night with a placid sea, a whispering wind and his little limpet colony nearby.

"Aye, aye, aye," sighed Limpic, pleasantly full and pleasantly sleepy.

There was only one thing left to do: he had been given one Starstone to send Horas home. Limpic walked about for a while looking for the elvern. He finally found him sleeping amid many folds of blankets, surrounded by equipment of every kind.

"Hmm, should I let him sleep till morning?" pondered Limpic.

His voice stirred Horas from his slumber.

"Wh—Who's there?" Horas stammered. "If you limpets don't go to sleep this instant, I shall ... be very, very cross!"

"It's me," said Limpic. "I'm back."

"Limpic!" shouted Horas, rising from his bed in great excitement. "I must say, I am glad you're back. Things have been mighty strange around here. First there was no water and I had to move the limpets further out, then there was lots of water and I had to move myself to higher ground, and then there was this bright light from the west and the whole world seemed to cry out. I remember feeling cold, so cold, like I was covered in ice. Cold right to my very core. It's nonsense, really, although I do feel rather stiff." He rubbed his back and frowned. "But then the cold sensation left and there was peace and tranquillity, as though the world was at rest. Is there peace and tranquillity now, Limpic?"

"Yes," replied Limpic. "There is much peace and tranquillity."

Horas sighed and settled himself but his face was downcast. "Zarkus saved me once, you know. When I'd poisoned myself with one of the medicines I was making. He climbed all the way to the top of Sleive Inver and found the plant containing the antidote – in the middle of winter and through the snow. I suspect I shan't see my old friend again."

Limpic opened his mouth then closed it.

Horas smiled. "I know everyone thinks I'm rather eccentric, but I know what goes on around the palace. More than many realise. I knew Zarkus had been acting strangely. He often spent

257

time with me on my nature walks and listened as I blethered on about this plant or that tree. He loved nature. And then one day I found him stripping a young sycamore sapling of its leaves for no reason whatsoever. When I challenged him he laughed and ran off into the woods. But I'd seen his eyes." Horas fidgeted with his belt. "I couldn't save the tree."

Limpic laid a hand on his shoulder. "In the end Zarkus saved everybody."

Horas rubbed his eyes. "That sounds more like my old friend. I'll miss him terribly." He looked up at the moon. "I can go home, then?"

"Only if you want to," said Limpic.

Horas was up and about in a flash, packing everything together haphazardly.

"Oh, I think I will, Limpic. I think I must this very night! It's not that I don't love it here, quite the opposite actually. I think it's wonderful and beautiful and magical," he stood up and fidgeted with his hands, "it's just …"

"Aye?" said Limpic.

"Well, it's just … the limpets! The limpets were awful to me. They're organised, Limpic. They know when you go to sleep and when you're awake!" He pulled up his tunic. "Look!" he exclaimed, pointing to several large dark circular patches on his skin. "The limpets did that! They came out of nowhere, Limpic. Nowhere!"

"Alright, Horas, don't worry yourself," said Limpic, trying to hide his amusement at the thought of limpets coming out of nowhere. "You can go any time you wish. I have a Starstone here for you right now."

"Oh, but it was awful. There I was, one moment minding my own business and wondering to myself, 'Horas, what's happened to all the water?' and then BAM! They're all over me and I'm running around blindly, bumping into rocks and tripping over seaweed, and, oh, my leg, my ankle, my knee, I gave it such a twist!"

"Calm down, Horas!" said Limpic chuckling. "You don't want to wake the limpets again, now do you?"

"My goodness, no!" exclaimed Horas, peering over his shoulder at the water. "I only got them to sleep. Out of nowhere they came."

"Well," said Limpic, extending his hand. "Thank you for everything. At least my flock was in safe hands."

"Eh, what?" replied Horas, staring suspiciously at some bubbles that had just come to the surface of the water. "Oh, yes, not at all, not at all, any time." He took the Starstone and looked up at the moon. "I'm glad there's peace and tranquillity once more," he said.

He gathered all his utensils close and popped the Starstone into his mouth. His eyes almost popped out of his head as he roared and shook violently. His dishes clanged together like some delirious marching band and then with a bright whoosh he was gone and the air crackled like frost.

"Peace and tranquillity," whispered Limpic with a rueful shake of his head. "Poor Horas." Limpic looked to where the bubbles were rising. "Get to bed, limpets!" he said sharply. "I'm coming to check on you this instant."

And so he did, and he relished the coolness of the water and listened with absolute joy as the sea told him all about poor Horas and what the limpets had done to him.

'But they were only trying to find me,' said the sea solemnly. 'They are not bad limpets, not bad at all.'

Limpic agreed, but he made sure they knew he was back and

that he wouldn't put up with any of their nonsense. They settled down then and gave no more trouble that night and were very glad that their shepherd had returned.

Limpic came out of the water and gave himself a shake. He was feeling exceedingly weary all of a sudden and felt like lying in a bed, so he took his boat and made towards the western current. It didn't take him long to find it, nor to speed across the sea towards the cove at Lunaport. Here was his family bothy, built from dislodged boulders and stones. The roof was made from the timbers of reclaimed driftwood and was covered with soil and moss. It was really a very cheerful little cottage indeed with three rooms, one with an open fire and the other two with soft, springy beds. Leaning up against the cottage was Limpic's tiny smokehouse. Despite having eaten at the banquet, Limpic felt a sudden pang of hunger that sent his drowsiness fleeing, and he heated some smoked salmon over a few coals.

As he was eating at the table he found a note from his siblings.

Called today. You weren't here. Are you still away fixing the moon? Hurry up. Will be back tomorrow with sis. Get the pan on!

PS – The clans are all talking about you and what you did. There's rumour of a flower involved. Everyone's very excited although Brona of the clan of the Grey Whiskers looks pretty grumpy!

PPS – Good job with the moon. Mum and Dad would have been proud.

Limpic smiled. There wouldn't be much peace tomorrow with those three eejits coming. He would have to get some eggs and make some potato bread and maybe even some soda farls. As for Brona, well that would be for another time.

After supper he yawned and stretched as tiredness came sweeping back in a most comforting way. He had a quick wash and lay down on his bed, but no matter how much he tossed and turned, he couldn't stop his mind from relaying his adventure over and over. He missed the feel of the ocean beneath his feet and suddenly the bed, though soft and springy, didn't seem to move as it should have.

And then there was the moon. Limpic desperately wanted to watch the moon for a while. He took some blankets from his bed and made his way outside, across the stony beach and down to the water's edge where his little craft sat askew on the rocks.

The sea seemed quite content to lie at peace and snuggle into the cove. Limpic threw his blankets into the boat and shoved off. The sky was so clear that he almost thought he could see into eternity again and his heart leapt a little.

The vast ocean all around shone like a mirror, and he suddenly realised that he was sailing among the stars and gliding towards that other moon. Only when it disappeared beneath his boat did Limpic settle himself back into his blankets and content himself to watch the sky. The moon peered down and seemed to glow with extra vibrancy. Limpic sighed and allowed another wave of tiredness to sweep over his body. His mind stilled and he touched the flower on his chest. He was hame.

His eyes grew heavier, and each time they closed it took longer for them to open. Finally, they closed tightly and Limpic was fast asleep, curled up within his blankets. The sea came shushing around and the moonlight fell upon his gentle sleeping form.

Everything was still and quiet. No one passing would have heard a sound; the only creature that could have was asleep. No one would have heard that gentle voice just above the stillness, the voice of a grateful moon.

"Thank you, sweet Limpic," it said. "Rest now and dream of beautiful things."

And he did.